It's just enough to be strong in the broken places,
It's just enough to be strong,
Should the world rely on faith tonight.[1]

Fiction by Susan McGeown:

A Well Behaved Woman's Life

A Garden Walled Around Trilogy:
Call Me Bear
Call Me Elle
Call Me Survivor

Recipe for Disaster
Rules for Survival

Rosamund's Bower

The Butler Did It

Joining The Club

Nonfiction by Susan McGeown:

Biblical Women and Who They Hooked Up With

Joining

The

Club

By Susan McGeown

Magnificent Cover Art courtesy of Laury *Ann* Vaden.
Including the beautiful quilt work that is part of the cover.
What a woman of many talents, huh?
magentaswan@patmedia.net

Published by Faith Inspired Books
3 Kathleen Place, Bridgewater, New Jersey 08807
www.FaithInspiredBooks.com

*However, I must state that the love and loyalty between friends
is real, live, and true.
I can only write about it because I'm privileged to experience it
from more than one source on a daily basis.*

Bibliographic credit appears at the end of this work.

To Linda Jo and Wendy Sue and Laury Ann

I no doubt deserved my enemies,
But I don't believe I deserved my friends.[2]

Three precious girlfriends the Lord has seen to bless me
with over the course of this life's journey.

Friends love through all kinds of weather.
Proverbs 17:17[3]

Table of Contents

There are ghosts from my past who've owned more of my soul
Than I thought I had given away
They linger in closets and under my bed and in pictures less proudly displayed [4]

Chapter 1: Skeletons In My Closet

"Minnie, I think the kitchen's on fire."

Not the sort of thing you want to hear your four year-old grandson say to you, but, hey, that happens a lot with me. Scrambling up off the floor as fast as my forty-eight-year-old bones would allow I rush into the kitchen to find the grilled cheese I had been cooking burned beyond repair.

Hey, I'm not the best of cooks but I *can* cook a grilled cheese sandwich. When I'm alone. Uninhibited. *Not* watching my potential terrorist of a grandson, adorably packaged in the non-threatening appearance of a chubby, ginger-haired, big-blue-eyed deceiving parcel of innocence. When I can give the frying piece of butter, bread and cheese my complete, undivided attention rather than having to remove shards of potential stitch-requiring glass resulting from the broken lamp in the living room.

"I didn't break that lamp, Minnie."

"I know, Liam." I say in a slightly tired and 'been-there-done-this-one-too-many-times' tone of voice. "It just fell."

"It did not *just fell*, Minnie." Implied in the statement was also the phrase *'and we both know it,'* an expression I've used a time or two with my precious, first and (thank God) only grandson. A phrase I've had to

1

eliminate from my vocabulary because of said grandson's penchant for repeating – tone and all – similarly voiced phrases in alternative scenarios that make my daughter give me a 'are you sure you're up to this?' expression of doubt and concern.

"Oh no?" I'm having fun now, despite the lingering aroma of burned food floating through the kitchen. "How'd it happen?" Sometimes disasters are all worth it just to hear the detailed explanations that get spun. I wipe the pan clean and efficiently begin to butter bread for 'toasty-cheese' take two.

Once the two sandwiches are busy toasting – *on very low heat* – I take Liam by the hand, sit him on the couch, and resume my diligent hunt for glass slivers. We've been to the hospital once … *okay, twice but the daughter doesn't know* … So far, I've been able to avoid stitches and I'd like to keep it that way.

"Goliath did it."

I don't bother looking up. Time enough for that later, as the story is just starting. "Oh?" I say. Another phrase Liam can imitate perfectly when he chooses, including the arch of his eyebrows and slight left tilt of his head.

"Yeah, you know, Minnie, the giant."

"I thought David killed him with his sling."

"Nah, he was wearing a helmet. He just played dead so that David wouldn't cut his head off with his big, shiny sword."

I sigh and look up at my grandson as he stares at me intently, waiting … How come boys always get the great eyelashes? Is he smart enough to bring up another one of my disasters in order to deflect attention away from himself? He's only four for goodness sake …

Liam looks at me and then glances at the DVD cabinet by the television. "Unless, I've got it wrong, Minnie." That little …

Okay, so I bought a fabulously expensive collection of "Great Stories Of The Bible" for Liam to watch. Mistakenly, I thought it would be a brilliant time filler when things are … heading out of control and I need the magic of electronics to flash and dazzle where I cannot … or will not go. The very first video we watched was "David and Goliath," which included a terrific cartoon reenactment of David having just slain the giant, climbing up on Goliath's body, lifting his very large, sharp, shiny sword and severing Goliath's head. Stunned with horror, I hadn't been quick enough to grab the remote and shut the movie off. Hence we were both treated to the sight of David lifting the bloody head by the hair and waving it around victoriously as blood dripped copiously from the decapitated ... Well, you get the picture. Despite the fact that I then *immediately* turned the movie off – *never to be viewed again* – my daughter heard about the brief showing – *for weeks* – and Liam has been reenacting the vicious decapitation ad infinitum with his father (who had a good laugh), his friends (much to their mothers' horror), his stuffed animals, and, in times of real desperation my cat, Harry. The fact that he doesn't have a sword (No Weapons Allowed) a ruler, pencil, wrapping paper tube or stick will do just fine, thank-you very much.

"You're not watching the video, Liam. It was a mistake that Minnie made and *will not make again.* It's too violent."

"Can't we watch a different one?" He gets off the couch, takes the long way around the glass shards and me to get to the video cabinet and selects a video: *Joshua And The Battle Of Jericho.*

Wasn't Joshua helped by a prostitute or something?

I make a decision to hide the entire collection *after* Liam's been picked up for the day. Satisfied that my glass shard removal is successful (I've already dust-busted, vacuumed, used damp paper-towels, and searched using my extra-strong reading glasses ... What? Trust me, it's not over the top. You Don't Know Liam.) I take my precious grandson's hand. "Sweetie, come into the kitchen with me. We'll get the stepstool and you can help me clean the grapes to go with our sandwiches."

Having lost the battle – but not the war – Liam concedes. "Okay, Minnie, I'll go get the stepstool."

Within minutes he's working at the kitchen sink washing grapes while we listen and wiggle to some of the Christian rock music I've been listening to lately ... "*Like a thief in the night, Like a runaway train, Like a first*

3

class, lightning fast hurricane, I'll keep my ear to the ground, And my eyes to the sky, I'm ready now but somehow, I know You'll take me by surprise [5] ... "

Welcome to my life ... now ...

I'm called Minnie not because of my remarkable resemblance to the famous rodent or the financially challenged southern old lady who wore price tags hanging off her clothes. It was the closest thing Liam could manage to "Grammie" when he was first speaking and ... well, it was cute. You do stupid stuff, things you swore you'd never do when grandchildren arrive. Trust me.

My daughter, Erin, picks up Liam promptly at three-thirty. She's a fourth grade teacher right here in town. A *poor* fourth grade teacher, struggling to make ends meet, which consequently means that she must teach summer school for the months of July and August to pick up some extra cash. I watch Liam on Tuesdays and Thursdays giving us an opportunity to bond and cause as much worldwide destruction as an old woman and a little boy can manage. The other days of the week some dedicated professional named "Miss Nancy" takes responsibility for him and the lives of thirteen other preschoolers who Liam comes in contact with. More power to her. Erin and I discuss our final week of summer vacation which will include her working up through Wednesday and only needing me for a final Tuesday. *One more day*, my head thinks. *I've only got to keep us both alive and unharmed for one more six-hour period.* I think I can do it.

With Liam and Erin's exit (and my full disclosure of the broken glass and kitchen fire – hey, Liam will only rat on me anyway) I morph back into the moderately capable, semi-competent, usually reliable ... vaguely lonely and uniquely insecure woman that I am.

With a nice tall glass of iced tea and today's paper that I never got to, I settle in the lounge chair on the back deck only to be interrupted by the phone. "Hello?" Not happy that I've had to traipse all the way back into the house I suppose I don't sound too welcoming.

"Lainey? That you?"

Great. My ex-husband, Paul. "Who else would it be, Paul?"

"You're crabby. Liam just leave?"

I have a policy with Paul. I try to never give him accurate information. He's one of those men who always thinks he knows everything about me. Which is highly annoying. Which was Reason Number One why he's my ex. How can someone believe they know you with enough forceful confidence to *argue with you* about it when you're not even sure you understand yourself? "No, Liam didn't just leave." *He left almost twenty minutes ago.*

"We need to talk."

Does that sentence ever bring about good results? "We are."

"No, I need to do it in person. Face-to-face. What are you doing for dinner?" *Not eating with you,* I think with firm conviction. "When was the last time you left that house, Lainey? Come on, tell me what day."

"Look, Paulie," I call him Paulie because he hates that name more than I hate Lainey, "you were annoying when we were married, now you're positively maddening. I talk with you on the phone because I haven't gotten around to caller ID. I will not subject myself to an in-person conversation while you try to psychoanalyze me and advise me on reducing my caloric intake."

"Have you ever tried that elliptical machine I bought you so long ago? Or are you still hanging damp towels on it to dry?"

Paul, the husband who never gave a gift that didn't have an agenda attached to it. Paul, psychologist extraordinaire who never met a person he couldn't somehow improve. "I'm ending this conversation now, Paulie. *Good-bye.*"

"Olivia called me."

Paul didn't elaborate. He just lets those three words do their powerful damage.

"*Why would Olivia call you?*" Olivia. My older daughter. The daughter who prefers not to speak to me unless her world is in flames. Olivia, my daughter, who hated her stepfather Paul with such a vitriolic vehemence it became Reason Number Two why he became my ex.

"She asked me to do her a favor." Paul lets the random thought patterns spin out in my head as I struggle to figure out what possible favor Paul could do for Olivia.

I stand there with the phone to my ear looking at the grade school hallway pictures of my girls. Pictures that successfully managed to hide a multitude of homebound disasters and personal demons. My lifetime of guilt – so large that it is now carefully and diligently maintained in a securely locked mental stronghold - begins to rumble. I sit down on the steps and rest my head in my hand. "What does she want, Paul?" I fight back an overwhelming urge to go to bed.

"I'll pick you up at six-thirty. Will that give you enough time to get ready?"

Get ready: a term, for me, that has nothing to do with my physical appearance and everything to do with how long it will take to get my expired prescription of Xanax refilled. "Are you taking me to a public place so that I will be forced to maintain a controlled level of behavior?"

"No, Lainey," Paul says in a patient, 'I'm a trained psychologist and you're a damaged piece of goods I can transform' voice, "I'm taking you to a nice restaurant, because I know how difficult things are between you and Olivia and, *if you'd let me,* I know I could help you untangle this terrible knot of a relationship. Plus, I know how much you hole yourself up in that house and it's good to get out and about now and then. I'll buy you a nice piece of broiled fish and a salad."

Ah, yes. Let's not forget the calorie count. The childish side of me – something that's regularly in control of my life when Paul is near – plans on buying the fettuccini alfredo and cheesecake. I sigh in defeat. "I'll see you at six-thirty," and hang up before Paul can upset me any more than he already has.

I stare at my forty-eight-year-old face in the bathroom mirror in my attempt to 'get ready' to have dinner. I wear my hair shoulder length and it tends to have a mind of its own, curling wildly all over my head. Of course, the hair gets 'touched up' every six weeks or so to hide that annoying gray. I have green eyes and a clear complexion with very few visible wrinkles …

yet. I've got that puffy darkness going on under my eyes that has begun to concern me. I like to describe the way I look as not beautiful but not scary looking either: *uniquely average.*

Despite Paul's opinion, I don't think I'm overweight. Oh, sure, if I had a wish or two I'd drop fifteen or twenty pounds, but who am I kidding? I exercise ... sometimes. I use that damned elliptical machine or walk or ... have really good intentions of exercising tomorrow. It's not anyone's business how I eat; I make an effort to be healthy.

Paul's idea of punctuality is to be five minutes early. My idea of punctuality is to get there ... eventually. Hey, I can get there on time if it's really important. Things just rarely are ... that important.

Six twenty-two p.m. the doorbell rings and I am stark naked. I read one time the difference between 'naked' and 'nekkid,' which always stuck in my head. 'Naked' meant you had no clothes on. 'Nekkid' meant you had no clothes on and you were up to something. I sigh. I haven't been up to anything in a very, very long time. I open my bedroom window and shout, "You're early," at Paul down on the front step.

Paul, dressed casually yet elegantly in tan trousers with a crease that could cut through steel and a dark blue dress shirt, open at the neck, looks up at me. Taking the time to remove his sunglasses to perhaps catch a glimpse of what my bare shoulders imply, he shouts back, "And you, *of course,* are late."

It feels fantastic to flip him the finger and shut the window without a word. Seconds later I hear him in my front hallway. "And you *still* don't lock your front door," he shouts up to me.

I sigh. It's going to be a long, painful dinner with no end in sight. I'll wear my favorite black, high wedge sandals, which will make me just slightly taller than Paul – something that always annoyed him. Black cotton trousers, a bright pink, loose summer top, and my favorite gold earrings and I'm as ready as I'll ever be. Especially without the Xanax.

Paul and I were married for three years, two months, and sixteen days. He was part of my 'maybe some class and style will rub off on me' stage. A stage that was both astronomically detrimental and amazingly insightful at the same time. During my time with Paul - being corrected, improved, and refined - I hit what was perhaps the lowest level of self-confidence that is humanly possible this side of suicide. Let's face it, when you reach a point where you don't feel sure enough of yourself to food shop, dress yourself, or speak unless spoken to, you're pretty bad. Imagine an untrained but enthusiastic puppy that gets corrected, leashed, shaved, caged, and trained to such an extent that it's afraid of everyone and everything and all it can seem to manage is to piddle on the floor when you look at it. That was what I became during my marriage to Paul.

But somewhere during those three years, two months, and sixteen days, I decided that my lack of class and style was perhaps exactly what was so critically important to what made me *me*. Why should I try to become the approved female version of a self-absorbed, abrasive, condescending man like Paul? Was I out of my mind? Apparently, for a few years I was. Which lead to the remarkably positive decision to embrace the uniquely bizarre woman that I really was and dump Paul, quick.

My modus operandi for the evening is to remain silent, cool, and alert. Something I've been unable to achieve *in this lifetime* but which is always a commendable goal nonetheless.

"Nice shoes, Lainey," Paul manages as we step out my front door and make our way down to his flashy BMW. I sigh mentally and think with fond regret that one of the best things I got out of my marriage to Paul was the alimony ...

Paul tries for small talk in the car. Psychobabble 101: *Relax severely damaged patient with casual conversation.* Will I be teaching fifth grade again in the fall? How many years have I been in the educational trenches anyway? Shouldn't I be aiming my sights higher for some type of administrative position? How much additional training would I need? Do I have any higher aspirations? How is my interesting hobby of quilting coming along? Have I ever made a sale? Completed a project? Followed a pattern? Have I formulated a business plan? Spoke with a financial planner? Applied for an 'LLC'? (Whatever the heck that is ...)

Does he realize that I'm not answering or is this so much a part of what he does day in and day out that he doesn't even realize? "Sometimes, silence is best, Paul. You should try it." We finish the remainder of the ride in silence mixed with my satisfaction and Paul's anger.

Dinner is filled with Paul's accounting of all the children he's saved, and the new things he has learned and feels a need to share, and his many stellar goals for the future. It isn't until over coffee and dessert (yes, I had cheesecake) that Paul unveils the primary reason for this farce of a dinner: Olivia's request. "Olivia has been seeing a therapist for the past few months. Did you know that, Lainey?"

I take a sip of my coffee and mentally gear up for The Challenge of the night. "No. We haven't spoken in quite a while about personal things and the last time we did talk it wasn't to disclose her need for psychotherapy."

"Well, I was very pleased to find out that she's been working with a very qualified woman by the name of Aileen Burkart. She's eminently capable of dealing with the *numerous* issues that Olivia has."

"And what issues are those?" I feel compelled to ask.

Patiently, he ticks off a pile of issues, enumerating each one with a well manicured finger, "Abandonment, anger, low-self esteem, alcoholism …"

"*What's the favor, Paul?*" I say through gritted teeth and for once he seems to actually read me correctly and know that I am at the end of my self-control.

"She'd like me to convince you to give her the name and last known location of her father."

A nuclear bomb detonates within my head and heart but I make the gargantuan effort of concealing the devastation. I begin collecting my purse and jacket, making motions to leave. "I don't know what ridiculousness Olivia and you are playing at. She knows the name of -"

Paul interrupts me. "Lainey," he says with some volume, "Olivia and Dean had a blood test," he puts on his solicitous, psychologist face and reaches out as if to touch me consolingly, "and it seems as if the time has come for you to be forthcoming about some of the … *secrets* … you seem to have been keeping about your past."

Like hell I will.

I leave him standing in the restaurant with the dinner bill and no disclosures about any of my closeted skeletons. Good thing I've got taxi money in my wallet.

All the pennies I've wasted in my wishing well
I have thrown likes stones to the sea...[6]

Chapter 2: Wishes And Other Things Useless

So you're probably wondering, "Who's Dean?" Well, Dean's my first husband. We were high-school sweethearts. Okay, *junior* high-school sweethearts, because by the time we were barely seventeen we were already expectant parents and married – *in that order.* I think, for two teenagers we did a bang up job of trying, even if that meant we were divorced with two small children by the time we were both twenty-four.

There were a lot of reasons why we didn't make it: we were too young, we got married for the wrong reasons, Dean was a messed up product of two alcoholic parents and I was a messed up product of ...

I hesitate here as I write this and find, not surprisingly, that not only can I not *voice* certain things about my past, but apparently I cannot *write* things about my past as well. Which is pretty funny considering the reason why I am taking the time to do this ...

I did love Dean. He was my first real boyfriend and I think that he really loved me, too. Until real life took over and extinguished everything like a tidal wave would put out the flame of a match.

When I discovered I was pregnant, we had already been dating for over three years. There we were, two teenagers: uneducated, unprepared,

11

and completely clueless. We moved in with Dean's parents (a highly unsuccessful situation when Dean was there on his own, disastrously multiplied by three once he brought home a teenage wife and a colicky baby). While I struggled to finish high school, Dean dropped out and started working construction, and his mother, Miriam, watched the baby.

Olivia was that baby. Even now, to look at those thirty-two-year-old baby pictures, I'm stunned at her beauty. Dark hair that grew in glossy ringlets almost immediately, real, honest-to-goodness *violet* eyes, eyelashes that had to be three-quarters of an inch long, and a perfect little dimple in her right cheek. When she wasn't screaming loud enough to make your ears bleed, she had a laugh that was completely infectious. I wish I had a dime for every time I've wondered what type of adult she would have grown up to be had I been a more experienced mother, or had Dean been a more ... sober ... father, or had I had the courage to Do The Right Thing and give Olivia up for adoption to a couple who could have given her a better life.

Hey, I never lied to Olivia. She never came up to me and said, "Mom, is Dean Kelly my *biological* father?" And though I *am* playing with semantics, she never asked if Dean Kelly were her father at all. And if she had, I would have answered – without hesitation: *yes* - because he *was* her father. Though he wasn't the critical sperm donor, though he was frequently too drunk to make it up the stairs to get to bed, though his inability to hold down a job caused us to have our car repossessed and never permitted us the luxury of new school shoes in September or getting braces for our girls' slightly crooked teeth, he loved Olivia to the best of his ability. He delighted in her first steps, he brought her pink roses on her third birthday (well, he was off by one day but it was the thought that counted), and he somehow managed to achieve a less-hated parent status than I did. Which should really make you wonder just how bad I was as a mother.

I did the best I could. Honest, I did. I loved her with every speck of my heart and made a concerted effort to not make all the mistakes my Mom had. I married Olivia's father, didn't I? I worked hard to love

Olivia's father, didn't I? I never, *ever* blamed Olivia for my mistake, did I? I worked hard to follow the career path I'd always dreamed of so that I'd never be bitter or resentful of what I'd lost, didn't I? I stuck it out being married to Dean for over seven years trying to make it work, didn't I?

Even to myself I sound like a whiny child who's refusing to take responsibility for her failures. Welcome to Guilt Vault Stronghold Number One. Okay, here's the truth: I was a lousy mother. I was a teenager who had an imaginary perception of what a fairy tale life as a wife and mother should be and I was a complete idiot for it. I spent a lot of time blaming Dean and his alcoholism, my mother-in-law for her interfering, my father-in-law for his lifetime of poor examples to Dean, my mother for refusing to help us when things started to really go downhill, and life in general for never cutting me even one small, miniscule break.

It took me decades to realize the reality was that none of us, not Dean, my mother-in-law Miriam, my father-in-law Taylor, or my mom had any clue what was the right way to raise a healthy child, nurture a happy marriage, or select the proper road for personal self-improvement. During my marriage to Dean the only thing I learned with any certainty was that doing the exact opposite of what *my* lousy parent had done to *me* only succeeded in my discovering a completely new way to screw up my own children.

Lying in bed, I fall asleep watching personal video clips of my repeated and abject failures as a mother with my precious, firstborn daughter Olivia. Once I am asleep the nightmares of her biological father began.

I'm awakened by the ringing of the front door bell and the unpleasant feeling of my cat, Harry, fast asleep on my chest, breathing open-mouthed catty-breath into my face. For one horrifying moment I'm afraid I've forgotten to pick Liam up at Erin's but then my befuddled mind recalls the kitchen fire and glass shards and I remember that it's Friday.

Looking out my bedroom window I see it's the world's most unfriendly meter reader at my front door. Just as I go to put the curtain down (and ignore the perpetually nasty man) he glances up at me and we make eye contact. Practically waving his fist at me he shouts, "Open up and let me read the meter!" Ignoring him will only make the next visit that much more unpleasant so I pull on a bathrobe and stumble down the stairs.

"Wipe your feet," I say. The compulsion to be polite and add "please" to my request has been lost over the course of the repeated times I've had to scrub my front hallway after he leaves.

"Don't tell me you were still asleep?" he says in absolute stunned disgust.

"*It's nine-thirty a.m.*" I say and then immediately think, *why am I explaining myself to the meter reader?*

As he goes to open the door I block the way. "Your. Feet." I say with firm conviction.

He takes two perfunctory swipes and gives me a look that communicates oceans of sarcasm and the phrase, *Happy?*

I look down at his feet – completely encrusted in mud because he not only is nasty but is also a destroyer of gardens – and look up at him. *No*, my equally sarcastic look says back to him, *not even close.* I take note of the salt and pepper hair that is curling around his head due to adverse heat and truckloads of sweat. As a trickle of perspiration trails down the side of his face from the oppressive summertime heat and humidity, I make a grand show of shivering from the cold of the air-conditioning and wrapping my bathrobe around me. His eyes seem to widen in disbelief.

He bends down, unlaces his boots, steps out of them and then stands on my front steps in his stocking feet. "I♥Yankees" is plastered all over his socks. I can't help it. "How 'bout those Mets?" I say with an evil grin as I open up my front door and let him in.

He comes equipped with his own flashlight so I don't bother to do the neighborly thing by turning on any lights as he makes his way down into the basement. We've done this dance before and neither of us feels compelled to speak. As he makes his way back up and out the front door, I make the motions of putting on my morning pot of coffee completely ignoring the fact that there is an absolute stranger walking through my house while I'm in nothing but my pajamas. But as I turn to see him sitting on the front steps putting on his boots, I make the magnanimous gesture of pouring him a glass of iced tea and bringing it outside to him.

"What's that?" he asks when I step outside and hold the glass out to him. He swipes his forehead with the back of his hand and squints dark brown eyes at me against the sun's glare.

"'Gee thanks,' or 'Oh, I really appreciate this,' or even 'No thanks, I don't take drinks from strangers' are all appropriate things to say." I feel like I am instructing one of my Neanderthal fifth-graders.

He has the grace to look a tad bit embarrassed by his lack of manners. "Thanks," he mumbles as he takes the glass and downs the entire contents in three huge gulps. "It's hot as blazes out here and it's not even 10 a.m. I'm going to be dead by one."

"One?"

"Quitting time."

"*You're done for the day at one in the afternoon?* When do you start?" Too late I realize that my response is less than polite as it exudes a pile of criticism regarding his lack of dedication or reason for complaining.

"You forgot to say," here he morphs his voice into some high-pitched annoying woman tone, "'no wonder my utility bills are so high if you don't work past one.'" Handing the empty glass back to me he takes the time to fish out an ice cube and rub it across the back of his neck. "See you in a month."

"No, you probably won't. I'll be back to work by then."

"Oh?" he says. "And what do you do?"

"I'm a teacher," I say with all the pride, power and defensiveness one acquires from such a profession.

"*A teacher,*" he says and shakes his head and then gazes up into the sky as if he's dreaming the perfect dream. "Ahh, to work only one-hundred and eighty days, get a full year's pay, and be done every day by ..." he looks at me for confirmation, "three?"

"Want another ice cube?" I offer with venomous sarcasm. "It's the last one you'll ever get from me *in this lifetime.*"

"No," he grins, apparently happy that he thinks he's gotten the best of me, "one is all I can stomach." I'm back in the house with the door closed before he's off my property. If I play my cards right, I shouldn't have to deal with him until next summer.

Fortified with two cups of coffee and a toasted English muffin, I sit and stare at the phone for what is probably an hour. I have to call Olivia. I know I do. Don't I? I mean a *good mother* – one that I wasn't always but I certainly strive to be now – would call right away. Do I have the courage to tell my daughter with whom I have an absolutely abysmal relationship the deepest, darkest, most horrible secret that I have in all these years *never told a living soul?*

No way.

I should call Dean. What must he be thinking? Even though we no longer have any type of emotional investment, what must he be going through right now? How is he coping with the terrible discovery of my ultimate betrayal? I try to imagine his feelings and find that my own volatile emotions will not allow room for anyone else's. He has every right to be livid with me. Then I worry: will he take his anger out on Olivia as well? I know what it is like to fight a parent's emotional demons that I bear no responsibility for. I realize as I imagine the many various emotional ramifications of all this that ultimately this will only make Olivia hate me all the more.

If that is possible.

So I call Dean. Which is even worse than you might initially think. First, I have to endure a strained but polite conversation with Dean's mother, Miriam, because I have no idea where Dean is or how to contact him. I think over the course of the entire ten minute conversation: *she knows ..., she doesn't know ..., she definitely knows ..., she doesn't know ..., maybe she's fishing because she suspects ...* I'm exhausted by the end of the call and need to have a scoop of extra-crunchy reduced fat peanut butter to get my energy back.

Finally, I can find no other excuse to avoid picking up the instrument of the devil also known as the telephone. I dial, listen to it ring, then endure Dean's voicemail, *"Hey, this is Dean. If you're calling for construction business, leave your name and number and I'll get back to you as soon as I can. All other callers don't bother. BEEEEEEP."* "Hey Dean, it's me. Elaine. I … well, I guess we should talk? About Olivia … and stuff? I guess it's about time we faced all this … Since you know … stuff … I suppose you need to talk with me … Can you give me a call? My number is …" I hang up and realize that I've effectively imprisoned myself to the house until he calls. No big deal. As Paul so aptly put it, I hardly ever leave the house anyway. My favorite thing in the whole wide world (besides teaching which I sincerely do love) is to quilt. I head upstairs to my workroom and get lost in the magic and wonder of fabrics and textures, color and patterns, creativity and accomplishment. I work through the afternoon, through dinner, and long into the night before I stumble bleary-eyed to my bed without even bothering to brush my teeth. How's that for escapism at its finest?

During the school year I'm up by five-thirty a.m., at school by six-thirty, teaching by seven-fifteen and done for the day by one-fifty p.m. (something Mr. Nasty Utility Man certainly didn't need to know) and in bed by nine. During the summer I stay up late and sleep late. I have no young children I have to care for, no job I have to run to, and no responsibilities other than watching Liam two days a week (with pick-up at nine a.m.). So it is unbelievably cruel and unusual punishment to be awakened from a sound sleep at five-fifteen a.m. on a morning I could have slept until whenever I liked.

This time Harry is stretched out on his back, fast asleep on my pillow and I'm hanging off the edge of the bed. I hear through my growing consciousness not only the doorbell being rung but the front door being pounded on as well. I lie there in bed and think about ignoring the whole thing, until I hear, "E! Hey E! Open up! It's me, Deano! Your ex-husband! WE GOTTA TALK ABOUT OLIVIA."

Many things become immediately apparent as I leap from bed and rush downstairs. Dean has probably been out all night. Dean is probably very drunk. And if I don't want the neighbors to get an eye- and earful I'd better move *fast*.

I open the door to see my ex-husband Dean, swaying on my front porch. "Hey, E," he says with a sloppy grin and a voice tender with affection. "Did I wake you up?" He's parked his construction pickup on my front lawn.

"Come in." I know I could say things like, 'you shouldn't be driving in this condition,' or 'have you been out drinking all night?' or 'why didn't you just call me once you sobered up?' or any one of a hundred other things, but no one knows better than me how useless those words would be. I guide him by his arm towards my living room couch and give him a slight push to get him to sit down.

"Got a beer?" he says with the same disarming grin and twinkling blue eyes that got me to give him a pile of things I never should have over thirty years ago.

"No," I tell him, "I don't keep alcohol in the house. You know I don't drink. I never drank when we were married either."

"Yeah," he rests his head back against the couch, "I remember. You stopped drinking when you got pregnant with 'livia." Speaking her name makes him remember the purpose for his visit and he makes the difficult effort of lifting his head up to peer at me through bloodshot eyes. "We gotta talk, E. About 'livia. Shit, E. She knows. She *knows* I'm not her father ..." His eyes tear up and his head drops back against the sofa and I watch his Adam's apple bob as he swallows. "I thought we'd take that secret to our graves ... I really did ..." His voice drifts off as he does what I knew he would do ... passes out.

I begin to shake and tremble and finally lower myself to sit in the middle of the living room while Dean mumbles and twitches in his alcohol induced dreams. I feel like I felt on a roller coaster one time when I went forwards, backwards, and upside down all in twelve point four seconds and when the ride stopped I didn't even know if all of my body parts were attached or functioning. I just cannot process this piece of information that

Dean has so casually thrown at me. *He knew.* All these years he knew that Olivia wasn't his.

Then I start to get angry and want to scream a thousand questions at him: How could he know? Where did he find out? When did he find out? Why didn't he ever talk to me about it? Dean burps, farts, and snores oblivious to my emotional breakdown at his feet.

I sit there in my living room at five twenty-three a.m. on Saturday, August 27th and come to the stunning realization that the big, dark, horrible, never-to-be-told secret that I have been spending my *whole life* keeping quiet from all those I know and hold dear has been floating around *unchecked* in the alcohol-soaked brain of my ex-husband Dean Kelly.

It would seem that the thing that I cannot speak of or even write about must now be discussed with the whole, damn world.

I'm afraid I'm not all that you see all along the coast of me,
I'm camouflaged, a desert mirage, a nobody.[7]

Chapter 3: My Personal Nitroglycerin Stash

My mom and dad never married. He was a horrible excuse for a man who disappeared as soon as I made my presence known. I was a nasty, life-altering disaster that happened to my mother when she was nineteen on a full ride scholarship to Princeton University. It was my arrival that caused all of my mother's hopes and dreams to be dashed to smithereens, never to be retrieved or resurrected. She went on to become a financial analyst in a small time office working for people who never appreciated her intelligence or ability. I grew up to be a disappointment of astronomical proportions because I was never contrite enough, appreciative enough, obedient enough, willing enough, quiet enough, fast enough, pretty enough …

Ah, hell. Give me a minute.

Sigh. I'm sure if you talked to my mother she would have a slightly different perspective. When I got pregnant at sixteen with what everyone assumed to be Dean's baby (and no, of course my mother didn't like Dean, she didn't like anyone) it was the final straw that broke the proverbial mother's back. She always *knew* I would amount to nothing and here I was, real-live proof (finally) of all she feared would come to pass. And in a way, that final straw was also the perfect opportunity to cut herself free of me forever. My mother did not attend my wedding and she never showed any interest in either Olivia or Erin (who arrived two years later when I was barely nineteen). With my marriage to Dean, my mother pretty much shut the door, locked the lock, and threw away the key. Bye-bye.

When things were at their very worst: Dean drinking, bill collectors calling, Miriam harping, and me breaking down, I called my mother. You need to know that *in all those years* that Dean and I were together I only called her *once*. Olivia was only three and Erin wasn't even a year old and I was at an incredibly desperate point. I called my mother and asked her if the girls and I could come and stay for a bit until I got on my feet. I told her quite bluntly that I knew I had screwed up and that she was right about Dean, but that I had the babies to think about. I explained that I was taking night courses to get my teaching degree and working as a receptionist in a doctor's office during the day. I promised her that I would have all the babysitting issues taken care of. The only thing I asked her for was a *place for my babies and I to sleep.* And she said no. No apology. No explanation. No alternative offer of help or support. Just no. And then hung up on me.

So I stayed where I was. Where else did I have to go? I did my best to make the most of a pretty horrendous situation. I tried to stay focused on my goal rather than get dragged down by the disaster that was my life. I stayed married to Dean almost four more years. To this day I don't know what was harder: accomplishing what I set out to do or keeping my sanity. Maybe they were equally difficult.

At twenty-four, I got my teaching degree, got a teaching job, and filed for divorce. I qualified for rental assistance and got a small two-bedroom apartment. I fed my kids through food stamps and free school lunches and a hell of a lot of spaghetti and peanut butter.

Those years with Dean were probably the hardest I ever had to live, *but I did it.* Looking back I realized that I might as well grab as much positive as I could from that time: I came out of those years knowing I could do just about anything I put my mind to. I realized that the kid my mom was never impressed with, never wanted, and downright resented was strong, determined, and smart. And if my mother couldn't see it, that was her loss. *Move on, Elaine. Move on.*

By the time I was twenty-six, Olivia was ten and in fourth grade, and Erin was eight and in second. I had been teaching for almost two years and had already signed a teaching contract for the next year. I got on well with my principal and colleagues and was liked by the parents and students. You could almost say I was a success, right? Life was pretty darn good. Give that girl a pat on the back for accomplishing all she did, huh? I'd managed to get a slightly larger apartment in a better part of town. The girls saw Dean less than when we lived with him but at a much higher ratio of him being sober. Despite what my mother had always thought, despite my less than stellar past, I had every reason to assume that all of my big mistakes were in my past. And then I got introduced to the newly hired school psychologist. Yeah, you guessed it: Paul Richardson. AKA Paulie.

Through all this time I carried the secret of Olivia's conception with me like a giant container of nitroglycerin. When someone commented on her unique eye color, her adorable dimple, her glossy black hair, or her volatile personality (*none* of which anyone in my or Dean's family possessed) it was almost as if my heart stopped beating and my lungs stopped functioning. I waited for someone to look me in the eye and say, "Surely you could not have conceived this child with your husband Dean."

But no one ever did.

Dean eventually rouses himself from the couch around ten-thirty. I've been upstairs quilting my way into nothingness once again since I woke up on the living room rug at about eight-fifteen a.m. But no matter how fast I cut, pin, and sew I can't seem to escape the reality of my life: my secret is no secret at all. The top two people *in the entire universe* that I would want to *not know* now do: Olivia and Dean. I hear him in the kitchen clanking around pouring himself a cup of coffee and cooking something in the microwave. When I come down into the kitchen from my workroom – having taken long, long minutes to gather my courage, he's leaning against the counter munching on a bagel.

"Got any Excedrin?" he asks. I find the container in the vitamin cupboard and watch him take four tablets with a gulp of coffee.

"Can I make you something else for breakfast?" I open the fridge and start taking out eggs and bacon. I will distract him with food. Now is probably the one time in my life that I wish I had a fifth of vodka to offer him.

"Hey, I never turn down a free meal," he says and walks around the kitchen island and settles himself in a stool. "You okay, E?"

For all of his drunkenness, Dean was always a caring kind of guy when he was sober. He always seemed contrite, solicitous and appreciative when he was straight enough to manage those emotions. I shrug at his question. "I suppose." Hey, I *have* been worse.

"I've been sober for eighteen months and eleven days. Then I got your phone call last night."

I stop scrambling the bowl of eggs to look at him. "So, you'd like me to take full responsibility for your falling off the wagon. Again." Notice it's not a question, just a statement from extensive past experience.

"Hell no. I just wanted you to know that I'd set a world record for sobriety. Maybe this next time I'll make the full two years and get a new big penny." AA awards time milestones with mementoes that look like big pennies. Dean's got a million of them for a week, a month, and maybe a few for the six-month marks. I know it's pretty stellar that he'd made it to eighteen months ...

It took me a long, long time to be able to look Dean in his handsome blue eyes and feel not a speck of guilt or responsibility for this grown man who can't control his personal demons. I've got enough hard work keeping myself on the right track.

I go back to making breakfast. "Why didn't you just call me back instead of going off to the nearest bar?"

He stuffs the last of his bagel into his mouth, sweeps the crumbs into the sink and leans back crossing his arms. With his blonde hair, blue eyes, and tanned construction worker muscles, he's one fine specimen of a man. Actually, sober he's about the sweetest guy on the face of the earth.

The key words being *when he's sober.* "This wasn't something we could talk about on the phone, E," he says with a stunning flash of maturity. "When I realized what you wanted to talk about I got right in the truck and headed on over."

There is a huge part of me that can't allow him – even for a minute – to assume a superior role between the two of us. Consequently I snap, "So, what? You drove up onto my lawn and proceeded to drink a case or two of beer sitting in your truck before you decided to ring the bell?"

He looks sheepish and gives me his patented 'ain't I cute' grin. "Nah, I got as far as The Exchange. I stopped in to have *just one drink* to shore up my courage." The Exchange is a bar almost within walking distance of my house, once you leave the development and get onto the main highway.

I need to give him one more slap. "You should have called your sponsor. You know the drill."

In a tired, defeated voice, Dean says, "Yeah, Elaine, I know the drill."

Dean has the ability, even after all these years, to make me feel sorry for him. Sitting there, now with his head in his hands looking down at the counter, I remember the handsome young man who was filled with charisma, golden-boy looks and athleticism. Heck, part of his appeal when we were first dating was that even absolutely drunk he was always kind, loving and attentive to me, which was a hell of a lot more than I got from my mother in any condition. Those early years together, I remember thinking that if I had to deal with his occasional drinking, at least he was still nice to me and acted like he liked me. How pitiful was that?

"Why'd you want to talk about this now, after all these years?" He's been looking at me, as I stand in front of him lost in thought, letting the eggs and bacon start to burn.

I turn to the stove to avoid another fire. "Well, since Paul told me that you and Olivia had a DNA test that proved conclusively you weren't her father, I thought it might be appropriate," I say with a pile of sarcasm.

"And since Olivia, through Paul mind you, has requested I provide her with *her father's* full name and last known address."

Dean blinks his big, blue, bloodshot eyes at me in confusion. "Paul? DNA test?" He shakes his head. "I didn't have any test." He tilts his head in puzzlement. "Doesn't Olivia hate Paul big time?"

"Yes, but apparently Olivia has relative degrees of hatred. Currently she hates me more than she hates Paul." Dean mumbles something about "and that's saying something." I continue without acknowledging his mumbling, "Hence she's willing to speak with Paul to get what she needs from me." I sigh and take the time to pour the last cup of coffee for myself and make a fresh pot. "Apparently she's been seeing a therapist. The therapist knows Paul. I'm guessing Olivia was encouraged to speak through Paul to me since she was unwilling to speak with me directly."

Dean looks at me with earnest sincerity. "I didn't have any test, E."

I snort. "Dean, I could shave your entire body of hair when you're asleep and you wouldn't know it. If Olivia wanted a sample for a DNA test, it would have been little trouble to get without your knowledge."

Dean gets up and heads out of the kitchen. I have the presence of mind to turn off the stove before I follow him. He wanders back into the living room where he collapses full length on the couch. With his hand draped across his eyes and his voice husky with regret he says to me, "I'm so sorry, E."

The last thing in the world I thought I was going to hear from Dean was an apology. I sit down in the chair next to the couch and say in stunned confusion, "What are you apologizing for, Dean? I'm the one who's got to say the words of regret. Don't you have a pile of questions? Accusations? Words of hurt and fury?"

He doesn't answer me and when I hear him sniffle I realize he's trying not to cry. And then, in fits and starts he begins to talk. And all I can do is listen. "You ... were so sweet ... when I first met you. Even with that ... bitch of a mother you were all smiles and giggles and joy.

25

When I hung out with you I felt like I was so much better than I knew I really was. For a while, you were a better high than drinking was. I thought," he shrugs, "... well, I thought ... maybe you could help me stay sober ... more often." He makes himself sit up and looks at me sitting in the chair.

"You ... you suddenly started drinking at the parties we went to. Remember? I'd yell and tell you no, and you'd yell back and say that if I could do it why couldn't you? I'm pretty sure they were our first fights. And then," again he shrugs, "well, then I figured hell, if she's going to drink then she won't give me a hard time when I do. So, maybe it was okay."

We're both silent for a long, long time lost in our own thoughts: some good, but mostly bad. I remember those times: the wonder of someone liking you enough to call you a *girlfriend,* the discovery of emotions and feelings that you didn't know existed, the power of beginning to play with adult situations ... For me there was the added attraction of being able to escape from my mother, defy my mother, have someone who wanted me more than my mother ... When you're a teenager *in love* the world and its obstacles are never as big or imposing as they really, truly are. The world takes on an illusionary façade that makes problems disappear, obstacles miniscule, and reality nonexistent. Come on, you remember what it was like.

You remember how stupid you could be.

I was more than happy to give Dean my virginity at fourteen. He took everything I offered with delighted abandon. *Sexual promiscuity* as my mother called it was just another piece of kindling I was happy to throw onto the conflagration that was our relationship. Hell, she had a pile of things she was already complaining about to me that I couldn't control (i.e. my existence) so what difference did it make whether I had wild adolescent sex with my good-for-nothing boyfriend? By the time Dean came on the scene I was already teetering on the edge of full-blown rebellion, anyway. Dean was just some excellent company for the ride.

Adding the sexual perk to our relationship ratcheted up Dean's and my perception of what was real and what was false into the stratosphere of fairy-tale la-la land. We would ride around in Dean's father's car and choose houses we'd planned to live in once we were married. We would get engaged in our senior year, Dean would work and I would go to college to become a teacher. We were going to have four kids and name all the boy's with Dean's same initials and all the girls with my same initials. Dean was going to open his own construction company and I was going to run my own private school. We were always going to be happy, healthy and financially secure. And, as a result of our all encompassing love, our woefully dysfunctional parents were going to morph into grandparents that were solid, loving, dependable, and supportive … Okay, I'll end this so you can stop laughing.

"You learned drinking from me, E," Dean says quietly. "You did it to keep up with me and feel a part of the crowd."

"I never felt a part of the crowd," I say glumly, "drunk or sober." Truth be told, I've never felt part of *any* crowd to this day.

Dean sighs. "Yeah, I know. But in the beginning you at least had *me*, though, didn't you? You'd hang on my arm and be all sweet …"

I can still remember that glorious rush of belonging and being wanted. That feeling of superiority or inclusion or … I don't know the right word … when Dean would grin at me and sling his arm around my neck to pull me close. That feeling of being *a part of.* "It was okay for a bit," I say, "but after a while I felt alone with or without you." Suddenly I feel like a lost fifteen-year-old instead of a mature, put-together forty-eight-year-old.

"That's when you started drinking," Dean states with certainty and I nod reluctantly. "To keep up with me."

Let go of my hand, Elaine Marie. Why do you always have to hang on me? Where was this bizarre time-travel conversation headed with my barely sober first ex-husband? "Dean, why are you doing this?"

He looks at me then, takes a deep breath and says, "If you hadn't been with me, drinking with me, going with me to those parties, you wouldn't of gotten …" he swallows and alters his words, " … ended up pregnant with Olivia."

27

I lean forward and say, *"How do you know how I got pregnant with Olivia?"*

Dean frowns at me and seems to be confused at my question. "We went to Frankie's brother's graduation party. Things got out of hand pretty quick, remember?" I let myself be pulled back into the flashbacks of my deep, dark past: escapism without quilting but instead with alcohol and a truckload of teenage stupidity. When I come back to myself I find Dean looking at me with an expression that is so intense I immediately feel sick to my stomach. "You were drinking Rolling Rock beer and Boone's Farm Strawberry Hill wine."

I cross my arms and glare at Dean. "What, were you keeping notes? I find it particularly spectacular that you can recall what I was drinking at a party almost thirty-five years ago, when during the same period of your life you lost at least three pairs of sneakers because you were too drunk to recall where you'd left them."

"For a little while there, E, I had trouble keeping up with you."

"That's a lie."

Dean doesn't answer me at first. He just sits there staring at me. "You started drinking the Strawberry Hill right off the bat when we got there. Since you'd already been throwing back the Rolling Rock, I tried to get you to stop, or at least slow down. You told me to leave you alone." Dean stops looking at me and stares out the living room window bright with morning sunshine. "I remember thinking, 'Fine, let her. She's not my problem. If she can enjoy herself, so can I.'" He shrugged his shoulders and looked down at his tightly clasped hands. "I figured what was the worst that could happen? You'd pass out and end up with a hell of a hangover. Besides, I still had almost a case of Rolling Rock. I knew where the good times could be had."

When Dean and I were teenagers, the drinking age was eighteen. There were always liquor stores that served underage teens, fake IDs that you could mail away for, or older siblings who would be happy to accommodate should the price be right. Dean had an older brother, a fake ID that he'd mailed away to Las Vegas for, and knew of at least three liquor stores in the area that he'd been going to long enough that he was on a first name basis with the owners. In other words, when it came to obtaining alcohol, Dean was set. Factor in the underground network that always let you know when and where there was a house available for a party and each weekend was always a good excuse to cut loose and drink back a few cold ones.

I remember quite a few parties with Rolling Rock beer and Boone's Farm Strawberry Hill wine. But that's about all I have ever chosen to let myself remember about most parties I attended back then. "What's your point with all this, Dean?"

"I got pretty smashed that night, E." Now it's time for me to stare and not say anything. "I didn't watch out for you like I usually did. I knew you were headed for trouble but I just wanted to let you learn a lesson." Dean gets up, shoves his hands in his pockets and looks out the front picture window. "I know that was the night you got pregnant with Olivia, E."

"Oh?" I say, shooting to my feet and walking around so he has to face me. "How's that? Were you *there*? Did you take pictures?" My fists are so tightly clenched I feel the pain of my nails in my palms.

His blue eyes look bloodshot and sorry. "I didn't take pictures." He lets the reality of his unspoken words sink in: *he was there.*

"So, *if you were there* what made you so sure Olivia wasn't yours?"

He clenches his jaw. "I didn't participate." Now it's my turn to turn and walk away. I can't stand the look in his eyes. He follows me and stands behind me. "I went looking for you. Some guys were laughing. 'Go stand in line,' they told me and pointed upstairs. I found you, upstairs … with at least three guys …"

I close my eyes and put my hands up to my ears to block out the words he's saying. Within my mind I see just broken flashes of particular moments: the musty smell of a bed pillow that I was shoved facedown into so that I had trouble breathing for a time, the confusion of too many hands in too many places, and the inability to say what I wanted to say to stop what I was doing, the male laughter filled with titillated excitement … the terror of the darkness and the whispered words telling me to be quiet, the agony of helplessness, the fear of the enormity of what my mother would say if she knew, and what she would think of me *then*. The inevitable feeling that would eventually steal over me that I wasn't *really* there ... it was all *just a bad dream* that I would wake up from all this if I just closed my eyes and went away ...

He takes my hands from my ears and forces them down and bear-hugs me from behind still holding onto my wrists. I struggle and fight, trying to get away from him but he just stands there like a block of stone. Finally I stop wrestling and just stand still letting the tears and snot run down my face. "I went wild, making them all ... get out," he says softly in my ear. "You'd passed out by then. I got you dressed, and took you home. You're mom was out so I took you upstairs and tucked you in. I figured it would just be our secret. *I never told anyone, E,*" Dean says with intensity.

I feel him shrug. "When you told me you were pregnant, I hoped she was mine. Even though we always used Mike's rubbers." Dean's older brother who fancied himself a ladies man and bought rubbers by the caseload, giving us an unlimited supply of birth control. "Olivia never looked like either one of us. It always seemed like there was a third person involved, ya know? But you never brought anything up so neither did I. We were both a part of the whole ... thing ... I just figured you wanted to forget that ... time just as much as I did." He turns me around and grips my upper arms tightly, giving me a little shake. "I loved her like my own, E. There was never a time that she wasn't as important to me as Erin was. *I swear to God.* I ... wish that I could have ... kept that from happening to you ... I always felt if I'd watched out for you better ... hadn't been so drunk ... I could have changed things ..."

I look up into his concerned eyes. How ironic is it that after all this time we are having such a precious conversation? A conversation that would put most sane people right over the edge. And yet I stand there and realize how fortunate I was to have had him be with me for this horrendous blot in my life. Who ever would have thought that Dean Kelly would be the *perfect person* for anything that involved comfort, love or support? For more than thirty-five years Dean has carried around the guilt of what he could have and should have done that night so long ago. For more than thirty-five years he's agonized over a guilt that could not be forgotten or drunk away.

I stand there looking into his eyes filled with anguish and sincerity and guilt and am overwhelmed with what a mess all this is. Do I tell him it wasn't his fault? Do I tell him the responsibility for all of this does not rest on his shoulders and never did? Do I tell him that there was nothing he could have done that night to protect me? Do I tell him that the night of that party I was already pregnant?

How could that not make everything only that much worse?

I'm lost and broken all alone on this road
The wheels keep turning but the feeling is gone ...[8]

Chapter 4: How Far Can Rock Bottom Really Be?

I finish cooking breakfast for Dean, and coward that I am I decide to let him go on thinking that had he been sober enough he could have done the knight in shining armor thing and rescued me. For a while anyway. Until I get my thoughts sorted out. Find my backbone. Build another mental room for this new load of guilt I've just embraced. Was it just last night I thought I was going to have to speak with Dean and tell him ... what I could manage about Olivia's conception? Instead, he's got his own complete account – including in-color, live images of what he believes is the exact time and place. And in addition, he's carried around the guilt of his failure to save me for almost as long as I've carried around my nitroglycerine secret.

"I think I know where Steve Cantilone lives," Dean says through a mouth full of scrambled eggs.

"Steve Cantilone?" I have vague memories of a hulking football player with no neck and really bad acne.

"Olivia's got his hair color."

My eyes just about pop out of their sockets. "Dean?!" I say, completely on the edge of hysteria. "We *are not* going to give Olivia a list of

32

names of high school boys I've slept with in a drunken stupor so she can go door to door and try to figure out which one is her biological father!"

"It would only be three," he says calmly, "Steve, Joey Antrobus, and Sammy Ventnor."

Can he really believe it's that simple? *Here Olivia, I got really tanked at a number of high school parties and slept around. Dean thinks it only happened one time with three guys, but actually, over the course of a number of weeks, it happened more like five times. I'm guessing — and my information is not completely accurate — that this list of fifteen names is the sum total of boys I slept with while I was dating Dean.* Except for the fact that the name of Olivia's true father would not be anywhere on that list of fifteen names.

I have a really strong need to go sew. I can almost feel the texture of the fabric between my fingers, hear the whir of the sewing machine, and feel the delightful glazing over of my thoughts as I get totally sucked into the wonderful world of creative oblivion. A stunning thought invades my mind: is this what Dean feels like just before he goes and has a drink? If it is, at least I can still drive after I sew.

Dean is looking at me as he sips his coffee. With utmost care I try to explain things to him. "Dean, this is something I have to do in my own time, okay? I would have been very, *very* happy to have never had to say a thing about this *forever.*" I take a deep breath. "But now I do." I take his big hand in mine and squeeze it tightly as I say with every speck of sincerity that I have, "You've been *remarkably* kind, patient, and understanding. I don't believe that there is another man on the face of the earth who would have done what you did so many years ago in the way you unconditionally supported me and Olivia. That makes you better than any other man I know. *But you're going to have to leave the rest of this up to me.*"

With his last bit of toast, Dean mops up any left over bacon grease on his plate. Nodding slowly he says, "Okay, E. I'll leave this between you and Olivia. But I'm not going anywhere. I'm still Olivia's father in my heart. That's the way it's gotta be."

I stand in the front door of my home while Dean starts up his truck and backs up off my lawn. Jim Marinelli from up the street is watering his moonflowers and watching with avid interest. Idling in the street, Dean leans across the front seat and shouts something to me. Since I can't hear, I wander down off the steps and out towards his truck. "It was good to see you, E! But don't call me anymore, okay? I'm going to try to make it to the two year big penny."

Good to see you, E. Like we've just had lunch at the mall after a fun morning of shopping for shoes. Jeeze.

My phone is ringing when I get back in the house. "Elaine? It's Callie. Did I wake you?"

Now here's a friend that understands that on a Saturday morning at eleven fifteen a.m. there is still a possibility that I may be asleep. "No, I'm awake."

"Oh good, because I need you really clear headed when I ask you this favor." Callie chuckles in the phone. "I don't want you to have any reason to change your mind."

"I can't guarantee how clear headed I am since Dean showed up at five a.m. this morning, parked his truck on my lawn, and passed out on my living room couch."

"Dean? As in Dean ex-husband Kelly?" Her voice is filled with amazement and not a little bit of juicy gossip intrigue.

"I don't think I know any other Dean but that one." I let a big, world-weary sigh pour out of my lungs. "It's been a long morning."

"You okay?"

"Yeah. No. Ah, hell. I don't know." I hesitate and then take a tentative step toward disclosure and nitroglycerin elimination in the most trusted arena I know. "It involves deep dark secrets that even you don't know."

That keeps Callie quiet for a good thirty seconds. I can just imagine her mentally scrolling through the list of amazing revelations I've shared with her over the twenty-four years we've been friends. We met my first year of teaching. For me to imply that there is still some secret in my past that she doesn't know is akin to me revealing that I'm actually the secret love child of Willie Nelson. "You want to talk about it?"

"Eventually I'm going to have to." Before Dean gets drunk again and parks on Olivia's lawn.

"But not now," says my wonderful friend who recognizes my tone and knows not to push.

Maybe I should practice getting up the courage to say it out loud to myself in the privacy of my own home first? "No, not now. I just can't. But, unfortunately, as I'm not currently hooked up with a therapist who can help me through this traumatic stage of my existence, you're going to be the one that gets to hear it first."

"Ooookay. Whenever you're ready, so am I." I hear Callie take a deep breath. "Can I still ask you what I was going to ask?"

"I think I am supposed to say 'no' for my own personal safety and sanity ..." Callie's a good friend. She waits. Grudgingly I say, "Yeah, okay."

"I need you to come with me tonight to the church concert."

I sigh. We've been here before: Callie trying to save my mortal soul by repeated invitations to various church functions. It's my fault, I guess, because sometimes I encourage her by going along. When I'm bored out of my skull, fed up with my nonexistent social life, and angry at myself for staying in the house by myself for days on end. "Callie, I really don't want to go tonight. It's been a long day and it's not quite noon yet."

"Elaine, *you've got to go*. It's that concert I told you about with James' band."

Actually, Callie's husband James' band is pretty good. They write some of their own stuff but also play a lot of other stuff. It's Callie who's gotten me to listen to something I never in a million years thought I'd enjoy: Christian rock. In the last few years I've gotten hooked on Jars of Clay, Jennifer Knapp and Audio Adrenaline to name a few. I find the words can sometimes cut right to the heart of everything that is honest ... and messed up about my life. Add in a good rocking beat and a block of time with my sewing machine and I'm one jammin', rockin', sewin' babe. "Why's my presence so important? James does concerts all the time without me."

35

"Well, you know how it is after the concerts with me running around and having to deal with all of the tearing down, packing up, hopefully selling CDs, and possibly booking some new dates. Tonight there's that new guitar player I told you about and James and I got talking and we thought that maybe afterwards ... well ... you could hang out with the guy and help him feel comfortable seeing as it's his first time with the band and he won't know anybody."

"This is a fix-up?!" I scream into the phone. *"No way!"* I take a deep breath and then say with fixed determination, "Callie, I've got just one more *week* before I'm back at work and one more *day* of watching Liam, and I'm going to grab all the enjoyable downtime I can get. That DOES NOT include making nice with some awkward, geeky musician who is alone because of *God knows* how many bizarre habits or untreatable issues. And if that isn't bad enough, this fix up is at a *church* concert filled with hundreds of people who are out to get their hooks into me. It's bad enough that a bunch of people at your church now know me already from the number of times you've conned me into showing up. NO CALLIE. NO."

Callie's laughter fills my ear. "Come on, Elaine, let it all out. Tell me how you *really feel.*" At my continued silence she starts with the sly, backdoor tactics that have had some success in the past. "I asked *you* because you're my *best friend*" (which is true, but only because I'm very selective and she's qualified in most areas) "and I thought it would be an opportunity for just the *two of us*" (this is a blatant con as it's always 'the two of us' as I refuse to be third wheel with her and her husband) "to have a little fun together. We've hardly seen each other at all this summer," (that's because she's a beach bum and my sewing machine does really poorly in sand and salt water) "and I just thought that now that I'm back home we could have some *quality* time" (as opposed to just plain ole useless time, I suppose) "together."

I roll my eyes even though she can't see the gesture. "How are we going to have this great, just-the-two-of-us quality time when we're sitting at a concert unable to speak, and then afterwards I'm forced to interact with some unattached Neanderthal?"

With the smarminess of a used car dealer, Callie says, "Well, part of the quality time is communing with God by enjoying the beauty of nature and spiritually uplifting music while making your best friend happy and solving all of her problems."

"I haven't dated since Richard, Callie. *There's a reasons for that.* I don't want to become involved with anyone, *not even for one lousy evening.* That's how I stay happy, sane, and safe."

Now Callie shifts into the tough-love friend. "Elaine, when you finished that grief counseling – almost three years ago I'll remind you because I know you're not keeping track but I am – you were told to 'get out' and 'make an effort to start living' again. Aside from ten months out of the year when you're a wild and crazy fifth grade teacher I don't see that happening. I see you hiding behind your sewing machine stitching your life away." At my silence, she tries one last ditch effort, "Come on, Elaine, it's important. James doesn't want to loose this guy and wants him to feel really comfortable with everything tonight. Apparently, he's a fantastic musician. I haven't seen James this excited in a long time."

I sigh and before I can give in and say yes Callie lets out a whoop of astronomical proportions. "Yeah! I knew you'd do it! We'll pick you up at five and go out for a quick bite to eat -"

"Oh no you don't! I'll show up at the concert – you can save me a seat - once it's dark and I don't have to look at all of his scars, twitches, and drooling. If he's sitting up there on stage scratching himself or acting like he's God's gift to the world then he can just keep company with his own wonderful self. I'll only be there at the end of the concert to "keep him company" if first impressions are tolerable. Take it or leave it. Don't even tell him I'm coming. That way, if I don't show he won't be disappointed."

"Uh … I … a, I can't do that," my very best friend in the whole wide world says to me. "Apparently, James has already mentioned that you were coming and kind of described you and well, Alec's looking forward to meeting you."

I puzzle over this for a moment or two. "What did James say about me that would have caused this guy to look forward to meeting me?" Is this guy so desperate that the fact that I'm alive and have my own teeth enough to make him start humming the wedding march?

"Hang on, I'll ask." I hear the phone being shifted and then Callie yelling, "James! What did you tell Alec about Elaine? She wants to know!" I can hear James' indistinct voice in the background and then Callie saying in a shocked tone, "You didn't!" and then more talking from James. Finally, Callie comes back on the line. "James told him that you have a great sense of humor and a quick wit."

Yeah, sure. That sounds exactly what one man would say to another man when describing a potential dating situation. "What else?" I've got my 'don't-mess-with-me-or-you've-got-a-week-of-detention' tone going on now because suddenly this is very, very important to me.

Callie says with great care, "He mentioned that you were pretty and that you didn't look your age."

Sure he did. "What were James' *exact* words, Callie?"

Callie takes on a rather desperate, pleading tone. The teacher in me knows I've got her where I want her. "I can't tell if James is kidding or not. You know he's got a wicked sense of humor. If this Alec is the same way then it would just be the way they would naturally joke around with each other. It wouldn't mean anything."

"*Callie …*"

"James says he told Alec that you were stacked, had been married a few times, and he was pretty sure you'd put out by the second date."

I let out an explosive burst of horrified laughter. *"James said that?"*

Now I can hear James shouting in the background and Callie covers the mouthpiece. Finally she comes back on and says, "I'm supposed to assure *you* that Alec knew it was a joke."

"Yeah, well, then James, Alec, and *the entire church* should get a kick out of the leather miniskirt, bustier top, and five inch spiked heals I'm going to wear. That should make me easy to spot in the concert crowd."

Callie giggles. "I'll tell James. The concert starts at seven-thirty. I'll save you a seat."

I can't believe I've agreed to this. "You both owe me one."

"Thanks, Elaine."

I take a nap so that I'm sharp as a rusty tack for tonight's fun. It is not an exaggeration that I haven't dated anyone since Richard's death. Nor have I had the desire to. I know, I know, who's Richard you're asking? Well, Richard Brockman was my third husband.

Sigh. That's it. There were only three husbands. I would like to think that the reason I've had three husbands is not because I was loose, gullible, or immoral but rather because I am eternally optimistic, full of hope for the future, and always willing to try to find the good in mankind. (Go ahead and laugh, I sure am.) From Dean I learned about my strength of character and my ability to accomplish things at all costs. From Paul I learned that rather than *try* to change to please others you should only *determine* to change to suit yourself. And from Richard I learned that your life is only as precious as you choose to make it.

Richard was quiet, studious, thoughtful and reliable. He didn't drink, had held the same job for almost twenty-five years when I met him, *was not* in the psychological field, and seemed for all intents and purposes fantastically normal and well adjusted. In other words, the exact opposite of my first two husbands. He wasn't handsome. He wasn't particularly outgoing. He certainly wasn't dynamic. We met on a blind date that a teaching colleague set up, and although there were never any wild, passionate sparks, we hit it off quite nicely right from the start.

My still optimistic heart looked at his solid dependability and thought *now here's someone that I can spend a lifetime with.* Sigh. Oh yeah, I also learned how much maturing I still had to go through during my marriage to Richard.

Life was pretty good (once again) for the girls and me when Richard and I first started dating. I was thirty-three (having divorced Paul after only three disastrous years of marriage at the age of twenty-nine) living in the luxury of a full time teacher's salary *and* a very nice bit of alimony.

Thanks to my time with Paul, the girls and I were living in a real, honest-to-goodness-mortgage-financed home. Olivia was seventeen and full of raging adolescent angst, anger, and hormones. Erin, at fifteen, had already realized that the path of being noticed through controversy had already been more than adequately filled by Olivia, and had chosen the studious, cooperative, shy route instead.

At the time that Richard came on the scene, I was working hard trying to salvage some kind of relationship with Olivia while at the same time preventing Erin from completely disappearing into the woodwork. In retrospect, I am amazed at my moronic perception of what I really needed in a relationship. Once again, I grabbed hold to the "exact opposite" mantra and decided to pledge my life (and my daughters) to a man whose greatest appeal was that he was nothing like my two strike-outs thus far.

Richard brought no chaos of drunken unpredictability into our life. In fact, he rarely wanted to leave his lifetime routine of faithfully working at a job he loathed only to come home to an existence that, in his words, "made no difference to anyone." Assuming the responsibility of being a husband to me and a pseudo-father to Olivia the Terror and Erin the Nonexistent taxed his already shaky grip on his painfully low self-confidence. In addition, where only a few short years ago I had struggled to exist with a man like Paul who felt my skills were so negligent that I needed instructions on how to choose a proper drinking glass and dress myself appropriately when going out in public, Richard felt I continually outstripped him in everything from car maintenance to professional accomplishments.

It became easier to not talk, not react, not make plans, and not cry. Conversation always led to blame, any reactions were always wrong, and any future plans merely guaranteed disappointment. When I found out that Richard kept track of my "tear ratio" as he called it (days I cried versus days I didn't) I knew I was in big trouble. Once again, my best intentions were obviously not going to happen as expected.

I hadn't honestly (to the best of my recollection) considered divorcing Richard. Yes, I was stunned at what a bad situation I'd gotten myself trapped in – yet again – due to my eternally optimistic search for that "happily ever after" ending. I had begun (through therapy) to recognize just how detrimental my marriage to Richard was to both the girls and myself. I had begun to realize that my emotional shutdown to avoid confrontations was not only going to fail but perhaps permanently sever anything I hoped to hold on to with Olivia. I had just reached a point in my extensive psychological analysis where I was prepared to sit down with Richard and set some non-negotiable ground rules. And then Richard took care of everything in one fell swoop.

He killed himself.

Some find their solace in a bottle of gin,
Some find it still better when their horse comes in,
It's a way to deal when life ain't grand,
You just a-pack-it-up, hang your head and fold your hands.[9]

Chapter 5: You're Never Too Old For Nasty Surprises

As you might imagine, Richard owns another entire mental guilt storage container. He wrote me a long letter that arrived in the mail days after he took every prescription antidepressant in the house: his, mine, and Olivia's. It's a rambling ten page (both sides) legal size handwritten manifesto filled with apologies, observations, accusations, broken dreams, lost hopes and … words of love for me. He quoted poetry and wrote about things he'd hoped we'd get to do one day … He remembered with poignant clarity our first date, the first time we made love, our wedding day, and the few early vacations we went on with the girls when we still thought things were going to go the happily-ever-after route.

It is a letter from a man whom in the entire five years of our marriage I never met even once.

How could that be? How could I have lived with, slept with, made love with a person that I never even *knew?* The inevitable thoughts of what I could have done differently, my culpability, and a thousand other depressing scenarios roared through my head for a long time afterwards. Years of therapy, goodly doses of Prozac, Callie's faithful friendship, and my *decision to never get involved romantically again* is what brings me here to who I am now: adequately confident, above average tough, cautiously cynical, and *happily alone*.

So why am I standing in my closet trying to pick out an outfit that will impress a man I do not want to meet? Why have I shaved my legs and armpits, spritzed on my favorite almond perfume, worked carefully at my make-up, and selected the black cropped trousers that I know my butt looks best in? *Why?* Because old habits apparently do die hard and I've still, apparently, got some wisdom to acquire.

Callie's church is a short drive from both our homes. I park in the gravel parking lot and the heavy base beat of the music drifts towards me across the humid night air. I hear a moment of silence and then a rush of clapping and wolf-whistles as one song ends and then another begins.

What am I doing here? I ask to myself as I make my way towards the action. *Doing a friend a favor,* my head answers back. Callie's faithfulness to me and the girls after Richard's suicide has, in truth, given her the right to request *anything* of me and still have me in the red.

I walk across the church lawn towards the lovely sounds of a lone guitar strumming a quiet ballad. Adults and children alike are sprawled on the grass on blankets and in lawn chairs lit by the casually strung white Christmas tree lights that have been draped in the surrounding trees. Sitting on the center stage is a man, hunched over his guitar singing quietly into a microphone. I cannot see his face, just his broad shoulders encased in a worn tee shirt. He taps his foot in rhythm to the tune that drifts out of his guitar. His warm baritone flows out across the ground towards me, wraps up around my legs and crawls right into the center of my soul. As I get caught up in the atmosphere and the words I feel a little like the toddler-in-arms next to me staring at the stage awestruck, drooling, and silent.

Did you smile when You made the moon and gave the sky its color?
Did creation dance in rhythm to Your song of life, I wonder?
Did the angels know You knew my name before I existed?
Did You tell them out of all You made why You gave me Your image?
Is it true I'm Your heartbeat and You love me more than anything?

43

What sacred delight!
What infinite wonder!
That I'm precious in Your sight, You love me like no other.
No other.
Oh, sacred delight.

Did You think of me the day You died that I would dare intend this?
Did You know one day I'd come to You in search of Your forgiveness?
Is it true I'm Your heartbeat, and You chose to die than to live without me?

What sacred delight!
What infinite wonder!
That I'm precious in Your sight, You love me like no other.
No other.
Sacred delight! [10]

There is another explosion of clapping, whistles, and cheers and I am startled to discover myself standing in what can only be described as a mesmerized stupor. I hear my name called over the clapping and see Callie waving frantically and pointing to an empty lawn chair set up right next to her. Weaving my way through the crowd I settle myself down as she grabs my arm and gestures towards the lone guitar player bowing to the appreciative crowd and then shuffling back to blend in with the band as it prepares for another number. "That's Alec," she says with a delighted grin. "He's not bad, huh? And *can he sing.* I've only spoken with him briefly, but he seems nice enough."

I look at Callie's smiling face and then back at Alec as he watches James count out the beat and start the next song. First, he stuns me with the beautiful song and poignant words, and then he stuns me with his face. I'm speechless in shock as I sit there trying to pull myself together. The new song is a rocking, hopping tune and soon the little ones around me (and some of the big ones) are bopping to the beat. "*Shine! Make 'em wonder what you've got! Make 'em wish that they were not, on the outside looking bored. Shine! Let it shine before all men! Let 'em see good works and then, let 'em glorify the Lord!*" [11]

Callie nudges me, needing some verbal confirmation. "Hey? Are you okay? Glad you came yet?"

44

I'm really not sure how okay I am or glad I came. I don't know what has me more flustered: the words to Alec's ballad or Alec himself. For you see, I had no idea that my nasty meter reader could sing.

I sit absolutely silent throughout the concert and never take my eyes off Alec. Seated next to Callie, it's obvious who I have to be, and I want him to have every opportunity to prepare himself for our inevitable encounter. It's not until towards the very end of the concert when our eyes lock and he winks at me that I realize he's already dealt with it and handled this nasty shock with hardly a thought.

There is a standing ovation and a demand from the crowd for an encore. The band confers and then Alec and James step forward to the mike with their guitars. "We're happy to have spent the evening with you," James says to the appreciative crowd. "Here's one last one to carry home with you." He and Alec then proceed to sing without musical accompaniment of any kind another beautiful ballad that their voices wrap around and throw out into the night:

> *"I can feel Your presence here with me,*
> *Suddenly I'm lost within Your beauty,*
> *Caught up in the wonder of Your touch,*
> *Here in this moment I surrender to Your love …*[12]*"*

Afterwards, there is coffee and cake, lemonade and brownies and a general churchy camaraderie that I always feel when I visit Callie's church. Early visits had me worrying that they were going to try to recruit me or convert me or something but I have to honestly say that in all the times I've visited here I've only just felt … welcome. Of course, tonight, I am loaded with tension over the fact that my nasty meter reader – AKA Alec – is my pseudo date and I'm supposed to make him feel comfortable and at ease in this unfamiliar setting. Considering how unsuccessful I've been in the comfort and security *of my own home*, I don't exactly have confidence going into all this.

"So you must be Elaine," I finally hear from behind me and turn around to look into Alec's intent gaze.

I nod. "Do we pretend we're just meeting for the first time or do we acknowledge that we have history?" I mentally cringe as I suppose that my initial comment sounds rather confrontational.

Callie is immediately there oozing enthusiasm and eternal hope for the future. She's caught my comment and frowns in confusion. "You two know each other?"

"Not by name," Alec says cryptically.

Since I've posed a question that he's not answered I stay silent. Finally, Alec volunteers to Callie although he's still looking only at me, "I'm her meter reader."

"Her meter reader?" Callie says with not a little bit of amazement. She turns and looks at me and I suspect is remembering brief moments in times past when I've complained about the "careless utility puke with the muddy boots who is rude, nasty, and a general pain in my ass."

"I'm disappointed," Alec says to me with a small smile. "I heard you were wearing leather and a bustier tonight."

"I usually save that for the second date when I put out." I hear myself say. As Callie gasps out a shocked laugh and claps her hand over her mouth I think, *God, this man brings out the absolute worst in me.*

"Guess I'll have to be on my best behavior to assure I make it to that second date then," Alec says with a lazy grin.

"Well, make sure it's not a church sponsored concert. I do have my standards, you know."

He grins at me again. "That's good to know."

I hear James urgently calling Callie's name. Even though Alec and I are still doing our stare down contest I can see out of the corner of my eye Callie look in her husband's direction and then back at us. "Look, James needs me. Are you two okay?" She grabs my arm and squeezes. *"Are you going to behave?"*

Alec arches one eyebrow intrigued, I suppose, with the myriad of possibilities implied by that question. "I always behave," I say to both Callie and Alec in a superior tone, "exactly the way I deem to be most appropriate at the time."

"Oh great," Callie says with real dread.

"More than I hoped for," Alec says with unexplained delight.

Awkward moments ensue with Callie's departure. I'm finally forced to observe, "You don't seem to be someone who needs the presence of another individual to be comfortable in unfamiliar situations."

"Is that why Callie and James asked you to come tonight?" he says as he gestures towards the food tables and then starts walking before I agree or disagree. Without offering, he pours us both a cup of black coffee.

"It's not the reason?" I smile and nod politely to some unknown woman who touches my arm and says, "Oh! It's so good to see you again!"

"It was nice of them to make the effort," is all he'll acknowledge. "Want a brownie?"

"No thanks."

He proceeds to help himself to one and with what could almost be described as sensual delight takes long moments to savor the entire crumbly, chocolately square. Helping himself to another *two* pieces before he walks away, Alec says to me, "I'm a bit of a chocoholic."

We settle down in the chairs that Callie and I had occupied earlier. We watch the ebb and flow of the people as they chat and laugh easily with each other. "Do you attend church here?" he asks to fill our silence.

Shaking my head vigorously, I say, "No, Callie's always trying to get me to come but I'm a master of avoidance."

"Except tonight."

I look at him. "Except tonight." I *will not* have him thinking that I'm desperate for some misguided match-up. "She called in a favor so I couldn't refuse."

"Must have been a big favor, huh?"

I shrug. "I've got a huge personal debt." I look at him. "You didn't seem too surprised to see me tonight. How come?"

Alec looks off into the crowd. He's got a nice profile: lots of laugh lines fanning out from his eyes, straight nose, strong chin, nice mouth … He's not what you would call handsome; he's got a seasoned look about him that says he's lived life to the fullest - had some good times and some bad. His hair – more gray than black is long enough that even though it curls it touches the collar of his tee shirt. "I gave up trying to control my life a while ago. Now I just drift along waiting for the inevitable surprises." He chuckles at an apparent private joke. "Here I am, for the first time *in ages* allowing myself to be fixed up with a woman, and it turns out to be you." He lets his head drop onto the chair back and laughs again, harder. And this time he shakes his head in apparent disbelief.

"What's that supposed to mean?" I say, not liking at all where he seems to be going.

"Well, it's not like we've endeared ourselves to each other any of the times we've spoken. What, we've had like five or six encounters over the past year. Has *any one moment* ever been positive? Polite? Friendly? In fact, I'd say we've got about as much potential for romance as Queen Elizabeth and Crocodile Dundee." Without picking his head up, he rolls right to look me in the eye. "Come on. You've got to have a nickname for me. Let's hear it. I've got one for you."

I'm trying to decide if I should be insulted having just been compared to the Queen of England who is decidedly stuffy, aloof, and in her eighties. I turn to look out into the night. "Yeah, I do. You'd better stick with Crocodile Dundee. It's a heck of a lot nicer."

He chuckles a deep, throaty sound that I feel all the way down to my toes. "I bet you do. Come on. Tell me. I'm a big boy. I can take it."

I look at him and he's grinning at me again. He is casual and relaxed and seems to not have a care in the world. Does meter reading really make you that miserable? Or, and here's a really terrible thought, is it just showing up at *my house* that makes him so miserable?

"I call you Nasty Meter Man."

He snorts. "Not too original. I'd expected much better from you."

I fight the urge to say 'what's that supposed to mean?' again since it did me little good the last time I said it.

"I call you *Criticóna*," he says with a perfect Spanish inflection.

Something tells me I'm not going to like the translation.

"It means 'sharp tongued.' I thought that fit you nicely."

To respond in the manner to which I so strongly desire would be to reinforce the nickname I find so objectionable. I take the high road and say in a snooty tone, "You get back what you give out." Glancing down at my empty wrist, I curse myself for not thinking to wear a watch.

"Almost ten," he says and then baits me with, "Gotta run so soon?"

"As the reason I was asked to come was specifically to keep you company and make you feel comfortable in this unfamiliar setting – despite my total aversion to anything even hinting of romance – it seems pointless for me to stay." I look around for Callie to wave good-bye.

"Now that doesn't make any sense to me," he murmurs, "since you *are* helping me feel comfortable in this unfamiliar setting *and* you should *never* count yourself out of the romance category. Although somehow Nasty Meter Man and *Criticóna* are even less of a potential love match than Queenie and the Croc guy."

"Have you ever been married?" I grind out.

"Nope."

"Long term relationship?"

"Nope."

"Ever lived for an extended time with the human race?"

Alec chuckles and nods. "Yes. I have done that on occasion."

"Was that time spent in prison?" I say with loads of acerbic sarcasm.

He looks at me pointedly for a number of moments but doesn't answer. I feel the spit dry up in my mouth as he sits up. "Now *that* question," he says leaning in towards me, "is something I only answer on a second date." He gives me a slow, sensual wink. "Once I've got the leather skirt and bustier off. *Once you've put out.*" And then he *kisses me* right on the mouth.

My sharp tongue rolls right up into the roof of my mouth and I sit there speechless as he stands, walks over to the stage, picks up his guitar and saunters away into the darkness.

The weight of worry is never worth the price
Of a world of treasures that can never satisfy.[13]

Chapter 6: There Better Be A Light At The End Of This Tunnel

Given what's happened over the last few days, you must be thinking that I lead an exceptionally interesting existence with all these men waltzing in and out of my life. Hardly. Remember, two of them I spent thousands of dollars to get rid of and one of them I've nicknamed *nasty*.

Sundays are pretty much the same during the summer break or the school year: I sleep late, catch up on necessary chores and then travel on over to Erin's for Sunday dinner. An exceptional Sunday at Erin and Dan's includes Olivia's appearance, few (if any) references to any one of my many personal catastrophes, and copious quantities of laughter. A disastrous Sunday at Erin and Dan's includes Olivia's enraged departure, an addition to the extensive list of my personal disasters, and Liam mentioned in the same sentence with the words fire, blood, or vomit.

I enter Erin and Dan's house to find Liam on a stepstool at the kitchen counter. "I'm cutting up vegables, Minnie!" he says with a huge pile of delight. All I can think of is, *they've given him a knife?!* I relax when he waves a piece of red pepper and a butter knife at me.

"Excellent, little man! Got a piece I can munch on?" He hands me a mangled piece of pepper that I immediately pop in my mouth.

"Hey, Mom." Erin gives me a kiss on the cheek and Dan gives me a welcome grin while handing Liam another piece of pepper to mangle.

"What's for dinner, Liam? Are you cooking?" I lean over to give his silky head a kiss.

"Daddy and me are making stir fry."

"That's what boys do," I say with a wink at Erin, "they cook!"

Never having excelled at, embraced, or even enjoyed cooking, my job at these Sunday dinners is always clean-up crew. I sit down at the kitchen counter and fall into the welcome pattern of idle chitchat with people that (for reasons I can't quite fathom) love me unconditionally.

If a complete video diary of my life were available, I suppose I would be able to watch it over and over again (with expert analysis and commentary) and figure out why I have a great relationship with one daughter and a lousy relationship with another. Even casual acquaintances would see some of the major differences between my two girls: Erin has Dean's coloring (dark blonde with blue eyes) while Olivia has … darker hair and eyes. Erin leans toward the 'willowy', while Olivia is deliciously voluptuous. Erin followed my passion for teaching while Olivia tackled Big Business and is a financial planner for a large accounting firm. Erin married, Olivia stayed single.

Spending even a brief amount of time talking with the girls will reveal even more differences. Erin leans towards listening and questioning while Olivia has a talent for sharp observations and is never at a loss for words. With Erin you can relax, while with Olivia you feel compelled to sit up straight. Erin says, "Mom, I bought you a new purse I thought you'd like." Olivia says, "Mom, that purse makes you look like a bag lady. How many years have you been hauling that thing around?"

I know *now* I behave differently with them. With Olivia I eternally feel like I am walking on eggshells. Let's face it; each conversation has the potential to cause death or at least dismemberment. Erin and I have loads of safe topics to delve into: marriage (her success and my failures), teaching (mutual joys and frustrations), and Liam (comic relief).

But what I'd like to view, in that impossible video diary, were times when the girls were little. How much of our relationship today is nature and how much of it is nurture? Surely during my time with Dean, even though the girls were young, Olivia has to have memories of tears, drunken displays, and screaming fights between every adult in the household. For me, focusing on surviving and *getting out*, I'm sure there were *years* where Olivia felt that the only one she had to rely on was herself. With Paul, Erin would have been young enough to just enjoy his novel male presence while Olivia, I'm sure, would have resented his stepping into Dean's shoes. Paul's greatest damage was to me, personally. So while I struggled with the mental and emotion destruction of who and what I was as a person, I can honestly say that the most I could do for the girls was to make sure they were fed and clothed. By the time Richard came on the scene, Olivia was already rolling her eyes at my ineptness at life in general while Erin was working hard at not rocking the boat anymore than it already was. Both girls were away at college when Richard ended his life.

Somewhere over that roller coaster of years I came to understand that Erin was always going to be easy and Olivia was always going to be difficult. And while I honest to God love them both equally, there were many ... times ... when I only had enough in me to deal with Erin's easiness. Which left Olivia ... alone.

Sigh. Welcome to the largest and most horrible of all my mental guilt containers. Were this one to be labeled, it would say *Toxic, Soul-Destroying Thoughts: Never Open.*

Sometimes I hope that Olivia won't show up at Erin's for Sunday dinner.

Sometimes I hope that Olivia will just completely give up on her relationship with me, flip me the middle finger, and walk off into the sunset.

Sometimes I wish ...

Oh, God. I was going to write: *sometimes I wish that Olivia was ... not who she is ... that she was a completely different child.*

A different Olivia could mean no nitroglycerin secret. A different Olivia could have meant no marriage to Dean, which would have meant no lost years struggling to maintain my sanity. A different Olivia could mean a substantial reduction in my mental guilt containers. A different Olivia could mean simplicity.

When I am foolish enough to open this terrible place in my head and my heart (hey, everyone does self-flagellation now and then), I force myself to follow the train of horrible thoughts right to the end. The eternally optimistic idiot that I am *must believe* that there *has* to be a light at the end of this horrible, endless, distructive tunnel that is my relationship with Olivia.

Am I one of those people that has to have brutal life lessons in order to grow and improve? One thing the therapist told me (after Richard's death) was at least I never repeated my mistakes. I didn't perpetually get involved with only alcoholics or personality destroying psychologists. No, once I burned myself on those hot stoves I stayed away for good. The therapist said that *that showed positive growth.* I took that to heart.

Which brings me to the concluding train of thought in the Olivia guilt box: everything I've gone through – good and bad – is worth it in the end if I continue positive growth for myself. Right? Right. And regarding *this* situation, while I'm working on my personal growth meter, if I gain an opportunity to make Olivia happy – even briefly – wouldn't that be an enormous success? As Olivia is still the toughest point in my life, if I can handle this, with my daughter to a successful conclusion, then that's *got to* bring with it a pile of positive growth.

At some point, I've got to be done don't I?

While we're laughing at a 'Liamism' as we call it, Olivia arrives. I watch my eldest daughter give kisses and hugs to Liam, Hollywood kisses to Erin and Dan, and a curt nod to me.

"Hey, Olivia," I manage with as much bright optimism as possible, "you're just in time for Liam's stir fry!" Liam waves his butter knife and a mangled piece of celery to prove his involvement.

Patting Liam on the head, Olivia says with regret, "I can't stay for dinner, Liam. I'm sorry. I just came to speak with Minnie and then I'm off." She looks at me pointedly. "Can we talk, Mother?"

"Olivia," Erin says in a low voice, "I thought you said you were going to talk with Mom privately?" She glances down at Liam then between the two of us. Clearly, Erin doesn't want her son to witness bloodshed at this tender age.

"I was hoping Mom and I could have a *quiet* talk in the living room. In the end, after thinking things through again, I thought that it might be better to have you and Dan nearby."

"But -," Erin begins to say but I interrupt her.

"It's okay, Erin," I say in a resigned voice. I can almost guarantee that this will qualify as The Most Disastrous Sunday Dinner Ever.

My daughter and I walk silently into the living room. She sits stiffly on one of the two matching wingchairs while I settle down on the couch. I just stare at her. It's her show after all, not mine.

"Paul said you refused to give him any of the information he requested." *Tell me something I don't know.* "Why?" Olivia demands.

I shrug. "It's none of his business."

"He was doing that as a favor to me." I want to ask, *Since when have you been on good enough terms with Paul to request him to do favors for you?* but I realize that won't benefit this current situation. So I stay silent.

"I've been in therapy for about six months now," Olivia begins, "and I'm working through a lot of my issues that are all firmly rooted in my childhood." I hear *lousy* childhood even if she doesn't actually say it. "One of my primary complaints is that I never, *ever* felt a part of the family in looks, behavior, likes, dislikes ... *anything!* It was my idea to have a DNA test done between me and ... Dean."

Again, what do I say? After a few moments of silence I finally say, "I know what you want from me, Olivia. But I'm sorry, I can't give it to you."

"It's just a name, Mother." Olivia hisses at me in a tone that implies I'm being purposefully cruel just because I choose to be.

54

I start to tremble, but if I hold my hands tightly clasped it doesn't show. "No Olivia. It is not *just a name*. It is the entire directional force of my life since your moment of conception." Doesn't she get that if it were *just a name* I would have sung it from the highest rooftops long ago?

"What?" she says in a harsh tone. "Aren't you sure? Are there a number of candidates?" She waves her hand and four golden bracelets jingle together. "Just give me a list. I'll take it from there."

I see Dean's tear-stained face the other day and hear him saying to me across the breakfast table, *I think I know where Steve Cantilone lives.* I have a flash of my mother's face, filled with loathing, as she says, *It's always about you Elaine, isn't it?* I look at my daughter's expression and find the *lack of* loathing or sorrow or any real emotion even more upsetting. *She's not surprised at all. She's always expected the worst from me.* "I will not give you the name," I stress the singularity of the word, "because I ..."

Why? Am I afraid? Embarrassed? Horrified? With my hands clasped in my lap to still their trembling, I feel my head start to pound and my stomach start to clench. It's fear, I realize. Fear of exposing the very worst of what I ever was in my whole existence. Something that's so bad I can't voice it or write about it *to my very best friend or even myself.* If I can't do that, how can I tell it to this young woman sitting across from me who seems barely able to abide the sight of me? If I'm going to rip my heart out and slowly bleed to death, I'd at least like to do it in the presence of someone who'd be sorry to see me go.

"Because why, Mother?"

I look at my daughter and say, "I love you, Olivia. Do you believe that?"

Olivia turns her head and looks out one of the front windows. "As much as you are capable of, yes."

Ouch. I mentally sigh. How many times in her life did she receive concrete proof of that statement? I close my eyes at the tidal wave of grief and guilt that washes over me. "Do you love me?"

She looks at me. "You have to ask?"

I nod. "Yes. Yes, I do." Before she can respond, I clarify. "Not because I don't know if you do or you don't. Just because I never get to hear you say it." Her silence just about kills me.

I sigh and press on. "I know you are angry with me," I say. "I know you are critical of my choices, unhappy with many of my life decisions, hurt by my poor performance as a mother, and, at times, I think you are downright embarrassed at the person I am." I shrug. "You make every effort to detail all of those emotions loudly and clearly. I guess I'm just wondering how much love is left in all that."

Watching Olivia's face flush with fury convinces me I probably should have just kept my mouth shut. "How dare you! I've tolerated your lousy maternal instincts, your blatant favoritism towards Erin, your one-sided loyalties to what only you deem to be important, and your convenient memories regarding your extensive array of personal disasters!" Olivia is now standing, hands fisted at her side, shouting. Erin has run into the living room and is standing wide-eyed watching as her sister has a full-fledged meltdown on her living room carpet. Olivia takes a step towards me in fury. "You've never gone out of your way to do one, single thing just for me! *I'm just asking for a lousy name!* You don't have to give me details, explanations, excuses … *nothing.* Tell me and I'll gladly get out of your life! Forever! What's the big, goddamned deal anyway?" Leaning so close to me I feel her spittle on my face, she hisses, "Why can't you just, *for once in your miserable life,* do something just for me?"

At some point, as Olivia is standing screaming at me I realize that *this precise moment* is probably just as bad as the nitroglycerin secret exploding. It would seem that I've kept such a tight hold on everything that it's just squeezed out between my fingers and oozed out all over everything anyway.

Olivia is crying. Erin is crying. But I stand there before my daughters absolutely dry-eyed. Okay, okay, you want the real picture? Here it is. In a flat, emotionless voice I say, "I can't give you the name of your father because I do not know it, Olivia. I wouldn't recognize him on the street today, nor would I have the day after … your conception."

"You were fifteen years old, Mother," Olivia says through gritted teeth, *"and you were already sleeping around so much that you couldn't even keep track of whom you were with?"* She shakes her head in disgust. "No wonder grandmother never wanted to have anything to do with you."

There's not a speck of redemption in your worthless existence, Elaine.

"Yes," I murmur as I stand and get ready to bolt, "no wonder." I fish my car keys out of my short's pocket and take a deep breath. My chest is a gaping cavity where my heart once was as I stand in the glare of my daughter's loathing. "The only thing that came out of that time in my life that had any redeeming value or potential for joy was you, Olivia." I sigh and feel the start of tears, which urges me with significant haste towards the door. "But as you can see, just like all other things that are most important to me, I've managed to screw that up as well."

Cursing the quest, courting disaster,
Measureless nights forebode …[14]

Chapter 7: Fears For Today, Worries About Tomorrow

Where does one go after a show like that? If I were a drinking woman I would have headed right over to the closest bar to down a few stiff ones. I think briefly of my sewing machine, but it is a measure of just how low I am that my home and all it's comforts do not appeal.

I drive aimlessly for quite a while. My cell phone buzzes a couple of times and, in the end, I shut it off rather than ignore it. I consider a movie. I consider shopping. I consider getting a tattoo.

And then I have the most striking of all thoughts: *I am free.* There is really no more secret to keep. There are the gory details, but who wants to hear all of those? The terror of discovery is gone. Suddenly, I feel lighter than I have felt in as long as I can remember. Like giving birth and finally having that wave of *thank God that's over.*

And literally as I think those thoughts, I stop at a traffic light and to my right is a sign out front of a store that says, "How Free Are You? Come Experience The Freeing Joy of God's Love!"

I kid you not. That's what the sign said.

Why not? My head said suddenly. Why not take a stab? Turn over a new leaf? Write a new page? Jump off a cliff? I pull into the parking lot,

58

and before I can rethink my emotional stability walk briskly into the building.

It's the farthest thing from a church that my mind could have conjured up. The building is really a storefront that's been converted into a church. Light spills in from the big front windows illuminating a room filled with people of all shapes, sizes, and ages. Everyone's laughing and talking, waving and smiling. It's a large open room with a lightly patterned carpet with about seventy-five folding chairs neatly arranged around a front stage. I say stage because at the front appears to be a rock band tuning up and doing sound tests. No big crosses. No minister in flowing robes. No choir sitting solemnly in the back, dignified and holier-than-thou. Not even any fancy flower arrangements.

I sit in the chair farthest in the back. I have no worry about my shorts and general casual attire as everyone's dressed casually in summer clothes and flip-flops. The band has finished tuning up and begins to play a low, thrumming beat. There is lots of laughter and joking by one and all alike. Finally, a young woman in a purple tee shirt with a big white dove on the front climbs up the stairs and goes to the mike at the center of the stage. "The Lord be with you!" she shouts into the mike and everyone shouts back, "And also with you!"

That seems to be a signal, because all the people find seats quickly as the young woman then says, "Let's get this evening started!" The band bursts into song and immediately everyone is standing and singing to the words projected on the front wall. Some of the songs I recognize from some of the Christian rock CDs that Callie is always giving me.

I let the music begin to seep into me – filling me with its rhythm, and I get caught up, as I always do, with the words that sometimes knock me senseless. I don't sing but I stand and rock slowly back and forth and read. Like an onion, I feel the layers of me that keep all the deep, dark, sad, sorrowful, regretful, and miserable parts of me slowly, methodically peel back one piece at a time while I groove to the God tunes.

A young girl, she can't be more than seventeen, steps out on the center of the stage and everyone claps with ferocious encouragement before she even opens her mouth. As she sings, I feel the last of my onion layers stripped away and I feel completely bare:

I am clay and I am water
Falling forward in this order
While the world spins 'round so fast,
Slowly I'm becoming
Who I am.
Nothing ever stays the same
The wheel will always turn
I feel the fire in the change
But somehow it doesn't burn
Like a beggar blessed I stumble in the grace
Reaching out my hand for what awaits.
I will live from my heart
And I will catch the lines of love as they come
Back to You I know they'll lead
And into You I know I'll lean...[15]

There is thunderous applause and I miss whatever signal is given to make everyone sit down and be quiet. The same young woman of the purple shirt comes out front again, holds her hands up towards all of us and prays. Some people seated around me say "Amen" out loud and suddenly I'm wondering what I've gotten myself into. How did I get from Olivia screaming spittle onto my face to being surrounded by a pile of "Amen brothers"? I search for an exit while everyone's got closed eyes.

"I'm adopted you know," the woman says after she finishes her prayer. "My birthmother abandoned me when I was two days old - left me in a church sanctuary with a note pinned to me that said, "This is Crystal." She grins and looks around at her surroundings. "I guess I was destined to be a preacher, huh?" I'm stunned that she finds a point of levity but it is, after all, her story.

"Although I was adopted by a loving couple and given a relatively stable home life, many of you know my story. I spent a significant portion of my growing up years being angry and trying to prove my worth to anyone or anything who would take the time to notice me." Crystal tilts her head to the side and her long brown hair swings out behind her. "I really

60

wanted that nameless woman who abandoned me to regret what she did. I wanted her to feel pain, sorrow, and a level of personal angst that was deeper and harsher than my own."

Crystal steps down off the stage and walks out amongst the crowd. "Tell me this: how many of you would have regretted giving up a child who got involved with drugs, alcohol, and a gang? A child who was so violently angry that she spent two of her teen years in a juvenile lock-up facility?" She grins at all of us sitting silent and unresponsive. "Don't worry, there was a significant period of time when *I* didn't even want myself."

Walking back up onto the stage, Crystal says earnestly to the crowd, "I just wanted to be loved. Wanted. Despite my adoptive family's love, I just couldn't get over the fact that my birthmother had thrown me away." In a whisper voice she says to us, *"Isn't that what we all want?* To be honored, loved, wanted ... *treasured?* To have someone who really matters say, 'Good job', or 'Well done', or 'I knew you could do it', or – here's my personal favorite - 'I love you just the way you are.'"

I think back on my life rooted in my mother's disdain, my father's nonexistence, and my mistakes – some my own fault and some not – that seem to confirm my complete lack of value towards anyone that mattered. What would I have given to have had my mother, or Dean, or Paul, or Richard say those things to me and really, truly meant them? *I would have given absolutely anything* to have heard those things. *Anything.*

"Take a look at this verse," Crystal says, and behind her, where the words to the music had been flashes this: *No matter which way I turn, I can't make myself do right. I want to, but I can't. When I want to do good, I don't. And when I try not to do wrong, I do it anyway ... It seems to be a fact of life that when I want to do what is right, I inevitably do what is wrong.*[16]

Whoa. There's my whole life in a nutshell, I think in stunned amazement.

"The apostle Paul wrote this about himself. He made some really enormous mistakes over the course of his life, too. Like hunting down the new Jewish Christians and handing them over to be tortured and executed.

Paul was so into his crusade – thought he was *so right with what he was doing* - that the only way for God to get him to be on the right course was to *blind him* for a time to get him to sit down, shut up, and listen to the truth." Crystal chuckles. "Many of us are like that you know. God speaks in a still small voice but sometimes He needs to use a baseball bat with us to get us to sit down for a moment just to hear."

Crystal shrugs. "I needed jail time to get me to sit down, shut up, and listen. When I was in juvenile lock-up someone took the time to tell me The Truth. Someone took the time to explain for me the ultimate reality that I needed to know." Another set of words shine up behind her. *And we know that God causes everything to work together for the good of those who love God and are called according to His purpose for them.*[17]

"What got me most about this verse was the word *everything*. It doesn't say 'the good stuff' or 'the smart stuff' or 'all good choices' it promises *everything*. I remember thinking to myself (and I'll clean up my language because back then it was rather colorful) 'Are you telling me that God can make *good* come out of all the *bad?*'" Crystal chuckled and shook her head. "Forget about those walking on water miracles, forget about those changing water into wine miracles, forget about those five loaves and two fishes feeding five thousand miracles. Making *good* out of all my *bad* was a miracle of unimaginable proportions."

Shrugging and shoving her hands in her shorts pocket, Crystal said, "Cynical whatsit that I was, I figured *Why not give it a try? What have I got to loose? I'll give it a shot and see what happens.*" She grinned. "That was called a conditional commitment. *And it's not good enough.*"

The screen flashes *For all have sinned; all fall short of God's glorious standard. Yet now God in His gracious kindness declares us not guilty. He has done this through Christ Jesus, who has freed us by taking away our sins. We are made right with God when we believe that Jesus shed His blood, sacrificing His life for us.*[18]

"Made Right," Crystal says to us. "Did you get that? *Made right.*" She gives her words a moment to sink in and then says, "When I told you that I was adopted, I wasn't referring to my adoptive parents Tom and Laury Sanders – who loved me and never lost faith that someday I'd wise up and understand The Truth. I was talking about that decision I made to commit to God and all the love He was promising *me* by being a part of His family.

"How about this for a question?" Behind her the screen lights up with *If God is for us, who can ever be against us?* [19] "What do you think about that? How's that for power, support, and unconditional love? Huh?"

"It's a simple but very serious procedure." Crystal holds up her hand with three fingers extended. "Ask the Lord to take control of you and your life. Believe that He is the only one who can get you and your life on track. Confess that there is nothing you have done in the past that is worthy of this wondrous gift. Once you do that you're His. God claims you for His Own and you cannot become separated from Him."

The screen displays: *And I am convinced that nothing can ever separate us from His love. Death can't and life can't. The angels can't and the demons can't. Our fears for today, our worries about tomorrow, and even the powers of hell can't keep God's love away. Whether we are high above the sky or in the deepest ocean, nothing in all creation will ever be able to separate us from the love of God that is revealed in Christ Jesus our Lord.* [20]

"Let's talk to the Lord." Crystal begins to pray but I stare at the words that still shine on the screen behind her. *Our fears for today, our worries about tomorrow* ... God, that is my life in a nutshell, isn't it? My entire existence has swirled around the shadows of my lousy past that have threatened to overcast my todays and my tomorrows. Who knew there was stuff like this being spouted by ex-juvenile delinquents wearing big purple tee shirts in converted store fronts in downtown central New Jersey?

I miss the signal that dismisses all of us and with the determination of a pit bull begin to head towards the exit door before I get caught by some well-meaning churchie. But no such luck.

"If I didn't know any better," I hear murmured from behind me, "I'd think you were stalking me."

I turn around and look into Alec's smug face. "Here's an opportunity for me to see how smart you are," I hear myself say before I can think twice, "*do you know any better* or are you just not that astute enough?"

"Ahh, *Criticóna,* it's so good to have you here in church with me," he says with a grin as he takes my arm. "Come and have a moderately good cup of coffee and an absolutely fabulous piece of pastry."

I've recklessly built all my dreams in the sand
Just to watch them all wash away. [21]

Chapter 8: The Pervading Themes Of Life

Side doors from the church space have been thrown open to show a pastry shop and delicious aromas waft through to us. I can't decide if the coffee shop is an offshoot of the church or the church is an offshoot of the coffee shop.

"This isn't like any church I've ever heard of or seen," I say to myself but Alec responds.

"It's not supposed to be. It's supposed to be different and unique to attract people who don't normally feel comfortable or welcome or interested in the traditional style of church. During the week the coffee shop is an actual business that advertises the church while providing spectacularly delicious homemade pastries, and on Saturday and Sunday evenings the coffee shop is a place to hang after the services are over. Some people come only to the coffee shop and never go to the church and vice versa." Stepping into the bustling coffee shop, Alec seemed significantly pleased with life in general.

"Pastries make you much happier than meter reading it seems," I observe.

He grins and nods at me. "Always." Not exactly the answer I was expecting.

We find a table and sit. "What brings you here?" he asks.

I have a flash of Olivia's and Erin's tear stained faces. "Life," I say miserably and begin to feel the drag of the disaster of my existence.

"I'm not positive," Alec says, "but I think that's the main reason that most people show up at a church – no matter what the style it is."

"Do you attend here regularly?"

Nodding he says, "Pretty steady for the last six months or so. Sometimes I join the band but I'm not a regular. That's how James found me. He spoke with someone in the band and asked if they knew anyone who could play guitar and sing. They mentioned me and I agreed to give it a shot."

"Why not play steady for this church's band?"

Alec shrugged. "They're pretty set with what they're doing. James' band doesn't play as regularly. It suits my schedule."

"Meter reading takes a big cut out of your day ..." I say with flip sarcasm.

He doesn't get annoyed though; in fact he seems to enjoy the verbal sparring. "You best be careful. Making snap assumptions can cause severe embarrassment you know."

"One of the pervading themes of my life," I acknowledge.

"I'll go get us some coffee. What kind of pastry do you want? There are blueberry and strawberry tarts, cream cheese coffee cake with a hint of apple, raisin and apricot scones, chocolate–chocolate brownies with ..."

"Whoa, whoa! Just coffee's fine."

"Just coffee?" He says those two words like I've said the most awful phrase on the planet.

I look at him. "Yes. Just. Coffee."

"Alec! I'm sorry to interrupt, but we've got a *situation* in the back. Can you come?" A frazzled looking young woman with a blueberry stained apron stands panting by our table.

In a rather resigned tone, Alec says, "Yeah, Marie, I'll come." He glances at me. "Give me a minute, okay? I'll come back with coffee and ... well, maybe something you can sample. I won't be long." He stands and walks after Marie who's practically running towards the back of the shop. A few people call out to Alec as he follows Marie. He acknowledges them with waves and smiles.

Sitting at the table I take in the mass of humanity consuming thousands of empty calories and sipping coffee and tea. I have to admit that the empty calories do look delicious. I see two preteen girls flirting and giggling with a boy all gangly and blushing with inexperience. I see a toddler, whose entire face is a complete strawberry mess, sitting in his stroller screaming for more. A young woman with the same dark, curly hair as Olivia laughs at something an elderly woman says to her and responds loud enough for me to hear, "Oh do I love you, Mom!"

Suddenly, I'm right back where I was such a short time ago in Erin's living room: low, broken, and hopeless. Just as suddenly, I can no longer stand the ambiance of this well-meaning coffee shop. I've got to get out. Get fresh air. Find a new distraction. Escape the reality of my life.

Within minutes I'm driving in my car trying to find another place to offer me some escape, while knowing full well the awful truth that there's no where that fits the bill.

By the time I drag myself home, it's dark and the motion sensor lights give me a brilliant welcome. As I pull into the driveway I can see a white bag sitting on my front step. Rather than go in through the garage entrance I wander around to the front steps. Inside the bag I find a number of things: a carefully wrapped slice of what appears to be cream cheese and apple filled crumb cake, two carefully folded pieces of paper, and a magnet that says *Agape Shop: Outstanding Food For The Soul.*

As I munch on the crumb cake, which is almost a religious experience with its moist, sweet, creamy flavors dancing around in my mouth, I look at the two papers. One lists all of the fellowship opportunities over the next month: music performances, small group Bible studies and their topics, and lastly the schedule of church services. I smile at the handwritten note at the bottom that says: *Nasty Meter Reader due in your neighborhood September 16.* The other paper is a print out of all the Bible verses that had been shown during the sermon with *Romans Rocks!* written in bold letters at the top. I scan down and remember, with a warm rush, the power I felt of both the written and spoken words during the service …

No matter which way I turn, I can't make myself do right …

God causes everything to work together for the good …

We are made right with God when we believe that Jesus shed His blood, sacrificing His life for us …

If God is for us, who can ever be against us?

And I am convinced that nothing can ever separate us from His love. … Our fears for today, our worries about tomorrow … nothing in all creation will ever be able to separate us from the love of God that is revealed in Christ Jesus our Lord …

I've never prayed. I've never felt a desire or a need to go to church. I'm not one of those people who ever blames God for all of my lousy breaks. I simply understand the truth that I am completely and utterly alone and I just regularly make bad decisions.

I think about the wonderful … peace I guess is the best word … when I listen to some of the music that Callie's given me over the years. It's a positive enough emotion that sometimes when I'm feeling really low listening to those songs is the only thing that cheers me up. I remember that wonderful feeling of revelation and discovery as that young woman Crystal in her purple tee shirt and shorts said, "Made Right. Did you get that? *Made right.*"

I've spent my *whole life* trying to do the right thing. Trying to repair all my wrongs. This feeling I have of being a complete and utter failure is because I have never, ever managed to compensate let alone fix my trail of lifelong disaster and destruction. *Maybe*, my head says to me, *you should try doing something you've never done in your entire life.* Maybe I'll try going to church to see if I can get another taste of this peacefulness. Even brief snatches are worth the effort, in my opinion. *What have you got to loose?* my head says to me. As I pop the last bit of crumb cake into my mouth I figure at the very least I can always have another religious experience in the pastry shop.

My last week of summer flies by. I survive my last babysitting opportunity with Liam. We pick concord grapes from the garden and spend the day making grape jelly and then eating it spread on the homemade bread I've made in my bread maker. When Erin comes to claim Liam we are both lying on the living room floor groaning with purple lips, tongue, and fingers. Erin and I play our game where we pretend that there is no Olivia. We've been doing it for years and given Sunday's debacle there's no reason to change our modus operandi now.

I tolerate the first two days of school with all of the meetings, announcements, forms, scheduling nightmares, and curriculum changes. This is my twenty-fourth year of teaching, so it's safe to say that I've got most of what I need to know and do down pat. Bulletin boards were up and decorated in June and covered with protective newspaper. I've got computer programs that do grading. I'm teaching advanced literacy, basic math, and double social studies classes with my partner teacher, Marlie. Marlie teaches the complimentary subjects of basic literacy, advanced math, and double science classes. Ten years ago she was a baby out of college and I was her mentor teacher. Now (evil, Dr. Frankenstein laugh) I've molded her into my perfect sidekick and we are a force to be reckoned with. Aside from the ragtag collection of fifty-plus eleven- and twelve-year-old fifth graders, not much changes from year to year.

Marlie and I put in our requisite two days of set up and preparation. By Friday afternoon, all systems are go. Monday is the Labor Day holiday and then Tuesday the school year begins.

"What are your plans for the weekend?" Marlie asks me as we make our way out to our respective cars. We've already covered any summer news with her traveling across Europe being far more exciting than my sewing and keeping Liam and myself alive and uninjured.

"I might go to church on Sunday," I say and wait for the nuclear fallout. Marlie, you see, is Callie's spiritual clone and has been trying since day one of our acquaintance to get me to go to church and become more godly.

She frowns at me through her purple-framed eyeglasses. She has blonde hair that has a life of it's own – a complete and utter explosion of tight kinky curls all over her head that nothing aside from a crew cut can control. "Don't joke with me about that stuff, Elaine. You know how important it is to me."

"I'm not kidding you, Mar. I went to church last Sunday and I think I'm going to try to go again this Sunday. Or Saturday. They have evening services on Saturday or Sunday."

"Where?"

"Over in Somerville. It's a store front connected to a pastry shop called Agape Shop."

More frowning. "What denomination is it, Elaine? I don't want you getting involved with something that's all right wing and crazy. You need to get involved with a *sound, Bible-based* church."

"I thought you'd be happy!" Marlie, young enough to be my daughter, regularly pretends to be my mother. Well, no, wait, she's not that horrible. She regularly tries to be *a wise parent*.

"You can't just pick any old church, Elaine! You've got to do research. You've got to make sure that they embrace the Bible *completely*, with no additions or deletions. You need to research and find out what the basic church beliefs are, who -"

"*Stop.* I went once. By chance. At a time when I was feeling very down and out. I enjoyed the experience and it gave me something to think about. I think I'm going to go again. If they start dancing with snakes, doing live sacrifices, or start asking me to sign my house over for the greater good I'll run. Okay?"

I can tell Marlie wants to say more but she restrains herself. I also know that the first thing she's going to do when she gets home is research the hell out of Agape Shop. Then she'll revisit this exact location with both barrels loaded. With a deep, defeated sigh, she says, "I'll see you Tuesday. Don't forget the Snickers bars." I keep a stash handy for those days when only a creamy, caramel, peanut nougat can do the trick.

Going to church *when you plan to* is a lot different than going to church just out of the clear blue. Suddenly, I worry about what I should wear, what time I should leave, if my earrings are too bold, and whether I'll have to deal with an Alec sighting again or not. The last issue – Alec - I decide to solve by going to church on Saturday evening instead of Sunday. Obviously, he's a Sunday-go-to-church-boy so I'll completely avoid him by going Saturday, right? Wouldn't want him to think that I'm stalking him or anything.

I arrive just as the band is starting to play. Every one is standing and singing and clapping and I slip into a back row folding chair. The place is hopping with everyone smiling and enjoying the music but I immediately know I'm in trouble when I recognize the guitar player on stage and he gives *me* a grin and a wink. I, stupidly, look behind me and to my left and my right to see if he's grinning and winking at someone else which only causes Alec to throw his head back and laugh at me. Great. Here I am: the amusement of mankind.

I follow the words and the music but feel self-conscious with Alec's continued scrutiny. Every time I glance at him he's watching me. He seems absolutely delighted whenever we make even the briefest of eye contact.

I get caught up in the analysis of the magnitude of coincidence of this situation between Alec and me. He's my nasty meter reader, whom I have openly disliked and found abrasive and rude. He's a gifted guitar player and singer who has the astonishing distinction of being the first man to kiss me in years. He's a man who brings out the very worst of what I've got to offer in sarcasm, sharp insults, and outrageous comments. And, since I'm admitting stuff just in the privacy of my own head, he's the first man I've noticed *as a man* in longer than I care to admit.

I stand there as the band plays on and think about leather bustiers, second dates, and putting out and suddenly I'm afraid I'm going to get struck by lightning right here where I stand. I'm still trying to get myself together when suddenly the man in question appears in the space to my right. Leaning over I get a wave of warm skin and aftershave as he says, "Decided to come hear me play, huh?"

"I didn't know you were playing tonight!" I hiss at him in outrage.

"Sure you didn't," he says smugly and settles in his seat with a satisfied smile.

As Crystal begins to talk, Alec crosses his legs, opens up the biggest Bible I've ever seen in my life, and casually drapes his arm across the back of my chair. I sit there stiff and indignant, trying to keep my thoughts on Crystal's point rather than the feel of warmth from Alec's arm.

She refers to a Psalm and Alec flips confidently through his Bible. When words begin to flash up on screen, Alec puts on a pair of wire-rimmed glasses and looks down. I can't help but notice that he's got things underlined in his Bible. Lots of things. When I make the slightest movement to see what's so important, he glances in my direction, gives me a small smile, and shifts a bit so I can see better.

It's Psalm 56 and I read all the underlined bits in his Bible: *But when I am afraid, I put my trust in you. O God, I praise your word. I trust in God, so why should I be afraid? What can mere mortals do to me? ... You keep track of all my sorrows. You have collected all my tears in Your bottle. You have recorded each one in Your book.*[22]

Collected tears in a bottle.

Keep track of all my sorrows.

That level of compassion, if such a thing is true, is absolutely staggering to me. I feel Alec looking at me and I look up from his Bible into his brown eyes. There's no joking or teasing, just complete seriousness in his expression. He nods his head just once like he's saying, *Yup, it's true.* I look off into the distant nothingness of the room to avoid anymore honesty. Or connection.

When the service is over, Alec says to me, "You're coming to have coffee and a pastry. You *will not* disappear without saying goodbye to me. *Tonight, we will talk.*"

"I can't stand aggressive, take-charge men."

"I am really attracted to abrasive, contradictory women," he throws back at me without a moment's pause.

That comment stuns me into silence. For a moment. "I'm afraid to ask if I fit into that category."

"Honey," he says to me as he leans in close, "you're president of the club."

72

As he drags me into the pastry shop, I struggle to remember the last time that a man thought I was attractive. I realize, with stunning self-discovery, that I'm not sure that that's *ever* happened. I'm pretty sure Dean liked me because I put out regularly and with great abandon. Paul liked me because he thought he could mold me into the woman of his dreams and, initially, I liked him for the same reason. Richard liked me because … hell, I don't know why he liked me. I know I married him because he was everything Dean and Paul were *not,* and in being so, I, like the idiot I was, thought that made him perfect husband/father material. Ha.

I've never felt sexy, attractive, or desirable to *anyone*; just passably acceptable. Kind of like in the category of: It Could Be Worse. I watch Alec as he glares at me as I sit down at a table by the window and he strides up to the counter to place our order. He's a rather good looking middle aged man with dark brown eyes and salt and pepper, too long hair. He's a few inches taller than my 5'6" frame with an athletic body, apparently supported by the strenuous demands of meter reading and guitar playing. Up on stage with spotlights, guitar, and a crooning baritone voice, the urge to throw a pair of panties at him is not as far fetched as one would think. Add in his mile wide streak of irreverent humor and how nice he smells and, well, perhaps I am in serious trouble.

When Richard … died … I was completely unprepared. Unprepared to be alone again, unprepared to face the reality of his suicide, unprepared to examine what level of culpability I needed to assume. Whatever emotional output I was capable of *before* Richard's untimely and unexpected demise was severely readjusted once I found myself in the unbelievable state of widowhood. The three-strikes-you're-out rule that is so critical in baseball made perfect sense in application to my love life. I faced the fact that as lonely and as desperate as I was as a single woman with two children, I was astronomically better off than trusting my appalling judgment in choosing men. I seemed to have radar that gravitated only towards: alcoholics, egomaniacs, or the suicidally depressed. What kind of mother was I to continually attach myself in holy matrimony to men such as that?

Unfortunately, by the time I came to that (wise) conclusion, Olivia had already come to a few conclusions of her own – all of which were unfavorably skewed against me and my abilities.

All of this thinking leads me to an astronomically important question since I've just admitted I'm attracted to Alec: *What's wrong with him?*

"Man, are you lost in thought." Alec sets down at our table a tray with two steaming cups of black coffee and three different types of pastry: one cheese cake confection with raspberries, one chocolate layer cake with what appears to be strawberry filling, and one square of what can only be shortbread topped with caramel and chocolate icing.

"At least I'm still here."

Alec nods in agreement as he empties the tray and walks it over to a bussing station near a rack of magazines and newspapers. "So, what were you thinking about?"

"You don't want to know."

"Sure I do."

I look at him, trying to communicate with just an expression what an idiot he is. He stares at me silently for a few minutes and I am absolutely positive he gets my message. But instead of getting angry, he just chuckles and shakes his head at me. Picking up a fork, he digs into the cheesecake and then holds it in the air like he's going to feed me. Oh, for the love of …

"I can feed my -," I start to say but am unable to finish because my mouth is suddenly full of cheesecake.

"Well?" He has such an expectant air about him that I take a minute to savor the joyous experience that's happening in my mouth.

I take the fork out of his hand before I open my mouth to answer, which makes him grin again. "It's good."

"Just *good?*"

"Actually, it's probably the best cheesecake I've ever had. Is that better?"

He nods, satisfied and helps himself to a bite.

"The coffee cake the other night was absolutely delicious, too. Thanks."

"I sat at the table waiting for about fifteen minutes thinking you were in the bathroom or something. When I finally realized you'd left, I decided to make a home delivery."

"It was nice to come home to."

"Are you okay?"

The question is more than just a casual reference to what I'm doing at this precise moment in time and there's no way in hell I'm going to answer honestly. "I'm fine."

"Like the cheesecake was 'just good'?"

I give him a wan smile. No way am I going to spill my guts or even flash him a glimpse. But I do decide to set him straight in regard to me, my abysmal track record in life, and how fortunate he is that I'm honest and straightforward. "Look, you've got the mistaken impression, it seems, that I've been seeking you out, trying to gain your attention, hoping for some ..." I shrug at my lack of proper vocabulary, "connection or something. I'm not."

"I know."

"No, you don't know. I've been on my own for ten years. *Ten years*. I've got my job, my hobbies, my friends, my daughters, and my grandson and my *card is full*. Just because we've run into each other a few times -,"

"Three, not counting the meter reading instances," Alec says with a wink.

"- is purely *coincidental*. I have no interest in any more relationships with the opposite sex because all it breeds for me is complete and utter disaster." I lean forward to drive my point home. "I am a *loser magnet*. Consequently the fact that I find you attractive must only confirm the fact that you are in the ignominious category of being a los -"

"You're attracted to me?" he says with a grin that just about splits his face. "Really? Since when? Was that why you gave me such a hard time when I was reading your meter?"

I close my eyes and take a deep breath. But I know to stay silent.

"Or was it when I was playing something on stage? Girls love that stuff. The tortured musician who finds inspiration only in his music and ... in true love."

He waits until I open my eyes and look at him.

I can tell he's having a blast, all at my expense. "Or *maybe* it was after I kissed you." He thinks for a minute and then seems to make his own decision since I'm still not talking. "Yeah, that was probably when. I must have knocked your socks off with my style and finesse. I've been a smooth operator with the ladies my entire life, you know."

The need to knock him down a few hundred pegs rears up in me wild and crazy. "Actually," I say, "it was when I discovered how delicious the crumb cake was. It was almost a religious experience for me. I thought, 'Now here's something worth pursuing. If this guy could just show up once or twice a week, deliver me pastry and *disappear* then he'd be the perfect man.'" His surprised expression eggs me to continue on and really blow his mind. "It's too bad you're not the pastry chef. Add in unlimited crumb cake to that whole second date promise with leather bustier and me putting out and you'd be able to just about write your own ticket to paradise."

Based on the stunned expression on his face, I feel a moment of intense satisfaction for getting in the last word. Then he throws back his head and absolutely *roars* with laughter. I feel a measure of my superiority slip as he stands, grabs my hand and pulls me to the back of the shop. We rush past the counters piled high with desserts, past the smiling counter help, and through the double doors that lead to the kitchen. Organized chaos surrounds us as we stand just inside the double doors.

I recognize Maria, the young woman from the Sunday past that came and got Alec because of the '*situation* in the back.' She rushes over as soon as she sees Alec and I standing in the kitchen. "Alec?" She says with real concern. "Is everything okay? I know you never come back here during church coffee hour unless we need you or you've got a problem with something we've done." She looks around frantically, seeming to take stock of people, ingredients, equipment, and, most of all, the pastries. Looking back at Alec, she says, "I'm certain everything's fine today. Have I missed anything?"

"No, everything looks good, Maria. I just wanted to show Elaine the kitchen."

Maria seems to notice me for the first time. "Oh! Hi! Welcome!" She glances at Alec, trying to read him I suspect. "Would you like a tour? You can let the boss man, here, do it or you can give me a minute and I'll be happy to." She points to two huge platters behind her. "I've just got to ice these last two servings of shortbread caramel." She winks at Alec. "The head pastry chef is a real nightmare if things don't go exactly to his specifications."

"What's the popular one today?" Alec asks as his eyes scan the room.

Maria smiles. "You need to ask? You called it right again with the shortbread. We can't keep it stocked out front it's going so fast."

"Great. I'll see you tonight. Usual time."

Instead of taking me back out front, Alec leads me out through the back kitchen exit. Once we're outside in the relative quiet and privacy of the alley, he turns and says to me, "So? When do I pick you up?"

"Huh?" I say, still trying to process the fact that my meter reader is a guitar playing, lead singing, *pastry chef*.

"I've got to get in my first official date with you because the second date," he sighs and closes his eyes like he's imagining complete ecstasy, "just can't come soon enough."

"Do two things for me," I say struggling to recover some of the acreage I've lost.

"What's that?" he murmurs, moving in a bit closer, his body practically vibrating with hopeful expectation.

"First, close your eyes." Alec gets this cocky, 'I know what you're up to but I'll play along' smile as he closes his eyes.

"Now," I say as I slip past him and throw over my shoulder, "hold your breath." I hear him chuckling behind me as I walk away down the alley to my car.

Down in the valley, dying of thirst
Down in the valley, it seems I'm at my worst.[23]

Chapter 9: Peaks and Valleys

"Elaine! *Elaine!*"

I hear hurried footsteps behind me and turn as I get to my car. When Alec sees that I'm not scrambling to get inside and lock the door he slows down a bit. Finally he stops directly in front of me.

"My full name is Alec Xavier Monroe. I'm fifty-three years old. I've spent almost my entire life on the wrong path, but recently, within the last five years, I've finally begun to get it right. I told you that first night that I'd given up trying to control my life. Instead, I focus on trying to fill my life, my head, and my heart with the things that are Right, and see where that leads me. I don't believe in coincidences. This," he pauses, obviously searching for the right word, "*thing* that's happening between us is a perfect example."

Since I'm not looking him in the eye, but rather staring at a remarkably fascinating candy wrapper on the ground at our feet, he bends down and gets in my face. When I sigh and look up at him he says earnestly, "I hear what you've told me, Elaine. About the no romance or dating. I understand that you're not looking for love or don't even miss it. But you're reasoning doesn't jive for me. This whole 'loser magnet' thing you've just spouted to me in the shop."

When I roll my eyes and go to turn away he catches my chin. "I *expect* you to have history! No one who's *lived* could possibly reach this point in life without a pile of bad and good choices under their ..." he grins and glances down at my legs, "skirt. But what I *need* for you to hear is what I'm saying back to you – and I don't think you are. I've joked and flirted and had a grand time verbally sparring with you. I love how I have to keep on my toes every minute we're together. I replay our conversations over and over and have fun imagining what we'll manage to say to each other the next time we meet. *I look forward to that.*"

His hand that held my chin now slides down to cup the side of my neck. Its warmth spreads down my arm to my fingertips. My toes curl. "Whatever life you've led, Elaine, I want you to hear me say that I like the woman that's the product of it. I'd like to get to know more of her. Okay?"

I nod, reluctantly, and am horrified to feel tears begin to build. Suddenly I need to get away, be alone ... sew until four a.m. One half of me wants to escape the warmth of his hand and his words and the other half of me wants to step into a male embrace the likes of which I suspect I've never experienced in my life. He seems to sense my distress and steps forward and tentatively, carefully pulls me toward him. I resist for a second and then give up the fight. *God he smells good* I think with my face pressed against his neck. One of his arms wraps tightly around my waist while the other one cradles the back of my head. Because I want to know what it feels like more than I want just about anything else, I hesitantly wrap my arms around him. He's solid and warm. *We make a good fit.*

"I'm joking about the second date. Just like you are. You know that, right?" he murmurs into my hair.

Mentally I sigh. *Yeah, I know.* I nod.

"I'd like to exchange phone numbers, or if you'd prefer, email addresses. I'd like to reach a stage where I can initiate contact so that I can have something more solid to look forward to. And, if that isn't something you want to do, then I'll just fall into your perfect man scenario."

I pull back in his arms and frown in confusion. He gives me a lopsided grin, "Dropping off delicious pastries once or twice a week and just disappearing."

When I step back even further and go to open my mouth, he quickly places a finger against my lips: a finger that smells strongly of chocolate. With his other hand still resting on my waist he says, "I don't need an answer tonight. You didn't come here expecting to see me. *I* came here hoping to see *you* with a pile of things I wanted to say." He reaches into his pocket and pulls out a business card. I wonder briefly if it lists all of his professions? *Meter Reader, Guitar Player, Christian Rock Singer, Pastry Chef* ... are there more? "Think about all of ... *this* ... and then call me. Otherwise, I'll see you next week at church ..." he hesitates and I look up into his serious brown eyes, "... right?"

Slipping the card in my hand, he can't seem to help himself and before I know it I'm getting a kiss. He's got one arm around my waist again and the other hand is cradling my face. It's not a slam me up against the car and have his way with me kind of kiss. It's just a I've-got-to-do-this-right-now-because-I-can kind of kiss. He touches my mouth with his thumb when he's done. "Thanks for that. You know. Not slapping me." I arch my eyebrow and he grins. "Or kneeing me. I've wanted to kiss you again since the concert so badly it's become quite a distraction. I don't want to loose my edge when it comes to verbal encounters with you. Gotta stay sharp and focused, you know." He lets go of me and takes two steps back. "Safe drive home. *Call me, Elaine.*"

As I get in my car and drive away I realize that in that whole exchange I've never said a word. Me, the Queen of Verbosity ... speechless. Now I know I'm in big trouble.

Sunday morning I call Callie. It's time I spoke with someone I trust who knows my history and will be lovingly objective. "'Lo?" a groggy, sleep filled male voice says.

"James! Did I wake you?"

"What time is it?"

"Seven-thirty."

"A.M.? As in morning?"

"Yeah, I'm sorry …"

"Must be bad. Hang on. I'll get Callie. She's already up." James, husband of my very best friend, who knows just how out of control my life must be depending on the hour I call. What a guy.

"Hey, girl. You okay?"

"I don't know."

"Want to come over?"

"Do you and James have plans today?"

"Nah, we're just hanging out. James has got a pile of stuff to do and I was just going to write up plans for next week." The weekend fun of every teacher.

"When can I come over?"

"What's good for you?"

"Aren't you going to church?"

"Nah, we did that last night. James and the band played. It was great."

"I'll come over now then."

Sitting on Callie's back deck, I struggle with how to start. There's the whole matter of Olivia and the fact that she's nominated me for Worst Mother Ever and I strongly suspect I'm going to win. Then there's the complication of Mr. Alec Xavier Monroe, who is the most distracting collection of coincidences I've ever experienced. Lastly, there's the whole God thing that suddenly seems to have begun to pervade my life and I'm uncertain as to what to do with it. I make a face of disgust and say, "I could be here for a couple of days, you know."

"Start with the easiest one," Callie says and I think, *Honey, you have no idea.*

"Okay. I'm glad you're sitting down." I take a deep breath. "I've been going to church."

Callie nods and says, "It's about time. Where?"

"Agape Shop. In Somerville."

My good friend frowns in concentration. "I've heard of that place ..." She thinks and thinks. "Isn't that that new place on Main that's a church and a coffee shop all in one?" I nod, waiting for her to connect the shocking pile of coincidences that have become my life. "James went there a while back because ... *ooooh!*" Suddenly, Callie has a delighted grin on her face. "Agape Shop's where James went to recruit Alec for the band."

"Yeah. I didn't know that, though, when I went.'

"But you know that now."

"Oh, yeah. I know that now."

"So? What's the problem?"

"Callie, do you really believe all this God stuff?" I watch her face, especially her eyes, because I can tell when she's conning me.

She leans forward so that I can see the flecks of gold in the irises of her hazel eyes. "Yes, Elaine. I believe every, single, solitary speck of it."

"I've been listening for a long time to the music you give me. Some of the words to some of the songs are really ..." I shrug for want of a better word, "... powerful. I find that sometimes, when I'm really down, they can give me a lift, you know?" Callie nods but doesn't say anything. "And then I went to church. Actually I've been twice. And I hear all of these amazing words about being made right, and God being for me, and nothing being able to separate us from God's love, and how He counts all our tears ..."

I can't sit down any more so I stand up and walk to the railing of the deck. "I've lived forty-eight years, Cal, and I've got very little to be proud of: three broken marriages, a nonexistent relationship with my eldest daughter, a daunting pile of regret and guilt regarding just about every decision I've ever made, -"

"Stop!" Callie demands. I turn to look at her, surprised at her tone. She spits words out at me as she advances towards me. "You have lived forty-eight years and have *much* to be proud of: you have a wonderful relationship with Erin and Dan *and* you have a spectacular relationship with your grandson, Liam. You have survived circumstances that would have destroyed a lesser woman, making you strong, capable, and resilient. Colleagues and parents alike value you at school. For over twenty years you have taught faithfully a collection of children who have loved and respected you for your honesty, sense of humor, and wonderful personal style. And you have *me* who loves you like a sister and refuses to let you stand here and tear yourself down."

What a good friend. Time to show her the real deal that is me. Let her know just how deep and dark the reality of my life is. "Dean is not Olivia's father, Callie. I've lied about it all these years."

She leans against the deck railing and crosses her arms. One of the things I like about Callie is she's careful with her words. If she needs the time to collect her thoughts, she takes them. "Okay," she says after a few moments of digesting my huge revelation, "I appreciate the magnitude of trust you've just given me in sharing that."

I wave my hand like it's no big deal. "Don't be. It seems the whole world knows: Dean, Olivia, Erin, Dan, even Paul."

"Paul! How'd he get into this?"

"You'd have to ask Olivia," I say miserably. "She apparently got in contact with him when Dean failed her DNA test."

"Oh, Elaine, I'm so sorry."

"Then Olivia told Dean," I look Callie right in the eye, "who *already knew* and offered to help me make contact with some of the high school guys he found me *involved with* when I was too drunk to help myself." Callie just stays silent because she knows there are no suitable words to say. "Surprisingly, the fact that I slept with a *significant number* of high school guys beyond what Dean knows doesn't complicate the issue though." I'm crying now, silent tears that run down my face and drip off my chin. "Because Olivia's father isn't any one of those young men."

Callie walks over and embraces me. She hugs me tight, rubs my back and says, "Shhhhh, it's okay Elaine," like I'm a baby.

"It's not okay," I say, "not by a long shot." Now that I've started to tell all of this crap about myself it's suddenly highly important that Callie *gets it.* She needs to understand just how *lousy* I really am. I sniffle and look into Callie's concerned face. "Olivia wants to know the name of her father. And I can't give it to her. She thinks I'm being selfish or purposely cruel."

"I know that's not the reason," Callie says with best friend conviction and loyalty. I try not to roll my eyes.

"No, it's not the reason. I really, honest to goodness, don't know."

Callie pulls a tissue out of her pocket and mops my face. "How can that be, Sweetie?"

I sigh. Here goes. "My mother ... she would sometimes go out ... when she got really down on herself and ... me. She'd go out and really tie one on and pick up a guy who'd make her feel all ... good, I guess." Callie's watching me, holding onto both of my hands tightly, as if she's afraid I'll disappear forever. "I knew to keep out of the line of fire and lots of times I don't think the guy even knew there was a kid in the house. She didn't go out all the time ... just now and then." I sigh and fly back a thousand years to those dark scary nights where my mother – who was never, ever close or caring or loving – would become an even more distant, frightening stranger. If I think about it, I can still hear her flirty high-pitched laugh and smell the perfume she'd douse herself with before she went out. I remember the strange sounds that, for a while, I didn't understand, and the horrible child like images I would conjure up to fill in the blanks. But much too soon I understood what was going on, sometimes right outside my bedroom door.

"Usually, the guys never stayed the night. I just had to lay low for a few hours and then they'd be gone. Mom and I never discussed it. It wasn't my business." *What Elaine? Why that look? Have you got something to say for yourself? Come on, little miss perfect. Let's hear what you've got to say.*

"One night ... one of the guys she brought home ..." I sigh again, suddenly so tired I can't stand up. When I sit down on the deck chair, Callie pulls another chair over, sits right down beside me and holds my hand again. "I heard them laughing and talking and ... finally going at it. I must have dozed off because suddenly everything was quiet and dark. I got up to go to the bathroom and the guy was sitting in our living room smoking a cigarette." To this day the smell of a certain brand of unfiltered cigarettes makes me want to hurl. "He was tall. Dark wavy hair. Big. I always imagined he had violet eyes but I never really saw them that night in the dark. He ... he decided since I was there that he'd have two ... of us ... for the price of one."

For a minute I think Callie's trying to rock me but then I realize it's me rocking myself back and forth. I make myself stop and sit still. "Did your mother even know?" Callie asks in an anguished voice. Her face, when I look at it, is awash with tears she can't stop.

I shrug. "Sometimes I thought she did and sometimes I thought she didn't. I certainly yelled enough and made enough of a fuss at the time to wake the dead. After he ... finished ... with me he just left. I don't know how long I lay there on that living room floor. Then I finally got myself into the shower. My mother finally shouted at me because I was using up all the hot water.

"Dean was away. Down at the shore with his family. He went every summer for a month. My mother wouldn't let me go. Said she didn't trust me to not get into trouble. By the time he got home, I'd already missed my period.

"After that I got real careless with things. Who cared how much I drank? Who cared if Dean and I used a condom or not? There was a bunch of times ... for a while there ... that I got too drunk to really care about anything at all. I pretended for a good couple of months that I wasn't pregnant, but eventually I couldn't ignore it anymore." I look at Callie and shrug like it's no big deal. "So, I lied to Dean. He proposed. I married him. My mother was well rid of me. Olivia arrived. End of story."

Callie gives me an impatient scowl. "The rape was never reported?"

Rape. After all these years to hear it called that. I roll it around in my mind for a moment or two. I look away, out into Callie's back garden. "I never called it ... that. I always called it the time I got pregnant with Olivia."

"You were sexually attacked, Elaine. That's rape."

"I should have stayed in my room. I knew better."

"You were fifteen!"

I shrug and look her in the eye. "I was a wise-ass, sexually experienced, belligerent teenager, Callie. Don't make me out to be some innocent. I wasn't."

"How many guys had you been sexually involved with before this happened?" she demands.

I can't look at her again. "Just one," I say. "Dean."

"You told me you loved him."

I nod reluctantly. "Yeah, I did. He was, hell he still *is*, kind and loving as long as he's sober. I learned about love from him." *Certainly not my mother* I think, but I keep that to myself.

"So this wise-ass, sexually experienced, belligerent teenager was also in love and experiencing love for the first time in her life with her one and only boyfriend. She was brutally attacked *in her own home* by a stranger her mother brought home. And during this attack in which the young woman 'made a fuss that was loud enough to wake the dead', her mother was either too drunk *or* too indifferent to make any effort to help. Don't you dare take any responsibility for this! *You were innocent!!*" Callie's yelling when she's done.

She still doesn't get it. "I knew the drill, Cal. 'Stay in your room and shut up. I'm bringing company home tonight and I don't want to be bothered with the likes of you.'" I look down at my tightly clenched hands and make an effort to have them relax. "Jeeze, it was almost a relief when my mother would spell it out so clearly for me. Usually I had to try to guess at her moods and anticipate how I was supposed to act. At least when she was going out, I knew the score."

"I never knew, Elaine." I look into my best friend's tearful expression. "*I never knew.* You never *ever* showed a hint of the pain and anguish that has to be hidden deep down inside. Even the fact that you never referred to that time as 'rape' puts Olivia's conception on a different plain. You've always loved that little girl with every fiber of your being. You've agonized over 'trying to get it right' with her more times than I can count. From my perception, you've shed more tears, had more sleepless nights, and sweated more drops of blood over Olivia than anything – or anyone – in your entire life – even yourself." She takes my clenched hands in hers. "That's true love, Elaine."

I make a rude noise in the back of my throat. "Tell that to Olivia. I think her exact words 'regarding my miserable life' were something like she's tolerated 'my lousy maternal instincts, my blatant favoritism towards Erin, my one-sided loyalties, and my convenient memories regarding my personal disasters.' All she wants from me is 'a lousy goddamn name.'" I start to shake and suddenly feel *so cold* and I know I'm rocking back and forth in Callie's plastic lawn chair but I can't stop it.

I gasp out, "The only thing she's ever really asked me for … the only thing she's ever wanted from me … and I can't give it to her." At last the dam breaks and I'm crying so hard that I can't speak anymore.

Again, the Queen of Verbosity is speechless.

*I'm lost and broken all alone on this road, the wheels keep turning but the feeling is gone,
When I fear I'm on my own, but you remind me I am not alone.*[24]

Chapter 10: Glasses Half Full And Half Empty

allie leaves me and my complete mental breakdown on the deck for a few moments only to return with a glass of iced water and a box of tissues. I blow, and blow again, and take a sip or two of water. The tears won't stop though. It's truly like I've sprung a leak.

"Can I talk to you about some things?" Callie asks hesitantly, and I realize that besides the tissues and water she's brought back something else: her Bible. "I'm only bringing this out because of the way you started, asking me if I believe all this stuff or not. I always try to respect your lack of interest and not make you crazy with my penchant for Bible-banging."

"It's okay," I manage. My voice is thick with tears and snot and emotions better left unnamed.

"You can tell me to shut up whenever you want. I'll try to be short, sweet, and concise …" She waits for a response from me and I give her a shaky nod.

"I can only explain things to you in the way I understand them best. Real faith – belief in God – is a personal, unique thing because it's woven up with the individual's life: his or her mistakes, victories, dreams, and private agonies." She touches my face and makes me look at her. "We all have those private agonies, you know. Some are just bigger and badder than others." I see her fight back tears. My precious best friend who has struggled, unsuccessfully, for almost fifteen years to have just one baby. My precious friend who, when she decided to give up on the natural route tried the adoption route only to be told her husband – ten years her senior – was too old to qualify as an adoptive father. I nod. I get it. *I know.*

Callie continues. "For me, God is the perfect parent – both mother and father. He encourages, chastises, loves unconditionally, champions, delights, and sorrows over each one of us. He's always willing, always available, and always right. He *allows us* to go on our merry way throughout life and make all of our own choices – with or without His guidance. He gives us loads of choices and loads of opportunities to get it right. He doesn't put us in a protective bubble – which wouldn't really be much of a life – but instead gives us a multitude of skills, talents, tools, and openings to choose the right path and make a success out of the life we've been assigned. He wants us to be happy, healthy, wise, and wonderful, but unless we do these things by our own means it's not our own life, is it?

I nod, for all this makes sense so far, take a sip of water, and blow my nose. Again. *Not that I'd know what a perfect parent looks like. I've never experienced one nor have I ever achieved being one.*

"Problem is, without God as our main directional goal, we pretty much are doomed to failure. We kind of flounder around randomly catching good and bad prizes, unsure of how we managed or why exactly we failed. We feel helpless, rudderless, and without any real purpose. Life just seems to constantly work against us."

Hello. Spotlight's now on me. Now we're getting into my life history here.

"Just like a perfect parent, God is watching and waiting for us. Earnestly desiring for our well being. Craving our love and affection. Wanting a personal relationship where we talk, share, laugh, love, and cry *together.* But He doesn't push. He's just patient …

"He doesn't care what we've done, how old we are, how broken we may be, how guilt-ridden or desperate we've become, how addicted or how emotionally destroyed … *He just wants us.* All of us. Not a piece. Not just until things improve. He wants the whole entire package. And here's an amazing, powerful thing that many people don't realize: He's actually more interested in our failures and weaknesses than He is in our personal strengths and talents."

I frown at her. *If that's the case, God must be itching like crazy to get His hands on me.*

Noticing my expression, Callie says with a smile and a nod, *"It's through your greatest disasters* that God makes the most momentous victories."

I look at my friend and she sits silently letting me digest this last sentence. My greatest disaster. That would be my failure with Olivia. I'm supposed to believe that God could make this my most momentous victory? *Yeah right.* I can hear the cheers now: Good job, Elaine! You had sex with one of your mother's many one-night stands and got pregnant! You deceived your faithful and unsuspecting boyfriend into marriage, causing him years of guilt and anguish! You've lived a life of lies with your eldest daughter so that she feels only anger, betrayal, and hatred at the thought of you! You're so horrible to live with you drove one husband to suicide! You have practically nothing of value to show for forty-eight years of living. Outstanding! Let's give this girl a hand!

"It's not a matter of believing, Elaine," Callie murmurs softly, interrupting my pity-fest. "It's a matter of *faith.*" For the first time, she opens her Bible and flips through the pages. She's like Alec in that she's got truckloads of stuff underlined and even things written in the margins. "Here," she says pointing to an underlined section. "Read this."

What is faith? It is the confident assurance that what we hope for is going to happen. It is the evidence of things we cannot yet see.[25]

"It all starts with faith. Jesus said if we had faith the size of a mustard seed we could move a mountain just by commanding it. I take that to mean that microscopic amounts of faith are all we need to get going." She grins at me. "I haven't moved any mountains lately." She goes so far as to chuckle briefly. "But then I never thought I'd be sitting on my back deck reading you stuff from my Bible, and you actually tolerating it. Guess I'd better step up my level of faith a bit."

She holds up her hand and counts off on her fingers. "Ask the Lord to help you on this life journey. Believe that you can't do it on your own. Confess that you've made mistakes and would like them to be forgotten." She smiles and holds up three fingers. "The A-B-Cs of a Right Life: Ask, Believe, Confess." She shrugs, "I like to add a D for Diligence. You've got to stick to it when times get tough."

Callie looks at me, seeming to determine if my eyes have glazed over yet. "One more verse." She flips pages, turns the Bible towards me, and points.

I read aloud, *"For I know the plans I have for you," says the Lord. "They are plans for good and not for disaster, to give you a future and a hope. In those days when you pray, I will listen. If you look for me in earnest, you will find me when you seek me."* [26]

Callie struggles to pull a silver bangle bracelet off her wrist, one I've seen her wear thousands of times, and holds it out to me. I take it and read, *For I know the plans I have for you, declares the Lord. Jer. 29:11.* When I look up at her she says softly, "Being on the right track doesn't mean things get easier," and I think about those babies that will never know her and James' love and affection. "This verse always reminds me where I need to head for a future and a hope. That's what I want more than anything else." When I go to give it back to her she smiles and shakes her head. "No, keep it. I bought two. I was always going to give you one but something told me you wouldn't be too inclined to walk around with a Bible verse on your wrist. Even if you don't want to wear it, at least now you know the emotions behind it."

I slip the bracelet around my wrist and it's still warm from my best friend's body. "I want to get on the right path," I say to her with complete sincerity. "I want my life to be in control, on track, purposeful. I want to know where I'm headed and *why*. I'm tired of floundering in the dark."

"Ask. Believe. Confess. Do you have a microscopic bit of faith, Elaine, to take the chance? Faith will grow with experience. I'm living proof of that. You know I've not lead a squeaky clean life. But *my mistakes are gone*, Elaine. Washed away. Forgotten. Nonexistent. If God's erased them from His book, why should I keep dwelling on them? Move on. Step forward. Look ahead. *"What lies behind us and what lies before us are tiny matters compared to what lies within us."* Ralph Waldo Emerson said that. Aside from a pile of favorite Bible verses, that's my theme. You can't change the past, Elaine. But you can surely take control of your future. Trust God for your future so that you can have that wonderful hope."

I see James through the windows of the deck in the kitchen going through the motions of making coffee. He's dressed but his hair is sticking up all over his head in an amazing display of morning bed head. "I better go. I'm intruding on your Sunday with James.

Callie looks in the direction I'm looking and sees the same thing I see and grins. "Most men go bald as they get older. I end up with one who just seems to get hairier! Don't worry. James' whole morning is taken up rehearsing with the band. They want to try some new arrangements now that they've got Alec on board."

I have a horrible wave of gut wrenching panic. "Does that mean Alec's coming over?" My voice squeaks out two octaves higher than normal.

Callie waggles her eyebrows at me and grins a wily grin. "Yup. Didn't you mention you've seen him at church a few times? *What an amazing set of coincidences!* First he's your meter reader, then he's your blind date, then he's at the first church you attend in *your entire life,* and now he's," she starts to laugh as she glances back into the kitchen, "helping himself to a cup of coffee in my kitchen."

I look into the kitchen at the man in question as he salutes me with a cup of coffee, takes a minute to blow it cool, and then takes a sip. I think he winks at me but my eyesight isn't that sharp to be positive. "Alec says he doesn't believe in coincidences," I say kind of to myself but out loud.

Callie's warm hand on my arm makes me look into her dancing eyes. *"Neither do I,* Elaine," she says with a low, throaty laugh. *"Neither do I!"*

James Danely, an accountant by day and Christian rock musician during all other times, has a fully equipped recording studio in his basement. Loved by musical friends, colleagues, and even vaguely distant acquaintances for his premier equipment, Callie's always been tolerant of the continual stream of performers wandering through her home. As we sit on the deck, I watch James and Alec make their way downstairs.

When I turn to speak with Callie, she's grinning at *me*. "What?" I say perhaps a bit too defensively.

"You like him."

"I *don't even know him.*"

"What you *do know* about him, though, you like."

I can't argue with that but I don't have to admit it. "He didn't need me to be there that first night. Why'd you go to all the trouble – even calling in a favor to *force me* to say yes?"

Callie shrugs. "You have to ask James. He asked me to call you and see if you'd go to the concert to help his new guitarist feel at ease and comfortable. He's never asked me to do anything like that before, so I figured it was pretty important. When I told him that you wouldn't be very favorably inclined to come along he asked me to try and convince you." She's studying me like I'm a bug under a microscope. "I've known you for close to twenty years, Elaine. I've been with you through Paul and Richard and I've seen and heard enough about Dean to feel rather well informed. I'm putting it mildly when I say it was rather fascinating watching you and Alec the other night." She leans forward intently. "Are you *always* like that when you're," she hesitates searching for the right word I suspect, "*encountering* a man for the first time?"

Ah, jeeze. If she only knew what I was capable of! I close my eyes and have a myriad of flashes: Alec winking at me from the stage, Alec kissing me, Alec's delicious scent, Alec referring to leather bustiers and second dates ... I know that I'm blushing furiously now.

"Holy Cow! You're blushing!" Callie says with genuine excitement. "What's going on that I don't know about?! Spill it!"

I open my eyes to see Callie looking at me and trying, with every speck of her being, to read my mind. Thank God she's not *that* good. "He brings out the worst in me, I'll grant you that. But, unfortunately, that doesn't necessarily seem to be a bad thing. I'd like to go on record as saying that despite my miserable track record, I've never behaved with such complete, in-your-face provocation toward any man. Despite what he's said to me."

"What do you mean *despite what's he said to you?*"

I look at my friend who's oozing intrigue out of every cell. "He told me, just last night, and, I might add it is the primary reason I'm here at this ungodly hour on a Sunday morning, despite all the other … crap …" I take a deep breath and close my eyes again remembering Alec's intense brown eyes, serious expression last night, and deliciously warm hand wrapped around my neck. I know I'm blushing again.

"What? What did he say?" When I look at Callie she seems to be making every effort to keep herself from shaking me.

"You know, I've done everything in my power – aside from showing him color photographs – to impress upon him that I'm not worth pursuing. Which he seems intent on doing, regardless."

"What. Did. He. Say. Elaine."

"He said," I sigh and suddenly feel a bit teary and wobbly again, "that whatever life I've led, he likes the woman that its produced … and that he'd like to get to know more of me." Wow, even repeated it sounds pretty darn good.

She sits back in her plastic lawn chair, stunned. *"Really."*

I nod.

We both mull this over for a bit and then I finally say, "I don't think I've ever been so brutally honest, in-your-face, *real* with any person in my whole life as I have with him. I always … shift or change to fit the situation. I walk on eggshells with Olivia, I shower love and affection and turn myself inside out to keep things positive with Erin, I stay self-contained and business like at school with the kids, I -"

"What do you do with me?" Callie interrupts, sitting forward with curiosity.

I look off the deck because I figure, after all these years and after all that I've shared so far with her today, she deserves my honesty. "I try to be … good … witty, cheerful, fun to be around … so you'll want to stay my friend."

"You think if you don't behave *correctly* I won't be your friend anymore?" Her tone implies she can't believe I'd think such a thing.

"Not so much that … you're too loyal to do that after all these years. No, it's more like," I sigh because I know how ridiculous it sounds, even though it's what I feel, "I've got to make sure I'm … *of sufficient quality* … to deserve your friendship so you'll maintain and continue it."

"What a load of crap."

I sigh. "Yeah, I know. With everyone," I stop and say with stunned hesitation, "except Alec …" I shake my head in disbelief, "I always have a running dialogue of snotty, in-your-face, offensive comments that I roll around and sort through. Depending on whom I'm with is what I let out – with Alec I've held little back." I glance at Callie's stunned face. "I love you too much and respect your goodness too much to let too much of that side of me out." I laugh a self-deprecatory laugh. "It would curl your hair to hear that smart mouthed persona in my head that is the *real* me."

"Give me an example."

I think for a minute and then sigh. "Well, like when Olivia was spewing out about my lack of maternal skills and common sense," *and that's putting it mildly,* my head reminds me, "I wanted to say something like, 'Hey, did I ever tell you my greatest wish in life would have been for you to never have been born? Did I ever say that the very sight of you reminded me of the worst moment I ever lived? Did I ever tell you that living with your ungrateful presence made me dream of the bliss of child abandonment? No? Well then count yourself lucky, sweetheart. It seems I've got at least one gigantic, friggin' gold star on my motherhood chart."

Callie is looking at me with her mouth hanging open in stunned shock. I give her a big, toothy, in-your-face grin that says, 'Aren't you glad

I kept my mouth shut all these years?' But she surprises me. "You're mother said all those things to you." It's not a question. Apparently, I've revealed far more about myself than even I intended. Crap.

I open my mouth to deny it but then just look away in silence. Welcome to my one and only greatest accomplishment: I'm not my mother. Instead, I acknowledge to Callie, "These past few days I'm pretty sure I need to either get back quickly to the shrink I saw after Richard offed himself, or I've got to find a new prescription med to go with my Prozac."

Callie ignores me and my poor attempt at humor. "Do you want to know why *I am* friends with you?"

No. Yes. Ah hell, I don't know.

Callie takes my silence as permission to spill. "I'm friends with you because I love your quick wit. I love how you look at things – regularly – from a uniquely different perspective than I would ever dream. You're irreverent at times, but always honest. You inspire me with your strength and determination to keep forging on no matter what life throws at you.

"As far as your mothering skills are concerned, I have always admired your fortitude dealing with Olivia and how you never even seem to *consider* giving up. She smashes you down with word or deed and after you finish reeling from the blow, you brush yourself off and forge right on towards her again. I've never been given the opportunity to be a mother … but I always have doubted if I would have had the same committed, loving, staying power as you have shown.

"There are a lot of times over the course of our friendship where I've gotten myself out of bed or managed a laugh and a smile because I know what you'd say if I didn't. You're my *best friend*. You're the sister I never had. One of the things I'm thankful for every night in my prayers is you and our relationship. My life would be so much less joyous without you.

"Now, you've sat here today and painted the full picture of your life and I … well I'm in awe that you're still sane and standing upright!" She grabs hold of my hand and squeezes. "You look back on your past,

97

Elaine, and see nothing but ruin. I look back on your past and am stunned at the brilliant successes that you've accomplished *all on your own*."

With nail digging intensity she says to me, "I'm proud to call you friend."

It's nice, these words she's said to me. Really nice. She's certifiably delusional, but it's still amazing to hear.

"Come in and help me make lunch."

I shake my head. "Oh, no. I'm outta here. With the mood I'm in, God knows what I'll say to Alec if he starts pushing my buttons."

"Chicken."

I just look at her. Does she really think that will work with me?

"My tough-as-nails, wise-ass, best girlfriend would never run from the likes of a few men. She's faced down evil mothers, brutal daughters, numerous sorry excuses for husbands, and – here's the most telling example of her strength and power – hundreds of ten and eleven-year-olds on a daily basis."

Trying not to laugh, I ask, "What's for lunch?"

She shrugs. Another way we've cemented our friendship is our complete abhorrence of anything involving serious cooking or kitchen responsibilities. "Sandwiches. I was going to make some egg salad and macaroni salad and some homebrewed iced tea. Maybe some brownies."

"Got any sour cream?"

Callie thinks for a minute. "Yeah, I think so. I was going to do a dip."

"Can I make a cake, instead?"

Callie shrugs. "Sure."

We go traipsing into the kitchen and the floor vibrates with the low bass guitar beat downstairs. Going over to the intercom, Callie flips a switch and we're treated to the practice session going on downstairs. While we bee-bop to the rhythm, Callie breaks out the eggs and starts boiling water while I try to remember my grandmother's famous sour cream coffee cake recipe to impress the rock singing, meter reading, pastry chef right below my feet.

A while later, I recognize Alec's voice, finally, over the intercom and Callie says, "Oh I love this one." As she mixes up mayonnaise, tuna, and chopped celery for the macaroni salad she begins to sing along with a surprising good, sultry alto voice: *Praise Him under open skies, Everything breathing praising God, In the company of all who love the King, I will dance, I will sing, It could be heavenly, Turn the music loud, lift my voice and shout, From where I am, From where I've been, He's been there with me, He's built a monument, His very people, So let His people Sing, sing, sing, And it's so wonderful, Just to be here now …*[27]

From where I am, from where I've been, He's been there with me. Has He? Is that why I'm, as Callie so aptly put it, still sane and standing? I think back over how many times Callie's come to my rescue with words, or deeds, or just five or six Snickers bars. "Thanks," I finally say as I'm pouring batter into a greased bunt pan.

"You're welcome. Why are you thanking me?"

"You're a good friend. Good God public relations material, too. In the past twenty years, if I let myself look back at the really dark times you were always there."

"Can I tell you something really Twilight Zone cool?"

"Yeah, sure."

"I knew to come to your house the afternoon that Richard killed himself."

I turn and look at her but she has her back to me as she's chopping up red peppers now.

"I had a dentist appointment that day right after school. You know me. I'm not bothered by dentists or anything but I had," she shrugs, "I don't know, it must have been a panic attack or something on the way there. It was so bad I had to pull over to the side of the road to get myself together. I remember thinking, 'What's this foolishness? I'm not afraid of the dentist! I'm not a big gigantic chicken like Elaine -'"

"Hey!"

She laughs. "That got me thinking about you and suddenly I felt *so powerfully compelled* to get to your house. Like putting the pedal to the metal, breaking the sound barrier, and getting there at all costs compelled. I didn't even know if you'd left school yet. I even started to head toward the dentist only to start flipping out again." She turns around and I can see that she's still really moved by all this. "I drove to your house. And you were already home ..."

I swallow and vividly remember. Through dry lips I murmur, "I was freaking out over the dead body in my bedroom." She nods and I can see that she's teary now as she silently watches me process what she's just told me. "I always wondered how you got to the house so quickly. I couldn't remember calling you ..."

Callie shakes her head. "You weren't capable of calling anyone. I called the police. And then we sat in the hallway outside the bedroom, holding each other and crying. It was one of the most powerfully spiritual times for me *in my life. God made me go to your house that day, Elaine.* How cool is that?"

"How come you never told me?"

She makes a face and goes back to her red peppers. Over her shoulder she says, "What would the *real* Elaine have thought if I'd told her sometime other than today?" I can tell she's smiling.

"After I recovered suitably enough to speak coherently?"

"Yeah. After that."

"I would have thought, 'I wonder if she's in as close contact with the tooth fairy and the Easter bunny. I've got some really critical questions I'd like answered.'"

Callie looks over her shoulder at me and grins, "See?"

"See what?" James says as he and a pile of heavy footsteps emerge from the basement.

"See how beautiful women can be in the prime of their lives?" Callie throws out an air kiss to her husband.

"You got that right," James says as he comes up behind his wife, nuzzles her on the neck and makes a grand show of trying to bite her. Letting out a shriek, Callie elbows him away and begins ordering everyone around: get the paper plates and cutlery, go wipe down the deck table, grab the pitcher of iced tea in the fridge and a pile of paper cups, grab the pickles and the mayonnaise, carry this and that out ...

I find myself seated at the Danely's large deck table. In addition to Callie, James and Alec there's Ed who plays drums, Rick who plays keyboard, and Manuel who was once introduced to me as The God Of Sound.

I've been to lots of parties before at Callie and James' and everyone is always very friendly and welcoming. It doesn't stop me from feeling like the outsider or, maybe a better term would be the Evil Heathen or the Devil's Own Spawn since I'm usually the only one not in The God Club. I don't always get the godly sense of humor that they have amongst themselves, making it seem like a private, members only alliance. Like there are cracks about "wives being submissive and subservient" (to which Callie always responds "quote me the scripture, Neanderthal") to everyone's delight. Or deep discussions will ensue about some point made by a minister or an author or a radio broadcaster that's got everyone all hot and bothered. Many have the ability to throw out a quote, I assume to be from the Bible, to make a point (funny or serious) that leaves me clueless. And phrases like, 'Oh, I'll remember you in prayer', 'God bless!', or 'Praise The Lord!' make me want to jump out the closest window and run screaming into the night. One time, Callie embroidered me a beautiful saying for my birthday and she and James just about fell on the floor laughing when I asked why a guy's name (John) was at the bottom. Turns out it was a *scripture reference* for the Bible verse – not a saying – she'd chosen for me.

Sitting at the table, eating sandwiches, chips, and salad, I watch these people who seem to have either a.) all simultaneously bought into some mumbo-jumbo stuff about living forever and personality transformations more powerful than a triple dose of the strongest psychotic drug, or b.) wisely discerned a spiritual reality to which I seem incapable of buying into due to my astronomically cynically/warped character. They laugh and joke and seem so normal and happy that I find myself seriously considering evaluating my moral fiber.

"This is the quietest I've ever seen you," Alec murmurs in my ear giving me a wash of goose bumps down my arm.

"I try to behave in these settings. Today I'm outnumbered six to one."

He eats a dill pickle as he scans around the table. "What?" He whispers again in my ear, "Because we all go to church you think we're perfect or something? You think we don't get jealous or angry, depressed or," he leans in and whispers, "horny?" with a wicked chuckle. I look at him and physically will myself to not blush or say the dangerous rush of wiseass words that are buzzing around in my head like angry bees. He gestures to the collection of people around the table and whispers in my ear. "We're regular Joes and Janes who have just given up trying to steer our own lives. We've let Someone take the driver's seat and we've just committed to do our best to listen to directions, follow the printed plans and make the most of the options we've been blessed with. We still have all our own foibles and we still all continue to battle our own personal demons. We've just got powerful help on our side now."

"Who says I've got foibles or personal demons?" Manuel asks with a grin. "I'm perfect. Just ask my mother."

"How about your wife?" James says with a bigger grin.

"Maybe not today," Manuel says and everyone laughs.

"My personal demon is my deep seated fixation on becoming the next Mick Jagger," James says with a straight face. "There have been times in my life when I would have given *anything* to experience the adrenaline rush of thousands of screaming fans and all the fame and fortune that goes with it." I actually think he's serious.

"Single malt scotch whiskey," Ed says with a shy smile. "I've already lost about a decade to it, so I'm trying to avoid losing any more time."

"Motherhood," Callie says looking me right in the eye and I know how bare and raw she feels acknowledging it out loud.

James drapes his arm around her neck, "But honey, you've got me. I try to remain as high maintenance and adolescent as possible so that you feel like you've got a child."

"And you do such a good job, too, baby," she croons back to him and rests her head on his shoulder.

"I'll bet you fifty bucks my demon is better than yours," Rick says and everyone cracks up laughing – another one of those inside jokes I don't get.

"Gambling," Rick says to me quietly with a wink once everyone settles down. Oh.

"See?" Manuel says to me, "We're not perfect. We're just forgiven." Everyone laughs and goes back to munching and talking.

It's another one of those jokes I've heard before that leaves me out of the club. Out in the cold. And the rain. Soaking wet and shivering.

Alec follows me as I go in to get my cake out of the oven. Watching me test my creation with far too much analytical interest, he asks me, "Do you have anything special going on tomorrow?"

It's Labor Day Monday. It would make perfect sense for me to say something like, *Yeah, I've been invited to a big celebration by one of my many friends.* Except I've got nothing planned. Except to enjoy my last free, uninhibited day to sew ad infinitum. Even Erin, Dan and Liam are away for these days of the final weekend of summer fun. I put the cake down on the cooling rack and hear myself say, "No, nothing special."

He tastes a piece of the cinnamon crumble topping. "Will you spend the day with me? It's one of the few day's I've got free."

"From meter reading?" He takes another taste and I'm just waiting for a critical comment. Paul used to do that. *Oh, Elaine, a nice try on the chicken. Next time, why don't you try a little more garlic in the marinade?* Here's a tip for you: soy sauce *does not* come out of men's white dress shirts no matter how many times you wash them.

"Nah," Alec says, "I get a lot of free days with the meter reading. It's the pastry chef job that I hardly get any free time from. Not that I mind. Agape Shop is closed tomorrow for the Labor Day holiday."

"Oh." I look at him and narrow my eyes. "Aren't you going to make a comment? Offer me a suggestion to improve?" I glance down at my crumb cake.

He looks confused. "About your coffee cake?" He shakes his head and then narrows his eyes at me. "What, is this some kind of test or something? So far it smells and tastes great. I'll do the same thing I'd expect you do to my stuff: say I like it, say I hate it, or even ask for the recipe." We stare at each other for a beat. Finally, after a moment of charged silence on my part he arches an eyebrow and says, "Okay?"

I'm being a colossal idiot. Alec doesn't realize it but there are more than just the two of us here in this kitchen. There's critical Paul, my soul destroying mother, and possibly Richard who was always worrying about his fat and cholesterol count and would never let me make my grandmother's sour cream coffee cake because it's like 8,000 calories a slice. This kitchen's way too crowded. I sigh. "Okay."

"Come on, Elaine. Spend the day with me. I promise I'll have you home early – like eight o'clock. I've got to catch some sleep before I go in to work that night."

"What time do you go in?"

"Usually between two and three."

"*A.M.?*"

Alec grins and nods. I scroll through the fact that he does that job and then must go right to his meter reading job. No wonder sometimes he's crabby by the time he gets to my house. I'd be as nasty as a flesh-eating virus.

"Okay."

He seems to work at containing himself from jumping up and punching the air in a victory salute. "Great! I'll pick you up at four."

Frowning I say, "Okay, but that's an awful short day if you're going to get me home by eight."

Shaking his head he says, "No, Elaine. I'll pick you up at four *a.m.*"

I laugh out loud. Is he out of his freakin' mind? I inform him, "I haven't been up at four a.m. since Erin was six months old. She's twenty-nine now." I lean into his face. "You *are not* picking me up at four a.m."

He has the audacity to look disappointed. "Just because I'm not working doesn't mean I don't get up at odd hours still. I could have said I was going to pick you up at two a.m."

In your dreams. "Sure, you could have said it, but it wouldn't have ensured you were going to be any more successful."

"Come on, Elaine. I'll bring pastries. If we get going at four then we can get to the place I have in mind to see the sunrise."

"I. Have. No. Interest. In. Seeing. Any. Sunrise. That. Occurs. Before. Ten. A. M."

"*Ten a.m.!* The day's half over by then."

I cross my arms and glare at him. "That's my final offer."

He looks down at my crossed arms and I realize I've got a pretty good cleavage display going on (which only happens when my arms are crossed, I'll confess). After a few lost moments on his part, he makes eye contact with me and asks, "If I bring coffee – *really excellent coffee* – and pastries, can I come at nine?"

"What do you mean by *really excellent coffee?*"

Sensing victory he smiles an oily salesman smile and says, "It's *Yauco Selecto AA* from Puerto Rico. I've got connections."

"Is that as good as Jamaican Blue?" Which I've had once, about thirteen years ago, and personally I didn't understand what all the hype was about but Alec doesn't have to know that.

He makes a dismissive sound, "Light years better."

Blatantly flirting, I tilt my head to one side, "What kind of pastry?"

Stepping in, he crowds me up against the counter. "A surprise. I'll bake it fresh. Since I've got *hours* until I'm allowed to show up at your house."

"Okay, nine o'clock. But not a minute earlier. *And it better be worth it.*"

If I hear just one more time that I should try and be more open-minded,
I think I'll scream
This world says this is all there is, yet I believe the One who says there's life after this,
Now tell me how much more open can my mind be?[28]

Chapter 11: Pages In The Book Of Life I've Never Read

I'm not a morning person. Actually, I'm not a late night person either. I guess I'm more like a late-morning/early afternoon kind of woman. Consequently, I know that it's going to require some significant work to look as stunning as I possibly can at nine a.m. which means my cursed alarm goes off at seven-thirty a.m. to begin the momentous task ahead. I lie there in bed, next to Harry and all of his fur and bad breath, and I doubt my sanity, my resolve, and any significant personal growth I think I've made over the course of my forty-eight years.

I wasn't kidding when I told Callie about not allowing the real me to ever appear. I learned early on with my mother to stifle things that would only make the situation worse. God only knows how early *that* started. I could morph into anything required under my mother's spectacularly erratic existence, always with the knowledge that no matter what I did, it wouldn't be right. My subsequent relationships – both married and otherwise – regularly drove home the point that no matter how bad the situation was, being myself would only make it worse. The magnitude of my vitriolic anger, low self-esteem, and gargantuan guilt makes me a perfect candidate for going postal one day. Good thing I'm not a mailwoman.

These last ten years of singlehood I've discovered the real, honest to goodness Elaine Marie Cummings nee Kelly nee Richardson nee Brockman. I like her, don't get me wrong about that, but she's definitely best served up in small, carefully managed dosages for the most successful result. Like strong cough syrup. Or Milk of Magnesia. Not intended for small children, not to be taken regularly, and never to be mixed with alcohol.

I take a long, lusciously hot shower and use my favorite almond bath gel in copious amounts. I make no effort to tame my hair with blow-drying or curling iron because knowing the man in question we're probably going to go skydiving or something. Which leads me to my next problem, what exactly do you wear on a date that starts at nine a.m.? I can safely eliminate four-inch heels (like I've got any) or a ball gown (ditto).

Looking out the window, it's an absolutely perfect day. Blue sky, no clouds, cool but not cold, no humidity ... Definitely a day for outdoors. I settle on my trendy pair of low-rise jeans. Olivia was relentless for a few months about my 'mom jeans' that were high waisted and made my 'butt look huge.' Erin bought me a pair of 'low rise boot cut' jeans for Mother's Day ... along with a pair of quite excellent cowboy boots. As I stare at my tee shirts, I feel an outfit coming together ...

I'm wandering down the stairs at eight thirty-five a.m. beginning to vaguely feel alert and refreshed, only to see a man sitting on my front porch reading my morning paper.

Not any man, of course.

I spend a few minutes debating on letting him sit outside and wait until *not a minute earlier* than nine a.m. but the reality is - I'm stunned to admit to myself - I'm quite excited about the whole day. Opening up the front door, I step out into the morning sunshine and lean against my house. "How long have you been here?"

Alec takes the time to check me out. From head to toe. He takes in my still damp hair, my purposely selected Mets tee shirt, my completely fashionable low-rise jeans, and my way cool boots. When he *finally* makes eye contact with me he answers, "Since a little before eight."

Harry makes a vocal appeal for release and I let him out. "The main man in my life," I explain to Alec as my cat saunters out onto the porch as if he's waiting for applause. "Harry."

"Hello Harry," Alec says and holds his hand out for Harry's close inspection. Alec starts to scratch Harry behind his ears and suddenly his lap is filled with a huge purring mass of orange fur. "I guess I pass inspection."

"I guess you do."

"Is that you that smells so good?" he asks as I settle myself in the second cushioned porch chair.

"Nah, it's Harry. How long have you been awake?"

"Actually, I didn't set my alarm so I slept until almost three-thirty."

That someone would *naturally* wake up at three-thirty is absolutely ludicrous. "What's the world like at three-thirty a.m.?"

"Quiet, dark, peaceful. It's nice, actually." He leans over towards me and takes a deep breath. "Man, you smell good. Are you wearing almond scent just because I bake?"

I turn to answer him and his face is *right there*. He doesn't smell so bad himself, I think as an aroma of coffee and aftershave drifts towards me. I can't help it and I grin at him. "I've always been into bakery-based pheromones."

His hand comes up and catches the back of my head and he gives me a kiss that rockets us both right out into the stratosphere. It goes on and on while we shift angles a bit and bump noses now and then. He finally ends the kiss and collapses back into the chair with his head back and his eyes closed.

"I don't want to sleep with you, Elaine," he says through gritted teeth.

Could have fooled me, I think. "Yeah, I've gotten that message loud and clear since the very first time we were formally introduced and you *kissed* me within the first half hour. Ever since then, you've been provocative and in-your-face with sexual innuendoes at every available opportunity." I glare at him. "And we won't even *begin* to discuss the looks you give me. Regularly. Repeatedly."

He runs his hand down his face and sighs. "Yeah, I know. I've been attracted to you from the very first moment you insulted me, standing looking at me through your front door in your pajamas *very braless and very cold.*"

I know the blush that flushes my face extends from the top of my head to the tip of my toes. *"What?"* I swallow and try to remember our first-ever meeting. *"When?"*

Alec shrugs. "Over a year ago. Maybe March or April of last year."

Shaking my head, I insist, "That's impossible. I only see you during the summer. Otherwise I'm at work."

Alec shrugs. "You must have been home, sick or something. I don't know. You came to the door in your pajamas all tousled and *cold,* let me in, complained about my muddy boots – which considering what I was completely distracted by was the *very last thing* I was thinking about. I was totally horrified by the directions of my thoughts and just wanted to get the hell out of your house as fast as humanly possible."

I have a vague, fuzzy recollection of a horrible sinus infection and a few days of R&R. Actually a head cold is almost the standard rite of spring for me.

"Every damn time I come to the door, you're invariably dressed in some provocative way -"

"I sleep in a tee shirt and boxer shorts!" I yell at him defensively. He makes it sound like I'm showing up at the door in a Victoria Secret thong, garter belt, and silk robe.

"It's not your fault, Elaine, it's mine. You could show up in fuzzy foot pajamas and I'd get all wrapped up in the fantasy of undoing the zipper." He winks at me. "The long, full length zipper that would slowly come down ..." He stops and seems satisfied he's passed on enough of the fantasy on to me. I look away.

Suddenly, he stands up, picks up a cool bag that I didn't notice until just now, and extends his hand to me. "Come inside. I'll make you the world's best coffee, serve you flaky, homemade croissants drizzled in chocolate, and tell you my entire life story." When I hesitate he adds with intensity, "I don't want to sleep with you, Elaine, because for once in my sorry-ass existence, I want to get a relationship right. Maybe, *please God*, if I can do this right, the next time someone asks me if I've ever had a long term relationship I can not only say 'yes', but I can say that *I'm still in it*."

I put my hand in his and allow him to haul me up. "Don't think I missed the Mets tee shirt," he says to me with a quick peck on my mouth. "One of the first things I plan to do is buy you a Yankees tee shirt to replace it."

"I'll only wear it without a bra," I say to him straight faced, "in the dead of winter."

Alec looks up heavenward and shakes his head. "This is my final exam, isn't it God? Pass or fail." Opening up my front door, he drags me inside.

He's one of those men who can make himself at home in anyone's kitchen. As mine is of the minimalist variety (no flair, main purpose to avoid starvation and malnutrition) it doesn't take a degree in brain surgery to find your way around. He's got the coffee brewing and has found pretty little dishes I never use because they're not dishwasher safe to put four luscious looking croissants on. I sit and watch him in his element.

"You going to give me your recipe for that coffee cake you made yesterday?"

"It's my grandma's sour cream crumb cake. I used to help her make it when I was a kid."

"Fond memories, huh?" he says with a smile as he sets two mugs down and pours out the coffee.

I shrug. "One of the few. You can have the recipe if you want."

He sits down next to me at the kitchen counter, breaks off a piece of croissant and holds it out to me. "What's with you and feeding me?" I ask taking care to not open my mouth wide.

He leans forward and says, *"I like to."* With cooperative resignation, I open my mouth and lose myself in butter, flaky pastry and dark, sweet chocolate.

It takes a moment for me to realize that I've closed my eyes in ecstasy. When I open them he's got such a predatory look on his face that I sit up straight and clear my throat. "Really good."

"I've been a player my entire life, Elaine. Calculating, concise, driven. I've looked out for number one," he thumps his chest, "and worked with unerring focus on achieving everything my little heart desired. Rules and laws applied to other people but not to me." He pauses in thought. "I don't think I necessarily thought I was above society's edicts, I just had a perception that they were only in place for people not smart enough or clever enough to find ways around them. You want to talk about personal demons and foibles? I can still look at any given situation I'm involved with and within minutes can calculate the maximum benefit – both monetarily and prestige wise – I could get out of it. It's like an addiction; it never really disappears, you just learn to control it better."

Suddenly I'm getting a really bad feeling. I squint at him. *"What, exactly, are you trying to tell me?"*

Seeming to gear himself up for the tough part of the climb, he says, "Even though it's not our second date, you *did* ask. I was convicted of fraud about seven years ago. Insider trading to be specific. Because I was able to afford an exceptional lawyer, I was sentenced to only one year in Butner Federal Correction Facility down in Raleigh, North Carolina. I was released after only four months and paid $350,000 in fines – which just about cleaned me out." My head says, *Oh, this is just priceless. Way to go, Elaine. A whole new category to add to your collection of loser men. This time you've outdone yourself. This time you've hooked yourself up with an ex-con!* Since I am completely and utterly speechless, he continues.

"I had an old childhood acquaintance – his name was Karl - who invited me to come and stay with him after I got out of prison. Our families had known each other; he'd watched me grow up and had kept track of my rise ... and my fall. He wrote to me when I was just about to get out of prison and told me his wife had died and he was alone, running a small, family owned bakery in central New Jersey. Said he could use some help if I was interested."

Alec laughs and looks out the window, I suppose lost in memories. "Talk about culture shock! It was a whole new way of life for me: casual, family based, noncompetitive … To my eyes, the shop was always in danger of bankruptcy but Karl was the most peaceful, content, happy guy I'd ever come across. He didn't want to hear anything about my ideas for expansion, improvement, or gaining a competitive edge. 'Why bother, Alec?' he'd say to me. 'I've got all I need. I'm happy. I sleep well at night. My kid's love me. I don't care about my bank account. I can't take it with me. I've just got to keep an eye on my soul account. That's the only thing that needs constant vigilance.'

"I slept on Karl's living room couch – it was only a one-bedroom apartment - for about nine months. I learned about fluffy pastries, family values, and how not to kill the yeast. But most importantly, I learned about the joys of silent prayer and quiet devotions at three a.m. while you're waiting for your cake to bake. Karl never shoved his faith down my throat. It was just *so appealing*, I couldn't help but finally ask about it. Karl tolerated scads of questions and he always gave me patient, meticulous answers. Sometimes he'd give me a smile and say, 'Now *that one*, Alec, I've got to look up.' Off he'd troop to his Bible," Alec gives me a smile, "much larger than mine, I'll have you know. He'd check his notes and flip through pages and finally say, 'Oh, right. Here it is,' and off we'd go on another discussion."

Alec is quiet for a long time. He takes a sip of his coffee, eats a bit of his croissant. "When he died, I helped his two daughters pack up his stuff and sell the shop. We found a big envelope addressed to me telling me to 'stay the course and keep the faith.' He left me all of his pastry recipes and a Bible verse." From under his shirt, Alec pulls out a heavy silver chain with a silver medallion hanging from it. I can see words engraved: John 14:25. Alec recites the verse to me while I hold the warm, silver disc in my hand, "*I am leaving you with a gift – peace of mind and heart. And the peace I give isn't like the peace the world gives. So don't be troubled or afraid.*[29]

"I could have gone someplace else, but it felt like home here. I got an apartment, managed to get a job meter reading, and started attending church regularly. When my church started Agape Shop, I was the one who pushed hard for the attached coffee shop. I committed to baking," he grins, "they made me prove my abilities, too!" So I do my paying job - meter reading - which gives me money and health benefits and then I go and do my dream job – as pastry chef - which keeps my soul on track."

When he falls silent, I ask him, "Where does guitar playing and singing come in?"

"Oh, I did the teenage rock band thing when I was young. I bought the guitar when I got the apartment and filled in the empty hours practicing. My church has always had a praise band and sometimes they'd invite me to play along." He winks. "Don't worry. I'm not like James dreaming of Mick Jagger glory and panties being thrown at me while I'm on the stage."

Alec leans forward and takes both of my hands. "Here's the thing Elaine. I've never had the time or interest for a real relationship with a woman. Now, don't get me wrong, I *love* women and have spent very fond times enjoying many of them. But the whole effort that was involved in a long term, monogamous relationship just never appealed. I had bigger things to do and see and become. After Butner … I really wanted to be *completely different* in all aspects of my life." He squeezes my hands and then amends, "Well, maybe not at first, but certainly once I bought into everything Karl shared with me about becoming a committed man after God's own heart." Letting go of my hands he stands up and walks over to the kitchen window. "Given my history with women, it was easier to avoid them all together. I laugh and flirt and tease but I never take it any further. It's just easier for me that way."

Thrusting his hands in his pockets he leans against the window and says softly, "Lately, though, I've been lonely. It's surprised me because I'm a gregarious kind of guy. I've got loads of friends and colleagues. I'm rarely alone, even baking at the shop I've got a bunch of assistants. The concept of *being* or even *feeling* lonely has never factored into my life." He snorts. "Not even when I was in prison." He glances at me sitting silently watching him. "It seems that I can kind of trace it back to this woman I met one *cold*, early spring morning on my meter reading route."

I know I blush, but I hold my head up high. He chuckles and shakes his head at me. He goes back to looking out the window.

"Maybe I was ready to meet someone, I thought. Maybe, this feeling of loneliness was God's way of saying, 'Hey, Alec. It's time you took a leap of faith and trusted that you could handle a real relationship like other normal human beings seem to enjoy.' I asked the guys in the band if they knew anyone. I stressed I didn't want anyone who was out of her mind desperate for a connection. I didn't want anyone who was young enough to want a white picket fence and two children. I just wanted someone who could appreciate my sense of humor and put up with the odd quirkinesses any fifty-three-year-old lifetime bachelor has *got* to have. I just wanted to have someone I might enjoy spending time with." Alec looks at me again. "James said he might know someone."

Walking over to me, he turns my counter stool around so that I'm facing him. "Even for me, all of this," he gestures between the two of us, "is a little too amazing. When I saw you weaving through the crowd toward Callie the night at the concert, I just couldn't believe my eyes. *No one* can ever convince me that God doesn't have a sense of humor."

"At least I wasn't cold that night," I can't keep from saying.

He steps between my legs, puts his hands on my waist and rests his forehead against mine. "No, you were far from cold that night. You joked about putting out, bustiers and leather skirts, and even teased me about having a prison record. You blew me right out of the park."

Shaking my head I say, "I didn't know ..."

His hands come up to hold my face. "I *know* you didn't know, Elaine. *I know.* I called James that night and flat out asked him. Demanded to know what he'd said to you ... or Callie. He denied saying anything to either one of you except that he'd asked Callie to ask you to come and keep the new guitarist company his first time out."

I feel it is tremendously important to add, "Well, James did tell me that he told you I'd been married three times and that he thought you had a pretty good chance of me putting out."

Alec lets out an explosive burst of laughter and then says, "I'm going to kill him."

Watching closely, I ask, "Did he tell you that?"

"I … He …" but Alec's expression is all the answer I really need.

"*I'm* going to kill *him*," I say.

I'm given the classic excuse. "We were only joking around."

Does he know how many times I've heard that in my twenty-four year career? "I'll *bet* you were joking," I say fighting to keep my eyes from rolling in sarcasm.

"About this putting out stuff," Alec begins and he's still holding my face. "I'm not saying I've got any set schedule or anything -"

"You've seemed awfully fixated on our second date," I'm inclined to point out.

He kisses me. "Hush." I open my mouth like I'm going to say something again, but it's really just so he'll give me another kiss. Which he does. Finally he says to me, "Let me finish. Please?" At my semi-cooperative silence, he drops his hands to my waist and continues. "I really don't want to mess this up. If there's one thing I've learned over the course of my life and *in particular* over these last bunch of years, staying on the right track with God is my surest guarantee for success." He sighs like he's almost in physical pain. "The fact that I'm *very* attracted to you," I waggle my eyebrows and he grins but keeps going, "makes it all the more difficult to do the right thing."

I think about all of the men I've ever been sexually involved with, and how *many* of them never had to wait until the second date to get lucky. Why stall the cow when the milk is guaranteed to come free no matter what? It's time I let Alec off the hook a bit. "I'd like the same thing, although not for such noble reasons." His thumbs are caressing my waist. "I want to stay on the right track, too. I kind of lose my … self … when I get sexually involved with a guy, and history has proven that I become a stark raving idiot. The fact that you're an ex-con isn't so amazing when you factor in my past relationships: alcoholics, psychological mind freaks, and the suicidally depressed. I figure if I can keep you out of my pants for long enough – something I've never managed to do in the past I'll point out – then I should be able to figure out exactly why you'd be completely toxic to me and my hard won mental stability."

He stares at me for a beat or two and then just starts laughing. Standing there between my legs, holding onto my waist, he just throws his head back and completely cracks up. "It's not that funny," I mumble, and only then does he sober up enough to kiss me again. He steps in even closer and I wrap one cowboy booted foot around his leg and snake my arms up around his back while he wraps both arms around me and squeezes tight.

When we come up for air, he sighs. "I'm trying to be completely honest with you, Elaine. It's a modus operandi that I've only recently embraced in the last few years and have *never in my entire miserable life* tried with a woman. I like you. I want you. I completely enjoy your smart mouth." He takes time to kiss me again quickly. "I crave - on a daily basis - getting to know you better: what makes you tick ... what makes you laugh ... what makes you cry ... what really pisses you off ... what you can't do without ... And I'm desperate to get this right."

I listen to this man say the most wonderful things to me. There have been periods over the course of my life that I'm pretty sure I would have donated a kidney to have someone say the things that Alec is saying to me. But I can't enjoy hearing them for even a moment because my head is saying, *Maybe the big bad thing Alec is hiding is he's certifiably insane.*

Okay, time for me to open my life, too. "You should know that a lot of the things you want to know are live mine fields for me. You'll probably need a biohazard suit or a flak jacket or something." He just looks at me. I laugh a kind of laugh that has attached to it the casual, airhead phrase, *whatever.* "You *cannot* be real. I've had a lot of experience with men and there's no way on the planet that you're as good as you sound. This whole ex-con thing is probably just a ruse to throw me off so I don't see the really bad stuff you're hiding." He's still looking at me but he seems to be enjoying my diatribe because he's got a tiny little smile going on now. Waiting for the next charmingly shocking thing that's going to come out of my mouth, I suppose.

"So we're on the same page?" he finally says after it's clear I'm done with my little speech.

Actually, maybe this could be fun. An opportunity to pull out all my stops and be as completely uninhibited and in-your-face as I've never been brave enough to be. I think about the brief feeling of freedom once the secret was out with Olivia. *Talk about complete freedom,* my head sighs in anticipatory ecstasy. All with the guaranteed reassurance that I won't loose my mind because he doesn't want to mess things up and end up between the sheets. It's a chance to really get to know this guy, while my head is sharp, clear, and sane, and discover just what deep down neuroses and top-secret faults he has hidden. So I can validate my uncanny ability to attract loser men of the highest order.

I run my finger down his chest, past his stomach and hook it in the front of his pants. He jumps like I've just Tasered him. Nodding, I say, "The celibacy page. A fascinating one I've never read while in the company of a man."

Dear God, surround me as I speak, the bridges that I walk across are weak,
Frustrations fill the void that I can't solely bear[30]

Chapter 12: Conversations I've Never Had

M y good friend Callie knows me too well when she says
in reference to my relationship with Olivia, *'She smashes
you down with word or deed and after you finish reeling from the
blow, you brush yourself off and forge right on towards her again.'* Which would
explain why, still on the high from my daylong date with Alec I am
considering contacting Olivia by phone or email. (I'm not brave enough to
try in person, usually.)

The first day of school is a half-day, which gets me over and done
with professional duties by one o'clock. Aside from one fifth grader who
had a complete psychological meltdown trying to open his locker, and
another who announced to the class that his personal preference was 'going
commando,' day one out of one hundred and eighty was rather routine.

I know, thanks to our day together, that by five p.m. most days
Alec is tucked away in his apartment fast asleep, phone unplugged, earplugs
in and blackout shades pulled. I also know that he rents an apartment
directly above Agape House, drives an Ford F150 pick up truck, and after
nearly twelve solid hours together seems even nicer than I first feared.
Conversely, he knows that I often stay at work until four p.m. because I
love what I do, have dealt with one shotgun wedding, one psychological

mind control husband, and one suicide. Plus he saw all my wallet photos of Liam, Erin, Dan, and Olivia.

After spilling his guts over croissants and coffee, we had an enjoyable day hiking some easy trails in a park in the northwestern part of the state. We stopped for sandwiches on the way and picnicked by the Black River, talking about anything and everything. The list of Alec's positive attributes continues to grow to such an extent that I went home and began to make a list.

Positives About Alec:

1. Says my sense of humor is enjoyable. (Thinks I'm <u>funny</u>!)

2. Says he's physically attracted to me

3. Wants to get to know me better (!)

4. Has all his teeth

5. Always smells good

6. Is gainfully employed

7. Has no apparent addictions

8. Is nice looking

9. Is physically attractive

10. Doesn't talk with food in his mouth

11. Doesn't scratch himself (at least in public)

12. Is on the God-squad (see #3 below)

Negatives About Alec:

1. I like him

2. Is an ex-con

3. Is on the God-squad (see #12 above)

Sometimes when I'm confused and struggling with life I like to write stuff down. For me, stuff in black and white, for some reason, is harder to ignore than stuff I can see with my two eyes. After Richard's death, the therapist I saw encouraged me to make lists to organize my head and, consequently, my life. Like, when I said something like, 'I had no idea that Richard was so unhappy,' then I was sent home to list all the positives and negatives that Richard shared over the course of our marriage. When I got finished with *that* list, I was inclined to reword my statement into something like, 'It's unfortunate I didn't realize the extent of Richard's depression which seemed to encompass every waking moment of his life.' Unfortunately, lists that have never been written by me, which would probably be the most productive such as 'The Things I Have And Haven't Done For My Daughter Olivia Over The Course Of Her Life,' or 'Resolved and Unresolved Issues With My Mother,' or 'Valid And Invalid Observations About My Personal Psyche Made By My Second Husband,' or 'Changes I Need To Make And Follow About Myself To Achieve Personal Success' will never be written.

Hey, I'm no masochist.

The list on Alec has a two-fold benefit. When the negative stuff starts to appear it will be much more difficult to ignore everything staring at me in black and white (benefit #1). *And,* should we finally end up between the sheets and I consequently loose my mind, perhaps I'll remember the list and make reference to it (benefit #2).

Driving home from school, thinking about my life, I inevitably end up thinking about Olivia. Popping in my earpiece, I dial her at work: a place that is a relatively safe place to call since she can't really scream or curse at me when surrounded by her colleagues.

"Olivia Kelly."

"Hey, Olivia. It's mom. Did I catch you at a busy time?"

There's that hesitation that communicates a pile of stuff and none of it's good. "No. It's quiet. There are still a lot of people out for lunch. Shouldn't you be at school?

"First day's a half day. I'm just leaving."

"How'd it go? Any potential criminals?"

Some years, the certainty that some of my students are future correctional facility inmates is rather frighteningly obvious. "So far, so good. Although one boy felt the need to inform us that he regularly goes commando."

Olivia chuckles. "I don't know how you do that day in and day out."

"It's the perfect place for me. If everyone else around me is wilder, crazier, and nuttier than I, it just makes me look that much more normal." At her silence on the phone I suspect I've stepped on incorrect eggshells, having reminded her that the woman that is her mother is not average or run of the mill. "Are you okay?"

"Yeah, Mom," Olivia says quietly into the phone. "Despite the fact that I've discovered that the man that I always thought was my father is *not* my father and despite the fact that my mother, for some reason known only to herself, refuses to name the man who really *is* my father, I'm okay."

I'd like to close my eyes at the magnitude of pain that rolls through my body but I'm currently driving sixty miles an hour down the highway. "I'm okay, too," I hear myself say and seem incapable of shutting myself up, "despite the fact that my daughter continues to rip and tear at a wound, that despite its age, is almost as brutally painful as the day it occurred. I'm okay, too, despite the fact that no matter what I seem to do, or how many times I seem to try, I never, ever get it right with you – despite my hopes, my dreams, and my best intentions."

I have no right to do this to Olivia while she's at work. None. And the moment the words finish coming out of my mouth I want to shout, "*I'm sorry! I take it back! Forget I said that!*" but of course I can't. There is a charged silence and I wait to hear the distinctive click of being hung up on.

"Grandmother's okay in the same way, mother," Olivia finally says.

"Grandmother who?" I can't for the life of me follow where she's headed.

"My *grandmother*. As in *your mother*."

"What do you know about my mother?" I ask in stunned confusion. To the best of my knowledge Olivia met my mother, her grandmother, just once and Erin not at all. Watching my mother talk down to me regarding my continuing course of bad choices and then hearing her disparage my violet eyed baby girl's less than auspicious start was something I chose to tolerate *only once*. Olivia had been just six month's old at the time.

"I contacted her," Olivia says over the phone, seemingly unaware of the host of cluster bombs going off in my head. "I figured if you wouldn't answer some of my questions about my past, maybe she would. We've met twice over coffee and spoke a few times by phone. She's told me some stories and been polite to me. Tell me mother, to what end did you choose to deny both Erin and myself this family connection?"

I can't speak. Clutching the steering wheel, I drive mindlessly down the highway, determined to get myself home before I completely detonate.

"Mother?" I hear in my ear. "Mother?" And then, finally, blessedly, I hear the distinctive click of the connection being broken.

Like a zombie, I make it through the first week of school. Contrary to what you might think, teaching school is a wonderful, mind numbing escape from the horrors of my life. It always has been. My life can be literally in flames, like after I moved out on Paul and lived briefly - for forty-eight hours - in my car with Olivia and Erin, or like after coming home and finding a man stone cold dead in my bed, and yet if I can *just get myself to school* I'm okay for the six and a half hours that I'm on. Consequently, finding out that Olivia has not only contacted my mother, but is in ongoing conversation with her, and will in all likelihood believe every single thing my mother tells her is still only like number three on my list of personal cataclysms.

The fact that I come home, eat, and invariably am fast asleep by seven p.m. during these three days, however, is a clue to me that I'm teetering on the brink of a meltdown not seen since Callie held me and we both cried that day in my upstairs hallway. Part of my feeling of impending doom is the realization that I'm going to have to go see my mother. Return to the scene of the crime so to speak, for she still lives in the same little ranch house that she lived in when I was a desperately unhappy child and tortured adolescent.

Friday evening, I realize I have one of two choices: sleep the entire weekend away only to get back on this same treadmill Monday, or drive over tonight, see my mother, and careen down a yet unknown path of destruction. Standing in my kitchen, I decide to bite the bullet and go see my mother.

God help me.

That thought, as I change into jeans and a tee shirt, brings me up short. Was that a prayer? I stand there with my pants around my ankles and decide whether I initially intended it to be or not, that I *will* make it a prayer.

"Hey God," I hear myself saying out loud in my bedroom as I tie my sneakers, "I don't think you've ever heard from me before. I'm Elaine and, well, it seems that you've surrounded me with a bunch of people that are all in Your Club. I have to be honest and tell you I'm not an official member … but I have to admit that lately the whole thing … the love and peace and forgiveness and stuff … well it's begun to hold quite an enormous appeal for me.

"I'm on my way to my mother's." I mutter under my breath, "You've probably never heard from her either." I sigh. "Anyway we have a relationship that really sucks." I hesitate here. Should I not be saying words like 'suck'? Am I supposed to censure myself just like I do with all those I care about most? Then I think, *what good will that do to guard my words when He supposedly can read my mind? I must have curled His hair long ago.* "Look, I'm just going to be myself with you, okay? You already must know better than anyone else what I'm really like deep down inside, so I don't see much sense trying to pretend I'm something I'm not with you."

Here I am, sitting on my bed having a conversation with God. Have I gone off the deep end? But I make an interesting discovery as I sit there pondering my sanity. I'm light years calmer than I was moments ago and I find that pretty amazing.

"I don't want to go, God, but I'm pretty sure I have to. She – that's my mother – is messing with my baby. Actually, she's not *really* a baby. She's a thirty-one-year-old gorgeous young woman who's having a hard time right now and I own most of her pain. I can't just walk away and let my mother ... screw ... with her. I just don't trust her. So, I'm going to go over and I'd ... appreciate your company. Now maybe striking my mother dead is too much to ask ..." I smile to myself and glance upward, "... like my sense of humor God?" I sigh. "Sorry. Could you help me out? Could you help me keep my big mouth shut and just say ... the best stuff that will help Olivia?" I nod, pleased at my request. "Thanks." Just before I walk out the door, I go over to my jewelry box and put on Callie's bracelet. Hey, I need all the help I can get.

Praying isn't so hard, I think as I drive. Maybe I'll try it more often. I kind of feel a little powerful driving to my mother's house. If this works out well ... man I could ... rule the world ...

My mother lives in a tiny ranch house that was cute and trendy during the time when it was acceptable to have children nicknamed 'The Beav' and 'Opie.' Sitting parked on the street looking at it, I take note of the faded blue aluminum siding and the neglected garden. Her car, a sporty but late model black Corvette tells me that she's still into attracting attention whenever possible. It's been over thirty years since I've seen or talked to my mother and it's a measure of just how poor our relationship is that I can't believe I'm back so soon.

Taking a deep breath, I haul myself out of the car and walk up the front walk. The front door opens before I can ring the bell and I stand there, face-to-face with what will probably be myself in another twenty years. Comparing our physical likenesses, you couldn't - unless you were legally blind - *not* mistake us for mother and daughter. Except she's got inch long red finger nails, hair cut and styled immaculately, and is wearing a black power suit that shows a touch of cleavage and is accessorized with three inch red high heeled pumps. "Still dressing to impress, I see Elaine," she says to me through the screen door. The urge to slouch and scratch my crotch to shock her is so all-powerful that for a minute I close my eyes and clench my hands. The thirty odd years slip away and here I am the know-nothing, eternally rebellious daughter facing the indomitable giant that is her mother.

"Hello, Mom. Good to see you, too. Are you going to invite me in or should we just duke it out on the front porch?"

She turns and walks back into the house without a response. I walk in to do what I came to do. On quick glance, there's not one single piece of furniture or knick-knack that I recognize. I note that the furniture, curtains, wallpaper, paint and even, as I walk into the kitchen following my mother, appliances are changed. "The house looks nice, Mom."

She ignores me, which I swiftly remember is the typical game. I make an effort, she blows it off, I loose my temper, and she proves her point. Her point being that I wasn't worth the effort in the first place. Mixing herself a drink – gin and tonic on the rocks – she gestures for me to help myself and then sits down at the small kitchenette built into the corner. She's ready for the show. So far, to the best of my knowledge, I've never disappointed. I hear my prayer, said not more than an hour ago, *Could you help me keep my big mouth shut and just say … the best stuff that will help out Olivia?* I strengthen my resolve and my backbone: there will be No Show Today.

Sliding into the bench seat opposite her, I ask, "How have you been, Mom?"

"Great. Couldn't be better. Job's great. Health's great. Life's great." She smiles an insincere smile and takes a sip of her drink.

The miniscule flash of hope that she might be remotely happy to see me dies a quiet death. Quietly I ask her, "Was there anything else, other than my never being born, that could have prevented the way things are between us?" I hesitate. "I'm honestly curious."

She sighs the sigh of a mother who has had more trials than is humanly fair. I recognize it, unfortunately, but that's my problem. "Elaine, I'm assuming you're here because your daughter has contacted me."

I want to say, *She's you're granddaughter and her name's Olivia* but God helps me keep my mouth shut. "Yes."

She arches her eyebrow, apparently stunned by my brevity and self-control. "She came looking for answers to questions I didn't even know had to be asked."

"Really?" I ask. "What questions were those?"

Making a broad sweep she says, "Regarding her paternity, your sexual history, and my memory."

Gee, give her an opportunity to say like five sentences and she's already going for the jugular. I love you, too, Mom. "Since I know the answer to two out of three of those, I'll just ask how your memory is."

For a brief second, there's a flicker behind her eyes. Like she wants to break eye contact with me, thinks better of it, and maintains. I think, *I'll be damned, she did know.* It's an answer that … I realize I probably could have done without. "My memory's fuzzy," she says with forced hauteur, "so I can only hazard a guess at your extensive sexual past. That's what I told your daughter, too."

"You could have told her the truth, Mom. You'd be better at the critical name than I would be." I watch her, unbelievably dispassionate, waiting for another flicker.

"I don't know what you're talking about." This time she *has to* look away, she can't stop herself. I think *she's going to need a fresh drink soon.*

"I think you do. But it's not worth the effort to beat it out of you."

"Get out of my house."

I do have to get out. I feel the repressed words and the murderous rage building up inside of me and I'm glad I don't have a weapon.

But I do have bare hands.

Time to go.

"Don't get me wrong," I say as I stand up. "I really would *like* to know what was going on in your head that night. Did you hate me so much that you just didn't care when you heard me crying out for help? Were you just so drunk that you couldn't do anything but lie there and listen? Did you care so little about me and my welfare that what happened in the dark of night once you were asleep didn't rate any concern on your part? Have you really and truly managed to make your memory 'fuzzy' enough so that you can blot it all out and pretend that it never happened? Is that why you could never deal with my pregnancy or Olivia? Is your general rule 'out of sight, out of mind' or something?"

My mother is now pale as death. Her hands look creepy with the blood red nails on the end of her pasty white fingers. I've rendered her speechless, which just might be one of my top ten lifetime achievements.

"I've made a good life for myself, Mom. I've got a good job and I am well thought of. I have two beautiful daughters, one almost faultless son in law and the cutest grandson *in the world*. I'm not perfect. I've made a hell of a lot of mistakes. But I haven't given up. I'm going to keep on trying to get it right until the moment they put me in a box and shut the lid.

"Olivia's my greatest challenge now. *I love her with all my heart* but I just can't seem to get it right with her. But I'm *not* going to quit. I'm not going to *let my memory get fuzzy* and forget that I even *have* a daughter. Even if she and I never reconcile, I'm going to go to my grave knowing that the only wish I had in this life was to have a good relationship with her."

I lean in across the table at my mother and she cringes back like I'm going to kiss her or something. "She's the only reason I'm here today, *Mom*. I *will not* let you hurt or confuse Olivia any more than she already is. If she contacts you again you have two choices: you either tell her *the whole ugly truth* or you *keep your mouth shut*." Through gritted teeth I say, "Have I made myself clear?"

I don't wait for an answer because I'd probably be here until next May. As I make my way through the living room, I hear a sound that makes me pause. And, it seems, I've added to my top ten list of things that have made me feel most like crap: the sound of my mother's sobs.

Sometimes I cannot forgive, and these days, mercy cuts so deep,
If the world was how it should be, maybe I could get some sleep[31]

Chapter 13: On Being Boring And Normal

I am suddenly conscious in the middle of the night.

Confusion swirls around me as I struggle to distinguish fact from reality, having just been in the middle of an intricate open-heart surgery procedure on my mother. Things were really starting to get hairy: how can you repair a heart in someone who doesn't have one? As all the bells and alarms start to go off in the O.R. I realize that, as head surgeon, I'm going to have a lot of explaining to do ...

The phone by my bedside rings.

Oh. I've been asleep.

Then I hear the doorbell ring. *Huh?*

My bedside clock says two-thirteen a.m.

I stand up and walk over to my bedroom window that looks down at my front door. By the dim light of the full moon I can see a dark shape. "Elaine?" I hear. "It's me Alec. Are you in there, Elaine?" My phone starts to ring again, and as I walk down the stairs my door bell rings again, too.

Opening the door, I stand looking at Alec who looks to be on the verge of complete hysteria. *"Where have you been?!"* He shouts at me. My house phone is still ringing because he still has his cell phone pressed to his ear.

"You can hang up," I say practically. "I'm here now."

Impatiently he flips his cell phone shut and shoves it in his jeans pocket. "Elaine, I've been calling you *for three days*. Where have you been? Why haven't you returned my calls? On the way to work tonight I all of a sudden thought, 'Oh Dear God, maybe she's *dead.*' That finally pushed me over the edge although I've been teetering on the brink since yesterday."

We stand there and stare at each other for a few moments. "Want to come in?" I finally ask.

He closes his eyes and sighs deeply. Then he drops his head forward and shakes his head.

"You don't want to come in?"

Wrenching open the door he stalks past me into the kitchen. Like he's done it a hundred times, when in reality he's only done it once, he goes through the motions of making a pot of coffee. From the way he moves and the set of his jaw I realize he's angry. Really, flaming, top of the scale angry.

"I'm sorry. Don't be mad at me. I've had a bad week."

It takes him long moments to calm down enough to speak. Looking at me as he leans both hands on my kitchen counter he says, "Are we a couple?"

I try to be funny. "A couple of what?"

Rather than appreciate the magnitude of skill it requires for me to be humorous at the ungodly hour of two-fifteen a.m., my comment only makes him drop his head down and groan in apparent agony.

I reach over and touch his back, making up and down soothing motions. Sighing, I acknowledge, "Yes, I guess we are. Only I didn't really think of us that way until just this moment." I lean in against him and wrap my arms around his waist. He's tense like a steel beam. "Hey," I say and I work my way under one of his arms and wriggle around until I'm leaning back against the counter with him still looming over me bracketing me with both his arms. I kiss his hot cheek. *"Hey."* I kiss his other hot cheek, then his nose and his eyes and finally his mouth. It's like thawing a glacier.

"I'm completely out of practice if you're annoyed at me for not behaving the way someone does in a relationship, Alec. And you should know that *even when I was in a relationship* it was never the kind that when things got rough I'd run to my man to comfort and protect me. I've always had to handle crap on my own. Whether you're a part of my life or not, what went down this week was something I needed to deal with by myself."

He looks up at me then. "So if I have a bad day or a crisis or just feel like crap I should stay away from you. Is that what you're saying?"

I frown. "No …."

He nods. "Sure it is. Because if you're telling me flat out that when life starts to fall apart you *always* operate solo, then that's the way I should operate, too."

I clunk my head into his. "Maybe I should say that *life's always taught me* that when things fall apart I've got to handle it on my own, and so I always do." He stays silent. "Maybe I need to learn a new way of doing things …" I nuzzle in against his good smelling neck and kiss it. When he remains silent I say, "Will you teach me?"

With a world-weary sigh he straightens up and pulls me into a tight embrace. "You scared the sh-," he catches himself, "crap out of me, Elaine. First, I thought we just missed because of my crazy schedule, then I began to think that you didn't want to see me anymore, and then -"

"- today you decided I had to be dead," I finish for him. "Nice. Some ego you've got, huh? Girl doesn't call you and you'd rather assume she's dead than she's blown you off."

"I don't really think I'm ready to joke about this yet. I was really scared, Elaine."

I pull back and look at him. He's got dark circles under his eyes and he looks exhausted. "Have you slept?"

"Not much," he mumbles and looks at his watch. "I gotta go."

"When are you done?"

"Sixish."

"Come by and I'll make you breakfast, then you can sleep on my couch, and then I'll tell you about my horrible week."

Alec looks at me, probably taking in *my* dark circles, *my* exhaustion, and the fact that I was obviously asleep in my clothes. "Are you okay?"

"No. Yes. Kind of in-between." I think about the confrontation with my mother, my rather stellar performance given past history, and the fact that I've had a conversation with God in the last twenty-four hours. Pretty darn momentous day if I do say so myself. "We'll talk. Later."

As he heads out the front door and down the stairs, I call his name. "What?" he says stopping and turning to look up at me.

"Thanks."

He gives me a slow, seductive smile. "You like me doing the knight in shining armor thing, huh?"

"I know it was just cause you were hoping to catch me in my sexy pjs again."

He nods. "It was that, too."

"See you later. I'll leave the back door open. Come on in and scream."

Harry's yowling at nine forty-eight a.m. wakes me and my first emotion is a wave of abject disappointment that someone didn't wake me at six a.m. When I finish in the bathroom, I pad down the stairs, let the beast out and head into the kitchen only to stop and stare at the man fast asleep on my living room couch. He's flat on his back, barefoot, and snoring like a bear. It's a wonder that I slept through the racket. My wave of abject disappointment is replaced with complete delight.

There's a familiar cooler bag on the kitchen counter and a pair of battered, flour covered sneakers by the back door. I break out my best coffee and start setting out breakfast. Minutes later I get a tingle down my back and know I'm being watched. I can *feel* him watching me. How wild is that? "How come you didn't wake me up?" I say without turning around. I peer into the cooler bag and it seems he's brought samples of every kind of pastry he must have made last night. Ecstasy on a plate.

"And walk into that den of iniquity?" he says, and his voice is deep and gravelly from sleep. "You actually think I'd be able to go *into* your bedroom, *kiss* you awake – because that's what I'd have to do, you know - and then be able to simply *walk* downstairs and eat breakfast with you?" He grunts. "Yeah, like that would have happened."

I look over my shoulder at him and he looks very cute all rumpled and ruffled from sleep. Leaning against the kitchen doorjamb with his arm's crossed, he's got a strawberry smear on the shoulder of his dusty white tee shirt and his hair is doing the happy dance across his head. As he stares at me with those sleepy brown eyes, I realize clear as a bell, that I hoped very much that he was going to come upstairs and *not* just wake me up and walk me downstairs to eat breakfast. I was hoping for a lot more. Deep down I realize I was hoping that his resolve towards the celibacy page wouldn't be as strong and determined. And with dawning horror I realize I've begun, already, to lose my mind over this man, and I haven't even gotten naked with him yet.

"Don't look at me like that," he murmurs. "Up until this moment, I've been able to joke and flirt and give you the bedroom eyes and you've just been flip, sassy, and flirty back with me. All of a sudden, I feel like fire alarms should be going off or something."

"Yeah," I say turning around to get the pastries out of the bag, "or something."

A weighty silence ensues as I lay out all the pastries, crumple up the bags, get two plates down, select two forks, and fold two napkins. The coffee perks and my back keeps tingling as he stares at me. I take stock of what I'm wearing, having been unprepared for company: boxers, a tee shirt, and bare feet. I wonder briefly if the phrase 'going commando' applies when wearing pajamas …

"I figured, since I was exhausted and you were exhausted *and already asleep,* I'd just catch some z's on your couch until you woke *me* up."

"Don't you need to sleep some more?"

I hear him pour two cups of coffee and then walk over and hand me one. "Maybe later. I'm good for now."

We stare at each other again in a haze of charged emotions. In the absolute silence there is a major battle going on between the forces of good and evil. I finally say, "So, you want to hear about my week?"

He seems to relax a tiny bit. Leaning over he kisses me lightly on the mouth. "Yeah," he says against my lips, "I want to hear about your week."

I start out telling him just the bare facts. I know it's the bare facts because I'm done in about eleven minutes. He watches me and I feel just like I feel when Callie examines me with her supersonic laser vision.

"So," he summarizes, "you and Olivia have been 'at odds' lets say for quite a while." I nod. "The Sunday you showed up the first time at Agape Shop you two had had a big, major blow up." I nod again. "Then, this week for the first time since then you called her and," he searches for the right words, "things that were already very poor hit rock bottom." I've stopped nodding but am just looking at him. "Part of the reason things are now at rock bottom is that Olivia has contacted your mother whom you haven't seen or spoken to in over thirty years. And knowing what you're mother is like, you finally Lone Ranger it over to her house to give her a piece of your mind. When I showed up last night you were in the throes of recovering from that." I nod, hopefully, for the last time.

He thinks for quite a while. I start to sweat because he's not a stupid man. "These issues you have with Olivia and your mother, is it one big thing or a whole crapload of many things?"

"It's not as simple as that," I answer slowly. "It's more like a big, tangled mass of yarn. There's a beginning, hopefully there's an end, but in the middle is one big huge knot that everything's tangled up in."

"Yarn," he says and I stare back at him. I can tell he's trying hard to stay with me. "So, is it correct for me to assume that Olivia's issue and your mother's issue are one in the same ... knot?"

"Well, the knots all mine I guess but there's yarn that comes out of the knot and goes to my mother and yarn that goes to Olivia."

He thinks again. "Is the yarn connected?"

Again I nod.

"And this … knot … it's something that's so big that it seems to have affected not only Olivia but your mother as well?"

"Actually, the knot begins with her."

"You're mother *made* the knot?"

No, not quite. But she brought the knot home with her. "Well, she didn't exactly *make* the knot, but she was the cause of it."

"But the knot has primarily to do with you."

You guessed it. I nod.

"And, it would seem, this … knot … is not something that most people care to discuss, examine, or reminisce about?"

"Right," I finally say but my voice is kind of dry and crackly.

Sitting at the kitchen counter, we've sampled a pile of lovely pastries and tarts. My fingers are sticky with raspberry jam and I've got a few of them in my mouth when Alec leans forward and says quietly to me, "Elaine? Why are we talking about yarn?"

I'm sure I've got a deer in the head light look about me. "Because," I manage to say after I've pulled my fingers out of my mouth and before I can think it all through, "it's easier to talk about than rape."

I watch him process all the information he now has about me. My 'shotgun' wedding with Dean at sixteen coupled with the realization of what I've just revealed about Olivia's conception. He can't possibly figure out where my mother fits into all of this but with our estrangement stretching over thirty years he's got to surmise she's had some culpability in it all. It's as much as I can tell him. As much as I can reveal about the horrible reality of who I am and what I am. And by the way I slowly begin to unravel sitting here looking at him, he very shortly will discover what a basket case I truly am.

He's quiet for so long that I have enough time to contemplate the enormity of what I've done. I've pretty much told this man, who only two weeks ago was a complete stranger, the most private and the most emotionally charged aspect of my life.

Am I out of my freakin' mind?

Yes I am.

And here we have it folks: a classic example of how I go completely insane when I get involved with a man. Exhibit #1 in the case to prove my complete and utter loss of common sense and self-preservation. A horrifying thought rises to the top of my bubbling mind cauldron: what state of mind would I have been in right now had he come and woke me up in bed this morning and done what I'd wanted him to do? Good grief.

Suddenly, I've got to get out of here. So what that it's my house. I've got to get away from this man so I don't have to deal with him ever again.

No nitroglycerin secret discussion.

No sex.

No insanity.

Back to my old, marginally stable, solitary existence.

I have irrational thoughts like securing a new identity and faking my own death. I'll just get up, pretend to go check something down in the garage, get in the car and drive away. I'll stop at the MAC machine, get a pile of cash, and drive until the car quits …

"Thank you," Alec says to me, slowing down my departure into the horizon by a moment or two. Leaving me just enough time to present the show for *him* that my mother was fortunate enough to miss.

"Thank you?" I manage. "I've just told you that the woman you've found so quirky and irreverent and compelling is still completely and utterly screwed up because of some horrible incident that happened over thirty years ago. You've been all lovey-dovey and in my face supportive about how you like the person I am because of the life that's brought me to this point. But you don't realize that all you see is just an illusion, haphazardly piled on top of a pile of putrid garbage." I hold my hands out for him to get a good look. "Ta-da. I'm a freakin' mess."

He blinks at me and tries to take one of my hands, which I don't let him do. He sighs. "Yeah. Thank you. Thank you for trusting me enough to tell me this. I recognize it as a compliment of the highest order."

I lean into his face, absolutely ballistic with unexplainable fury. "You are *so noble*, Alec."

He chuckles and shakes his head. "Noble? Hardly." As I sit there panting with rage he says through clenched teeth, "Elaine, will you listen to me please? I'll say it again: *I don't care* about your past. I'm an ex-con, remember?" Shaking his head he says, "You barely even *blinked* when I told you the other day that I'd done time. That's pretty," he imitates me, "*freakin'* huge for most people to come to terms with. I knew then that whatever 'history' you continually hint at had to be something big, and bad, and hard for you. When we went hiking, I listened to you talk about your past marriages to Dean the alcoholic, and Paul the psycho mind melter, and Richard the depressed and you just rattled them all off like it was no big deal. Even *then* I knew that there had to be something bigger and badder because hardly anyone ever talks about the really awful stuff *willingly*."

For some reason, all the anger has gone out of me and now I feel like a deflated balloon. A teary, deflated balloon. "So when you just started talking about yarn and knots," he says softly to me, "I had a pretty good idea that we were heading toward the punch line." He gives me one of his sweet smiles. "I didn't think you'd spell it all out so plainly when I asked, but was so overwhelmed that you'd trusted me when you did. I had a crisis for a brief moment, because you might not remember, but *I* certainly do, that I've never, *ever* gotten a relationship right. For a few moments, I got all caught up with what I should and shouldn't say, how I should or shouldn't say it, and where I was supposed to go to get it all right." He takes my hand, and this time I let him, and he pulls me toward him. "So I started with what I felt the most. In awe that you'd trusted me. So I said thanks."

I'm standing between his legs now, wearing men's size medium boxer shorts and a tee shirt that says *Sanity is back-ordered Sarcasm is in unlimited supply* (a gift from Callie). He's holding both my hands and looking at me intently, I suspect trying to gauge just how far I am from the edge.

"It's always there with me," I say to him through my tears, "reminding me of what I really am as opposed to what I want to be. I see it in my mother's eyes when I remember how she always said I wouldn't amount to much. I see it in Olivia's eyes when she looks at me with her lack of love and respect. And I see it in my own eyes whenever I look in the mirror and know the awful truth."

"And what is that awful truth?" Alec says as he stretches and grabs a napkin, and when I go to take it from him he won't release it and instead mops my face himself.

Huh? I look at him confused, my head full of snot.

Patiently, Alec says, "One awful truth is you had a lousy childhood. That was your mother's fault. Another awful truth is that you were raped as a teenager. Rape is *never* the victim's fault, *ever*. Another awful truth is that for your entire life you've been trying to escape the pain of your past which, as far as I'm concerned, isn't really an awful truth as much as a tremendously noble goal. So what I'm asking you, Sweetie," he says softly as he wipes my face again because the tears don't stop, "is what exactly is the *awful* truth about you that I need to know?"

I stand there looking at this man and I think *there is absolutely nothing else to tell him that is awful about me and he's still here and now he's calling me Sweetie.*

At my continued silence, he stands up, takes my hand and leads me into the living room. He pulls me down onto the couch beside him, tucks his arm around me, and kisses the top of my head. "I had to learn a lot about forgiving and forgetting because I had to apply it to myself, Elaine. And I didn't learn it until I made a spiritual commitment with God. Until then, the whole business of forgiving and forgetting was not only impossible it was *unwanted*. I needed, in my competitive, driven, old self, to keep track of all that crap so that I always had the edge. I was always scheming. When I *finally* got the right focus, all of it became so unimportant. It just dragged me down.

"How does always looking at the bad help you? Really? You talk about your friendship with Callie. What would she say about all this? What *does* she say? I bet if she were here right now she'd be cheering me on."

I look up at him. "If she were here right now she'd be telling me to marry you."

He grins. "I'm a new person, Elaine. Instead of letting the old stuff drag me down anymore, now I'm just proud to be such an alter image. I want people to hear all about my past and look at me in stunned confusion and go, '*You?* You were that mean, egotistical, success obsessed, bastard? Wow. What a change. I don't see any similarities at all. That's amazing.'"

"Callie says all the same stuff," I say with a resigned sigh.

"Then why aren't you listening?"

"Because I'm an idiot."

He tilts my head back and gives me a lovely kiss on the mouth. "You mean because *you were* an idiot."

When I give him a smile, he rests his forehead against mine. "Will you do me an *enormous* favor?"

Anything. "Sure. What?"

"Will you *please* go upstairs and get out of these fantastically sexy pajamas? Now that you're not having a crisis anymore, I'm afraid *I'm* going to have one."

Stunningly cooperative, I stand up and head toward the stairs, "Want to do something really boring and normal like go to a movie?" I throw over my shoulder.

"Sweetie," he says to me and I turn to see he's sprawled and at ease on my sofa, "no matter what we do together, something tells me we are *never* going to be boring *or* normal."

I'm smiling as I walk upstairs. Being crazy and abnormal has suddenly never sounded so appealing.

Chapter 14: Batman Is My Hero

"So, when are you going to try to contact Olivia again?" Alec asks me as we drive in his truck on the way to lunch. We've decided to skip the movie, since Alec tells me honestly that if I put him in a dark theater he'll be asleep inside of five minutes.

I really like that he says *when* as opposed to just *are you* with that question. Sighing, I acknowledge, "It might be a couple of months this time. Usually, I manage to keep my temper in check, but I said some pretty hard things to her over the phone – *while she was at work.*"

"You could invite her to meet you at this really nice new pastry shop that's just opened in Somerville called the Agape Shop. You could tell her that the pastries *are to die for* and promise her that it will be well worth her time to stop by."

"Probably if I promised not to be there, she'd come." Even to myself I sound like a whiny, pouting child.

"Have you ever thought that as hard and as diligent as *you* have been in trying to keep things open and positive with Olivia, *she's* been doing the same thing with you?" Before I can make a flip comment he says, "Has she ever refused to see you or speak with you? Changed her phone number so that you couldn't contact her? Moved without leaving a forwarding address? Not returned a message you've left?" He's glancing at me now with each question, a little smile turning up the side of his mouth. "Returned mail unopened? Avoided parties or gatherings she knows you'll be present at? Blocked your text messages? Cut out all your photos from her family album?"

I'm looking at him and he glances in my direction when we both become silent. "What?" he finally says.

"Are you done?"

He grins and nods. He seems to like pushing my buttons. A lot. "Yeah, I'm done."

"No."

He glances at me and then back at the road. "No? She's never done any of those things?"

"Not once."

"Isn't that good?"

I look out the window at the passing scenery. "I've never really thought of it before in the positive. I've always just thought of it as her way of pushing and pushing until I'm taken away in a straight jacket drooling at the mouth."

"I bet it would be a lot of fun sitting and listening to what she has to say about you."

"Your ears would probably melt or something."

"Or something." He reaches over and takes my hand. "I know I'm real new on the scene, Elaine, but from my point of view I see two women who love each other but can't seem to find the right spot that's safe ground. She's coming into the game with her issues, you're coming into the game with your issues and nothing ever gets discussed because too much information is always swirling around confusing everything."

"Every Sunday, we go to Erin and Dan's for dinner. We've been doing it for years. Come hell or high water, just like the postman, the both of us make an appearance."

"Always?"

I nod. "Yeah, usually. Sickness or business or vacations might keep us apart, but no matter how bad the last get-together was, she and I *never* don't come just because we can't stomach the sight of each other. Despite the fact that on numerous occasions it's probably true." I laugh a laugh that holds no humor. "Oh no, we always show up. I'm sure there's been times when Erin and Dan wished they had metal detectors at all the entrances."

"Why do you show up?"

"Because the moment I stop showing up, I'm doing to Olivia exactly what my mother did to me: kissing her off and waving goodbye," I grind out fiercely. "And *no matter what*, I am not going to let Olivia think that about me. *I love her.* She may not believe it, I may have done a really sucky job at showing it, but I do."

"She must show up for the same reason, huh?"

"I don't know," I mumble. "She could just be showing up to spite me. Liam's absolutely adorable – especially when he's under Erin and Dan's control – so that's always a big draw. The food's always good."

"Elaine ..." Alec sounds like a wise but frustrated parent.

"You know what?" I hear myself say. "Tomorrow's Sunday. Why don't you just come along with me to dinner and witness all the fun."

"I'd love to," he says without a speck of hesitation. Suddenly, I feel as if I've been completely played and he's gotten exactly what he set out to get.

After lunch, Alec goes home to get some much needed sleep. I spend the afternoon hours and into the evening lost in my sewing. Harry breaks me out of my trance howling on the front step looking for dinner. When I realize it's almost nine o'clock and I've been sewing for *almost six hours* I decide to quit. I sit at my kitchen counter eating a scrambled egg and toast while Harry sprawls out in front of me like a gigantic hairy centerpiece. We have an agreement, Harry and I. He can sit on the counter when it's just the two of us and I don't make a fuss, but if he jumps up on the counter when people are over I say in a horrified voice, "*Harry! Get off the counter!*" like it's the most disgusting thing I've witnessed in years.

Just before I go to bed, I call Erin. "What am I bringing tomorrow?" I ask.

"What would you like to bring, Mom?"

"A man."

Despite the fact that she's been born and raised on my humor I can still catch her now and then. There is an awkward silence and then she quietly says, "Really?"

I sigh. "Yeah." I don't say stuff like 'he's nice' or 'he's good-looking' or 'I think you'll like him' or any of the trite phrases I used to use when I brought home a date ... fifteen or more years ago when Erin and Olivia were teenagers. Back then it was wishful thinking and maybe a little bit of post-hypnotic suggestion to my kids. Alec will have to fend for himself with no help from me.

"Are you ... dating him?"

"Yeah. He says I'm supposed to say we're a couple."

"Where'd you meet?"

"The unemployment line."

She laughs a tiny bit. "Mom, you're not unemployed."

"Yeah, I know, but I heard there were a lot of available men there."

"The last I checked, you weren't looking for any available men either."

"I'm still not."

"Does that mean he's not available? Please don't tell me he's married, Mom."

Great. She thinks the first time I'd take a trip on the Love Boat in over ten years I'd head toward married officer's quarters. "Hmmm, I've never tried *that* category."

"Mother ..."

"I *meant* that I wasn't looking. He just showed up. On my doorstep."

Now my daughter groans. I can be a trial, at times, I guess. "Come on, Mom, stop teasing. How'd you meet him?"

"He's my meter reader, Erin."

"Oh ... God."

"It's not as bad as it sounds. I hated him when he was my meter reader. It was after Callie and James fixed me up with him that I kind of started to notice him."

"Callie and James?" In Erin's eyes they are The Voices Of Sanity And Reason. Alec's rating increases significantly.

"He also plays in James' band."

"Really." Now she sounds intrigued.

"And he's a pastry chef at the new coffee shop in Somerville called Agape Shop."

"Gee, he's busy!"

"He's got a cute butt. And he's an excellent kisser."

"TMI mother."

My fifth graders have educated me marginally in text lingo: *too much information.* "So is it okay if I bring him?"

"Sure. As long as you bring an appetizer, too."

"Maybe I can get him to bring some pastries for dessert." I hesitate, but glutton that I am I have to ask. "Have you heard from Olivia?"

Erin sighs into the phone. "Yes, Mom." I *try* to not make Erin choose sides. I *prefer* for her to listen, speak, and learn of my numerous disasters from her sister rather than from me. Why you might ask? Because I ...

I was going to say because I am an idiot. But I can hear Alec saying *because you were an idiot.* Sigh. So now I'll say, because it's what a good mother would do. And I am *determined* to be a good mother.

Alec does not disappoint in any category. He shows up promptly at my house, looking a little too yummy for words with dark blue slacks and a white button down shirt open at the neck and cuffed up his forearms. He tells me he's brought a big bag of "day old pastries" that I know for a fact would still be for sale at Agape Shop if I drove over there right now. I've cut up forty-five pounds of vegetables and made my famous onion dip.

Alec stands in my front hallway as I run around trying to get everything ready to go. When I pick up my tray of veggies and step into the hallway, he says to me, "You look fantastic."

"It's just because I'm wearing a dress," I say dismissively.

"Dress, three inch heels, make up," he leans in and sniffs my neck, "and that almond perfume that makes me want to take a bite out of you." The visual image makes me a little quivery around the knees.

"You forgot the thigh-high stockings, garter belt and Wonderbra," I say to level the playing field and try to gain back some necessary ground.

He gives me that intense, smoldering look that makes me glad I can't read minds because I just might go up in flames. "Put down the vegetables, Elaine."

I laugh. Nothing has ever sounded so dangerously sexy. "No."

"*Are* you really wearing a garter belt?" he asks.

Absolutely I am. Would I kid about a thing like that? Balancing the platter of veggies in one hand, I slowly, inch by inch, draw up the hem of my dress until ... bing! ... there is the start of the top lace of my stocking. I look at him and grin a huge, evil grin.

He looks ... terrified. "Oh dear God." I think he's praying just like I did the other day in my bedroom.

This is so much fun. "I just wanted to make sure that no matter how wild and crazy things get at Erin's you'll still have your eyes ... *and your thoughts* ... on me."

"Don't you want me able to function and provide polite, articulate conversation?"

I look him right in the eye and answer with complete honesty, "Not necessarily."

He swallows. "Put the damn tray down."

I shake my head and laugh again. "No. We're going to be late. Dinner is always on time. And I want to be there before Olivia. She's almost always late by a few minutes."

He steps in, steadies the tray with one hand and wraps his arm around me with the other. I know what he's doing. He's feeling for the garter belt. Sure enough I feel his hand dip down and stop. I look him right in the eye. "I'm having trouble staying on this celibacy page, Alec."

He gives me a huge, open-mouthed kiss that communicates loudly and clearly his difficulty as well. We only stop when the veggie tray starts to slip and fall and we both scramble to catch it, slamming it up against the wall in the hallway. With both of our hands holding it against the wall, he looks at me sheepishly and says, "Is the dip on the plate with the veggies?"

I shake my head. "It's in the plastic container behind me on the kitchen counter."

He sighs in relief. Slowly we lower the tray and my artfully arranged vegetable display is now a sloppy, tangled mess under the plastic wrap. "Still looks good to me," I say and Alec bursts out laughing.

Liam is the first to greet us, dressed in a Batman tee shirt, Batman sneakers, Batman shorts, and strapped to his face is a big black Batman mask. Alec looks at me straight faced and says, "This has *got* to be your grandson."

"Minnie!" Liam greets us, his eyes wide with disbelief, "Mommy says we're having *a man* for dinner today!"

I glance at Alec and he arches his eyebrows. Squatting down I say, "I don't think we're going to *eat* him though. He's just going to sit at the table and visit with us *while we eat dinner together.*"

Liam processes this while Alec says under his breath, "He seems disappointed. Should I be nervous?"

"Are you the man?" Liam asks, peering at us through black plastic eyeholes.

"I certainly am. Hi, Liam. My name is Alec." Alec holds his hand out for a slap five and Liam, delightedly slaps with all the force his four-year-old body can produce. "Yow!" Alec shouts and shakes his hand as if in pain. Liam's face splits into a huge grin and I'm pretty certain Alec now has a friend for life.

In actuality, Liam is *thrilled* to have a new victim, and Alec seems more than happy to climb up onto the sacrificial altar. Within minutes the two of them are on the floor snaking wooden Thomas The Tank Engine tracks all over the family room off the kitchen while Erin and Dan try to discretely check him out. Does Alec know that the way to a parent's heart is through the child? Whether he does or he doesn't, when Liam says to Alec, "You wanna wear my Batman mask?" and Alec reverently straps it on I see my daughter and her husband exchange significant glances.

Olivia makes her entrance just after this, and I'm thankful for these few brief moments of bonding. We were *so wise* to have chosen to take a.) the family friendly route, as opposed to b.) the sacrificial burning of the celibacy page in my front hallway route.

At Olivia's entrance, I hear Alec say to Liam, "Give me a second, okay buddy?" as he stands and heads towards the kitchen. I decide, right then and there, that I could fall in complete love with this man when he *does not* take Liam's plastic Batman mask off but chooses to greet Olivia incognito.

"Olivia," I hear myself say, "this is my friend Alec Monroe."

Extending his hand, Alec says, "Hey, Olivia. Please excuse my disguise, but Liam's given me the tremendous privilege of wearing his Batman mask and I don't know how much longer I'm going to be allowed to enjoy the honor."

I realize, as my daughter gives him a thorough once over and then extends her hand towards Alec, that not only has Alec stormed another barrier of *my heart,* but he's also, effectively leaped over a significant pile of obstacles with Olivia. All because of a plastic Batman mask. "Welcome, Alec. Any friend of Liam's is a potential friend of mine." Translation: be glad the kid likes you because that's all that you've got going for you right now.

"Aunt Livvy!" Liam shouts from the family room. "Come play trains with me and Alec!"

"Please, do," says Alec with a smile. "We're having a little bit of a structural challenge with the track. You don't by any chance have any formal architectural training do you?

"Last time I watched Liam we managed to use every single piece of track," Olivia says with pride. Under her breath she murmurs to us,

"Although I worked on that blasted thing for about two hours after Liam went to bed just to prove I could do it."

I watch my daughter laugh and smile with Alec, casually with no tension and hidden agenda, and I feel a wave of longing so acute that I must make a strangled little sound in the back of my throat. Drawing attention to myself. "Mother." Olivia acknowledges with a nod.

"Hey, Olivia," I manage. "Its good to see you."

"Mom!" Erin calls. "Would you do the drinks?"

"Sure, honey."

Dinner goes smoothly. Conversation flows from newest Liam escapades (coloring both feet completely green with Erin's permanent marker in an attempt to become the Incredible Hulk), to Alec's life story (mercifully sanitized sans prison time), to questions about my latest sewing project (asked by Erin to draw me into the conversation), to Olivia's plans for next week (travel to California for business). Alec's presence dilutes the festering cauldron enough so that it's at just a slow, manageable simmer. The 'day old' pastries are delicious and evoke exclamations of rapture. As we sip second cups of coffee, Alec finally says, "It's been so nice sitting down to a home cooked meal. You have no idea what it means to a bachelor like myself. But I'm afraid we've got to get going."

"Are you off to start baking?" Olivia asks politely.

"No, that's not till around two a.m. when most normal people are fast asleep. We're off to church. I've got to be there a little early because the church praise band has asked me to play with them. Their regular guitarist's wife just had a baby and he's home. I'm helping out."

"Church?" both Erin, Dan, and Olivia say at once.

Alec grins. "Yeah. Didn't Elaine tell you? That's where we met. Well, actually, it was at a church sponsored concert, but we really started talking when she *coincidentally*," he glances at me and winks, "showed up at my church a few days later."

"I only go for the pastries," I feel inclined to say when three pairs of eyes look at me like I've announced I'm joining a convent or something.

"How long have you been going, Mom?" Erin asks.

148

"Not long. I haven't officially joined the club yet or anything."

Alec pipes in with, "But she is considering a lifetime membership. She's intrigued by all the fringe benefits."

It's a club joke. Actually, it's the second one since I caught the inflection of Alec's voice on the word *coincidence*. I remember him saying, *I don't believe in coincidences* and I think about this *thing* that's happening between the two of us. But this second club joke is the kind that I've heard at Callie's house a million times, only this time *I get it*. I think lifetime membership = eternal life, fringe benefits = joy, peace, forgiveness, hope … I turn and look at Alec and he meets my gaze. I give him a blinding *I get your club joke!* smile and he winks at me, probably completely clueless.

Olivia's gazing at the two of us, taking all this in I suppose, with the inside jokes, winks, and smiles … "Good for you, Mom," she says.

I look at my daughter, still high on my feeling of inclusion, and smile at her sincerely and say, "Yeah, I think it really is good for me, too."

Driving to church I sit in contented silence. "You okay?" Alec finally asks me.

I smile at him. "I'm *great*."

"Why great?"

"Olivia and I talked and smiled and said a few nice things to each other. The afternoon didn't end with tears or furious departures. *No nasty words were said.*" I grin at him. "And you were absolutely fabulous."

"Huh? What did I do that was so terrific? I just hung out, talked and tried like heck not to think of you and that darn garter belt."

Actually. I'd forgotten about that. I reach down to hike up my dress a tiny bit and he claps his hand on mine, moves it away, and then firmly holds it in the center of the bench seat between us. "I forgot about that," I admit. *Until you reminded me.*

"Yeah, well I didn't, thank you very much. I feel like your friend Callie in that I need to tell you to *behave*, okay?"

"You want to know what my favorite part of the evening was?"

"Yeah." He seems relieved that I'm going to cooperate for the moment.

"When you greeted Olivia in the Batman mask."

"Well," he explains, "I knew what a big deal it was that Liam let me wear it. The look on his face when he said, 'You wanna wear my Batman mask?'" Alec shakes his head. "Man, talk about being honored. I didn't want to just blow Liam off, so I figured heck, she's his aunt, she should be okay with it."

"She was. You got *huge good guy points* for that."

"Good guy points?"

"Trust me. You arrived with me. You needed significant assistance to simply get up to *zero* to start with."

"She's nice. Olivia I mean. Of course, so are Erin and Dan, but I knew Olivia was going to be the tough one."

"It was a good visit: no fire, blood, vomit or personal disasters."

Alec chuckles. "Olivia has your sense of humor, you know."

I look at the window, silent.

"Talking to her," Alec says quietly, "I had to stay as sharp and as alert as I do with you. Erin's got the whole maternal, comfort thing going on. She's easy."

It's something to think about. Is Olivia the way she is towards me because she's annoyed and has a pile of issues, or is she the way she is towards me just because *that's the way she's made?* "So I'm hard."

It's a provocative comment, along the lines of 'so I'm fat', or 'so I look old', or 'so you don't like this dress.' I throw it out so that he can contradict me and make me feel better about little 'ole poor me. "Hell yes, you're hard," Alec says with firm conviction. "You're the toughest woman I've ever dealt with and that's saying something. You're smart and sharp and not at all shy or hesitant about speaking your mind. I'm sure you've eviscerated lesser men. I'll bet you that husband #2 – Paulie – was so darn threatened by you that he lay awake nights coming up with lists of things to criticize you for just so he could gain an edge."

My mouth is hanging open in shock. I don't know whether to be completely insulted or … to start preening a little bit, because I'd love to have made Paulie feel even a bit threatened.

He glances at me as we pull the truck into the Agape Shop parking lot. "You really have no clue, do you?" He turns towards me and leans his arm across the back of the truck. "Dean hooked up with you because he was drawn to your strength. Except no one can be strong clinging onto someone else so he failed miserably. Paulie hooked up with you because of your dynamic, in-your-face style of living. It's never once occurred to you to give up, has it? You just keep plowing through the crap, sorting through what's worth keeping and tossing over your shoulder what's worth throwing away. You don't have the time or the inclination to examine the why's or the wherefores; you just *act*. That's attractive, Elaine. Some men might even call it *sexy*. Richard," here Alec shakes his head in apparent pity, "he saw you as his last, great, white hope. He did the same thing Dean tried to do. When he realized that being with you wasn't going to make anything better *for him*, and then he watched himself drag you and your girls down into the pit *with him* ..." Alec doesn't finish his sentence but he doesn't need to.

"So why are you with me?" I've decided to take all this "being the toughest woman he's ever dealt with" stuff as a compliment. Why the hell not, right? *Now* I'm going to hear some mushy stuff, I'm sure.

Leaning across the seat of the truck he hooks one hand around the back of my neck, the other hand around my waist and hauls me toward him. I feel his hand slide under my dress and touch the top of my stockings and slide up one of the straps of the garter belt and he gives me a steamy kiss. When we come up for air he says, "I'm here with you because I've got what you're missing ..." His mouth travels down the side of my neck and I shiver at the pleasure of it all. "You're here with me because you've got what I'm missing ..." His hand has traveled around underneath my dress, touching, feeling, exploring. Now it rests high up on my thigh, above the top of my stocking, his fingers touching the elastic of my panties. "And when we're together we're appreciably better than when we're apart." I feel him flex his hand on my leg and then he kisses me again. "Right?"

I'm sitting in a church parking lot with a man's hand up my dress and thinking anything but heavenly thoughts. Alec's brown eyes look at me with intensity, waiting for my answer. I struggle to get my brain functioning enough to speak. "Yes," I finally say and lean forward and kiss him tenderly on the mouth. "You've got Life and I've got love."

He nods, satisfied. "Welcome to The Club," he says with one more brief kiss and then he's gone, reaching to get his guitar from the back of the cab.

You make an ordinary girl shine bright
In a world that needs salt and light.[33]

Chapter 15: Giving Up

"X-man!" I hear shouted as Alec walks ahead of me into the empty church sanctuary. "It's about time!" When I appear behind him, I hear shouted, "What were you two doing, necking in your truck?"

I'm glad it's dim because I'm sure I'm blushing. I hear Alec say good-naturedly, "Absolutely. Wouldn't you be?"

There is an enormous black man standing one step up on the stage, well over six feet, with a guitar slung over his shoulder. "Elaine," Alec says as we walk into the lighted area, "this is Tiny Tim."

"God bless us every one!" I say extending my hand.

He laughs delightedly at my joke. Grasping my hand he hauls me up the step and plants a big, wet kiss on my cheek. "Welcome to Agape Shop. Are you our new lead singer?"

"Only if you want to pack in a crowd just like the one you've got now."

"She's quick," Tiny Tim says to Alec whom I catch rolling his eyes and mumbling, "You have no idea."

"Who-ho! Don't tell me the Great X-man seems to have finally met his match with a woman! This should be fun to watch."

Alec's up on stage opening up his guitar case, getting ready. Head down, I can't see his expression and he's uncommonly silent. "I warned him to wear a flak jacket or body armor. So far, he's not done it though."

"Honey," Tiny Tim says, "nothing is better than going down for the count all because of love."

Alec snorts. "He's just eager to see another mighty one fall."

Tiny Tim nods in complete agreement. "Got myself married just eighteen months ago. I highly recommend it if you haven't tried it."

Alec's standing now, tuning his guitar. Without glancing up at me he says, "Took him thirty-nine years to finally tie the knot. Now he's the biggest darn cupid you'd ever want to meet, trying to push every man he's even casually acquainted with down the aisle." Finally, he glances up at me and winks.

I sit down in the front row and cross my legs. "How many single men do you know, Tiny Tim?"

"Truckloads," he says with a twinkle in his eye. "Single guys stick together. Kind of like a herd. We protect the weaker ones, keeping them to the center and only the strongest and fiercest are allowed along the outer edges of the pack."

"What's that say about you then, if you're married now?" I ask with a grin.

"It says I finally wised up," he says with a contented sigh.

"Any kids?"

"One's on the way," Tiny Tim says proudly. "Due in December. I'm going to be a daddy on the wrong side of forty but it's better than being no daddy at all."

"Do you know what you're having?"

"A little girl," Tiny Tim says with a grin as wide as a baseball field. "We're going to name her Jennifer Louise after both Katrina – that's my wife – and my mothers."

"Where's Benny and Tonya?" Alec asks now that he's all tuned up and ready.

Tiny Tim laughs. "Benny's been here, set up, and gone for coffee next door. Says if you're late and he's got the time, the best way to spend it is to eat your pastries. Tonya's late as usual."

"Actually, I ate two," says a voice that belongs to another hulking behemoth of a man who materializes out of the dimness. "Coconut something or other and some chocolatey-cheesy thing."

"Coconut crumble tart and dark chocolate cheese cake," Alec corrects him absently.

"Liked the coconut thingy better."

"That's because you've never gained the discernment to understand the magic and mystery of chocolate."

Benny rolls his eyes at me and steps forward with his hand extended. He's not quite as massive as Tiny Tim, with smiling blue eyes and brown hair collected in a haphazard ponytail trailing down his back. But his most distinguishing features are both his arms which are completely covered in intricate tattoos. "You're Elaine," he says with a smile.

"I know," I throw back.

Benny grins and points over his shoulder at Alec. "It was fun watching him have a meltdown about you the other night. More entertaining than pay-per-view wrestling."

As Benny heads towards the elaborate drum set, Alec says with a growl, "Shut up, Benny,"

Tiny Tim laughs delightedly.

"I'm here! I'm here!" calls a breathless voice hurrying up toward the stage. "My car ran out of gas. Thank goodness I was still in my driveway!"

"Only Tonya could run out of gas in her own driveway," Benny says under his breath and both Alec and Tiny Tim laugh.

"What's so funny?" Tonya asks as she jumps up on stage. She's young, maybe mid-twenties, with a pierced nose, long blonde hair and an impressive pair of breasts tightly encased in a tee shirt that says 'God Rocks.' "Hi," she says, glancing at Alec, and then to me. "You're Elaine."

Looking at Alec I say, "Did you tell everyone that I have regular problems remembering my identity?"

"No," Tonya says, "he just told everyone *about you* period: band people, bakery people, church people …"

"Let's get started. We've got less than an hour before people start showing up and I'm not sure what I'm supposed to be doing tonight," Alec says obviously eager to change the subject.

I'm looking at him intently as the band members talk about what songs they're going to play and which one they're going to practice first. When Alec finally risks a glance at me I've got my arms crossed, just waiting. As Tiny Tim counts out the start of the song Alec gives me a small smile, a shrug, and finally a tiny air kiss.

While the band practices, I think. I think about Alec saying *when we're together we're appreciably better than when we're apart.* Is it true? If it's true, I've never had a relationship where that was the case. I basked in Dean's adoration and the joy of having someone actually like me, want me, and love me. In return I piled all my problems up with his and ended up carrying two loads instead of one. That wasn't better.

With Paul, I immediately sold myself short being in awe with the fact that *a man like him* (translation: so much 'better' than I) would actually be interested in a person such as I. In doing so, I devalued whatever good qualities I did have, dragging myself down to a bottomless pit of worthlessness. That *for sure* wasn't better.

Richard's greatest attraction for me was stability, which in retrospect could, possibly be the greatest joke of my life. The belief that *at last* I could quit trying so hard and just coast along on the easy train ride was tremendously appealing. If I'd tried harder would we have had a better chance at success? The constant fluctuation of moods and the never-ending battle against the 'dark side' in dealing with *everything* exhausted and discouraged me. Never did I feel more like a failure than during my time with Richard. And that was before he killed himself. That certainly wasn't better either.

I look at Alec laughing at something Benny has said. I think about the way I am with him. That feeling he continually exudes that he's *interested* in hearing my thoughts, encourages me and makes me work towards thinking more carefully. The fact that he finds me attractive - having even used the word *sexy* in a sentence regarding me - is mind blowing. How's *that* for a confidence booster, huh? But, I realize as I sit here lost in thought, the most compelling thing about Alec Xavier Monroe is he knows my deepest, darkest demons and couldn't care less about them. There's nothing I have to hide or pretend about. In fact, he's said that he *likes* the person I am as a result of my rather psychedelic past. How unbelievable is that?

You've got Life and I've got love. That's what I said to him minutes ago in the truck. *Welcome to the Club* he said back to me. In my statement I acknowledged The Truth of all the words that he, and Callie, and Marlie and all the other well-meaning Bible-banging Christians have been subtly and unsubtly waving in my face. It's momentous for me to discover that I *recognized* what they've been telling me to be *The Truth.* I stand up and walk back into the darkness of the church because I think I'm having a crisis and I don't really know how demonstrative I'm going to be about it.

Leaning against the back wall, looking out the small, grimy window that reveals a side alley between the two buildings, I picture Callie's laughing face, James' perpetually teasing one, Marlie's perpetually sincere one, Alec's intense one ... and all of them have a peace and solidness about them that is very attractive. *I want it* I suddenly think fiercely to myself. *I want that peace and solidness, that confidence and assurance, that freedom and hope.*

I want to wake up each morning with a clear, honorable purpose so that I can travel on an unwavering, confident path.

I want the relief in knowing that when bad things happen I'm not alone and when good things happen I can be confident that *they will happen again.*

I want the knowledge that my past is not only my past but *gone and forgotten* and *incapable of controlling me any longer.*

I want to let it all go.

My whole life I dealt with the truth of things: either hiding from the facts or facing them. But one thing was certain: I never denied them to myself. I always knew the miserably flawed person I was, the totally inept mother I was, the bleakly disappointing wife I was, the high maintenance friend I was ... I spoke about it loudly and regularly to anyone who was unfortunate enough to be within earshot.

It's time for me to face this new Truth that I recognize and decide what exactly I'm going to do with it: hide from it or face it.

I believe that there is a God. How could there not be? How can I look at this beautiful world with its miracle of life and not acknowledge that there must be a higher power out there somewhere who is in control of it all? I've got to do some more reading of this Bible. There's too much profound wisdom in just the few brief things I've read for it to be nonsense. I decide that for me, the Bible *has* to be the word of God. Other people may disagree, and I probably am incapable of arguing a suitable case to prove my conclusion, but a woman's got to start somewhere, doesn't she? Could such a book last with such amazing completeness over all of these centuries? Not without some major miraculous finagling on God's part, I think. And if I choose to believe that the Bible is the word of God then, consequently, I have to believe that what's in it has to be the truth.

More truth to face or hide from. Jeeze.

I hear Callie saying, *The A-B-Cs of a Right Life: Ask, Believe, Confess.* I realize that I've already got the 'believe' part down if I believe in God and believe that the Bible's His Book. But I guess there's a bunch of people walking around like that. "I believe in God." "Yeah, I have a Bible and I read it." People in The Club seem to have a lot more going for them than just that. Kind of like the people that say, "Yeah, I know smoking's bad for me," as they blow nicotine in my face. There's believing and then there's Believing ...

I asked God for help the other night when I went and saw my mother. I don't think I'll be running anytime soon to repeat the experience, but it was certainly the best encounter I've had with my mother in four decades if not more. Wouldn't it be nice that the next time I'm facing something that's causing me to want to get into the fetal position if I could request help and get it just like that?

Alec says *I don't believe in coincidences.* I'd like that to be true. I'd like for there to be less … randomness in my life. I'd like to think that I can pray and ask sincerely and that the wheels of my life will grind into motion with God at the controls. Kind of like I can submit requests and, after things have been extensively evaluated by the big Boss, they'll either be approved or denied. Let's face it, if I believe that God is the God of the universe, then He probably knows better than I about absolutely everything, right? I should probably trust His judgment over mine, right? And if all that's the case, wouldn't it make sense, rather than asking God for occasional help now and then when things are really … poor … that I should ask God to just take over the whole kit and caboodle? Just take it all, God. Every lousy piece of paper that is in the messed up book of my life. Take it all, organize it, throw out what needs to be tossed, refresh what's salvageable, remake stuff that needs to be stripped right down, I don't care, but *take it all.*

I give up.

Standing there in the dimness, surrounded by the loving strains of the band's tunes, I think to God, *I want to climb into Your arms or Your big chariot or the very palm of Your Hand, curl up and give it all over. Right this minute.*

As soon as I think that I feel … contrite. I feel compelled to apologize for all the time it's taken me to get to this point in my life where I'm finally willing to listen. Talk about thick! Talk about procrastination! Talk about stupidity! Talk about a trial! I've been the epitome of the terrible twos, the rebellious teens and the obnoxious, know-it-all adults all rolled into one very difficult forty-eight-year-old package. *I am so very sorry, God.* I feel that emotion right down to my toenails. *Help me do it better. Keep me on track. Make me listen. Show me clearly. Heck, paint big black arrows on the ground, God, and I promise I'll follow them.*

I feel like crying and laughing at the same time. I feel … different. Which, considering who, what, where, when, why, and how I've been for this life of mine, feeling *different* is a pretty grand thing. I think *ask, believe, confess.* "I think I've covered all the bases," I murmur to myself. "Except the diligence, part." Callie's voice in my head says, *You've got to stick to it when times get tough.* "That'll be easy," I say with my best attitude: sarcasm.

"Elaine?" Alec says from behind me, his voice filled with concern. "You okay?"

I'm standing here talking to myself. He must be thinking I've at last gone around the sanity bend. I turn around to look at him and have to sniffle because, I seem to be crying. I smile through my tears and say, "I'm absolutely fine," and for the first time in my life I really mean it.

The music for the evening is better than ever. Benny shouts into the microphone as the growing crowd shifts, and says, "Hey! All you out there! Stand up and dance for joy!" The band explodes into a hopping song that I sing right along with as the words are projected up on the screen:

You are the child that I love in you I am well pleased ...
Nothing high, nothing low could separate you from me,
You are the child that I love in you I am well pleased
You've got nothing to prove
In you I am well pleased

And when you walk through the dark
I'll be a light unto your feet
And when you cry in the night
I'll be the comfort that you seek
Long before you spoke a word
Or your face was ever seen
Your every breath, your every move
Was ever visible, ever visible to me

When you need me I'm already there
I hear your every prayer
And every step you take I take with you
And every move you make I make it to
And when you walk through the dark
I'll be a light unto your feet
And when you cry in the night
I'll be the comfort that you seek
Long before you spoke a word

Giving Up

Or your face was ever seen
Your every breath, your every move
Was ever visible, ever visible to me³⁴

I can't help myself and in my mind's eye I picture the image I'm projecting of this happy, smiling woman singing Christian rock tunes at the top of her lungs. When the song ends everyone is clapping and someone wolf-whistles in the back. Benny bows and says, "Want some more?" and the crowd goes wild all over again.

This is my church I think as I dance at my seat. *That is my guy* I think as Alec winks at me from the stage. *I am a part of this Club.*

The music, rocking and rolling at the start, slows down gradually to get us all calmed down and in our seat so Crystal can do her thing. Tonya and her impressive God Rocks tee shirt steps up to the mike and begins to sing with Alec and Benny playing quietly in the background:

Beauty for ashes,
a garment of praise for my heaviness.
Beauty for ashes,
take this heart of stone and make it Yours.

I delight myself in the Richest of Fair,
trading all that I've had for all that is better.
A garment of praise for my heaviness.
You are the greatest taste.
You're the richest of fair.³⁵

The angels of heaven could not sing any sweeter. As Tonya bows her head and the band falls silent, Crystal opens with prayer.

Alec slips in next to me just as the prayer is ending and slides his hand across the back of my chair. He's concerned about me. I can see it in his eyes as he looks at me, never having heard me talk to myself in a dark corner before I suppose. "The last song that Tonya sang was beautiful," I sigh to him.

He's got his gigantic Bible again and out it comes. Flipping through pages he finds what he wants and sets the massive thing on my lap. He points and I look down. *Psalm 63* it says, *Good News for the Oppressed.*

161

He's got stuff underlined again, which I take to be the best parts, so I read that: *To all who mourn in Israel, he will give a crown of beauty for ashes, a joyous blessing instead of mourning, festive praise instead of despair … I am overwhelmed with joy in the Lord my God! For He has dressed me with the clothing of salvation and draped me in a robe of righteousness. I am like a bridegroom in his wedding suite or a bride with her jewels.*[36]

He's waiting for me to look at him I can feel it. When I finally do, along with a small smile, he frowns, takes a moment to tuck a wisp of hair behind my ear and then whisper to me, "Are you sure you're okay?"

I rest my head on his shoulder and take a deep breath. Turning, I whisper back to him, "I'm really, *really* wonderful. I gave up and joined The Club. I'm just getting used to things."

His arm, resting across the back of my chair now pulls me closer while his other hand reaches up to cradle my face. I feel him kiss the top of my head while he rocks me back and forth gently in our seats.

We are travelers on a journey, fellow pilgrims on the road,
We are here to help each other, walk the mile and bear the load.[37]

Chapter 16: The Inevitability Of Life

Isn't there a song about rainy days and Mondays getting a person down? How about if the Monday in question *is* a rainy day *and* you are forced to sit through an hour-long teachers' meeting after a full day of work *and* the person running the meeting is your ex-husband? What kind of emotion qualifies for that kind of day?

Paulie and I do a pretty tremendous job of avoiding each other in the daily grind of work but sometimes it's just unavoidable. Like, if I've got a kid in my class who's blatantly masturbating under his desk *regularly.* (Sigh. Yes. It happened.) Or I've got a girl who wrote an exceptionally well-written essay on how exactly she planned to end her life. (Yes. That, too.) In each case, Paulie and I were able to sit down, surrounded by other colleagues who comprised the Child Study Team (and who know some - but thankfully not all - of our rather awkward past) and behave like the civilized professionals we pretend to be.

Sitting in the back of the school library, listening to Paulie outline the new district guidelines for flagging and eventually classifying new cases of emotionally, neurologically, or communicationally handicapped children I doodle on my note pad and try to look like I'm cooperatively interested. Marlie, who at these meetings takes notes that are so detailed they could be published as minutes on the district website, is scribbling frantically to keep up. It's rather comical that teachers, in meetings such as this, regularly regress into the identical behaviors that we continually battle against with our students: subtle disruption, blatant disrespect, obvious boredom, and passive disregard.

When the meeting breaks up, I pack away my things (today I fell into the passive disregard category, I suppose, although all four behaviors have at times been my particular specialty) and say a casual goodbye to Marlie. Somewhere over the course of my wandering thoughts, I've decided to go to a local bookstore and buy myself a Bible. Having made this decision, I'm almost as excited as I would be at the prospect of buying a new pair of shoes. How weird is that?

"Elaine? May I speak with you privately?" I look up into Paulie's eyes. *Nervous* eyes. What? Does he think I'd embarrass us both here? Now?

I'll bet you real cash money that husband #2 – Paulie – was so darn threatened by you that he lay awake nights coming up with lists of things to criticize you for just so he could try to gain an edge.

Alec's words float through my head and I realize that this expression that Paulie bears - one of extreme tension - is something that I'm quite familiar with. *Holy cow.*

"Okay," I hear myself say. "Where?"

He blinks, obviously surprised at my neutral and cooperative tone. "Could we go back to your classroom?"

"Yeah, that would be fine."

"I'm not keeping you from anything, am I?" he asks solicitously as we make our way out of the library.

I look him in the eye. *I'm sure you've eviscerated lesser men.* I smile at the delightful thought. "No, nothing pressing. I've got a few minutes."

"Oh. Great. Fine."

We walk silently back to my classroom and wander over to the table at the front. There are already a couple chairs there so we sit down. "How are you, Elaine?"

Just the tone and the question pisses me off. What? Is he my therapist now? We've been divorced for almost twenty years. Why should he care? "Can I ask you a favor?" I hear myself ask.

"Sure," he says, startled and not a tiny bit wary.

"Will you cut all the whole guarded, psychological crap and just get to the chase? I'd much prefer your honesty than your cautious hesitancy."

Paulie looks out the classroom window and swallows. Then he looks back at me. "Olivia doesn't return my calls. I know better than to even *bother* with calling you. I didn't ask to be dragged into this *thing* between you and your daughter, but I was. You can believe it or not but I really would like to provide help to both Olivia and ... you ... if possible. I can't just walk away without feeling I'd done my level best to ... assist. So, I thought I'd risk it today and ask you if you were okay."

It took a lot of guts, actually. He knows damn well I've never been happy or receptive towards his *assistance*, even when things were their best between us. He can't help it that he seems to ooze superiority and condescension with every word he utters.

Suddenly, I have a strong desire to have a successful conversation with this man ... along the same lines as I had with my mother. I have no expectations of us becoming best friends or even me seeking him out the next time my life goes out of control, but I can at least walk away from this with the feeling that I did a good job.

I will take everything he says at face value, I think. *Give him the benefit of the doubt and not twist up anything he says with our history. I started fresh yesterday. I felt different yesterday. I will be different today.* "Wow, what a novel thought," I say out loud to myself.

Paulie jerks like I've slapped him. "That's not fair, Elaine! Just because you never believe what I sincerely try to communicate to you every time we're together -"

"Stop." I interrupt Paulie's tirade with my hands upheld in supplication. *"I believe you."* As an after thought I say, "I was talking to myself, actually, not you."

Now Paulie looks like I've stripped nude and propositioned him.

I sigh. I look upward, I guess hoping there will be a big black arrow or a sign in day glow letters that advises me what to say or not say. No such luck. Paulie's still looking at me, now perhaps frightened at what I'll say or do next since, apparently, all bets are now off. Beginning with great hesitancy, I murmur, "It was really ... big ... of you to be willing to help Olivia when, to the best of my knowledge, she's never said one kind or decent thing to you in her life. I guess the fact that she *did* call you and ask for your help was a measure of how upset she really was, huh?"

Paulie nods, trying to determine how he ended up here, in The Twilight Zone.

"I ... we talked ... Olivia and I. At Erin's. Not too successfully." I give him a wry glance. "Surprise, surprise, huh?" I look out the window. "She's been talking to my mother, too." I look at him again. "If it makes you feel any better that was worse than her talking to you." When he starts to say something I hold up one hand. "It would probably be better if you didn't say anything. Just let me ramble for a bit, okay?"

Getting up, I go to the classroom door and shut it. It's now pretty late in the school day and the building's probably empty. But still ...

Leaning against the door I say, "I can't tell Olivia the name of her biological father because I never knew it, Paul. He was a man ... that my mother brought home ... one night. He ... wasn't someone I ... I didn't choose to be with him ..." I can't say the word 'rape' but I don't have to as I look at Paulie and his face has drained of color. He's sitting at my reading table, his mouth partially open as if he needs help drawing in a full breath. "Dean doesn't know the whole story but it turned out that he always knew he wasn't Olivia's biological father." I smile a tender smile for the big, drunken lug. "I've got to give him credit. He loved Olivia like his own. I never realized he knew even part of the truth.

"I thought my mother didn't know ... but," I sigh, "after talking to her now I'm pretty sure ... she always did." I shrug. "Not that she admitted it, I've just got that feeling, you know?" Paulie nods.

"I've carried this horrible secret with me almost my whole life, Paul. Through three marriages and the birth and upbringing of my two girls. I've been running and running and running ... always looking back, making sure it didn't catch up with me. But I'm so freakin' tired." I shrug. "At first, when you called and all this started to unravel, I thought, 'This is it. Now my entire life is just going to implode.' But it hasn't. I feel ... kind of free. Almost relieved."

Walking over I sit down with my never-before-silent-for-this-length-of-time second husband. "I still have to tell Olivia the whole thing. I don't know how I'll do it. I don't even know *when* I'll be strong enough or courageous enough to do it. But I will. Eventually. And since you had the courage to risk asking me how I'm doing, I figure I owed you the courtesy of answering. Honestly. With as little venom as humanly possible."

We sit in silence for a long collection of minutes. He goes to move his hand, stops, sighs, and then with fixed determination reaches over and takes one of my hands in his. "Don't get angry at me for holding your hand, Elaine. This isn't part of my 'psychological agenda' you always accuse me of. This is who I am: a man that spent a period of his life with you. This is who I am: a man who's always wondered why he can always seem to say and do the right thing with *everyone else on the planet* except his own wife. This is what I do with friends and those I care about when I want to ... *I don't know!* ... connect with them, I guess. I'm always so damned uncertain around you, Elaine! No matter how hard I try, I almost always walk away feeling inadequate. This time I really want to get it right. So this time, I'm only going to say: you're some woman. I'm in awe of you. Please if there's anything I can ever do to help you, Olivia, or Erin, you know where I am." With one more squeeze of my hand, he stands up and leaves my classroom.

I sit for so long, my butt goes to sleep. Finally, I stand up and wander around my classroom straightening desks and ... spending a few moments wondering why Johnny has a pair of boxer shorts in his desk. Maybe I don't want to know. Part of the reason that I've always enjoyed teaching in middle school was because it was the last part of my childhood that was relatively innocent. Oh, I knew life wasn't television - mother had already proved that to me time and time again. But, in middle school I still believed that life wasn't … impossibly hard. When I look at the faces of these kids I teach and who suffer through my twisted sense of humor and warped perception of life, I glimpse at times that wondrous naiveté that separates children from adults. There is no specific age or time when one crosses over that line. Some cross it too early and, I suppose, some cross it too late. But if I could have just one wish, it would be that every child got to cross that line at *just the perfect time.*

I pick up my cell phone and dial Alec. He answers with a voice that doesn't sound completely sleepy. "Did I wake you?"

"Not yet. I just crawled into bed."

"How was meter reading today?"

I think he yawns. "Wet."

"How many houses did you track mud into?"

"The question you should be asking is how many houses saw my sexy 'I love Yankees' socks."

"How many?"

"None, I save those for when I'm trying to ultimately impress someone. I'm not interested in impressing anyone but you."

"Hmmm."

"You okay?"

How come Alec can ask me that question and I get a rush of warmth and Paulie can ask me a question and I fight the urge to spit? "Yeah, I just wanted to say, 'sleep tight'." He yawns again. "Go to sleep. Would you be interested in having a very late lunch or a very early dinner after you finish meter reading and after I finish teaching tommorrow?"

"Are you asking me out on a date, Elaine Marie Cummings? That's awfully forward, don't you think?"

"No, *forward* is putting your hand up a woman's dress in the church parking lot."

"Oh thanks, Elaine. *Now* I'm going to sleep soundly."

I laugh. I sigh. I smile. "If I leave the back door to my house open, you could go there after work and crash. I'd meet you there."

He's silent for a moment. "Are we still on the same page?"

I hesitate. "Do you want to be?"

Now he sighs, a great breath of frustrated air. "I'm forcing myself to say yes. But it's almost impossible."

"My life has never been so … right, Alec. Never."

"Right back at you, Sweetie."

"I won't wear a dress or garter belt tomorrow." I pause. "And I won't shave my legs." That's helpful, isn't it?

He chuckles. "And I'll be all sweaty and smelly from hiking around neighborhoods, going into dark dank basements, reading meters."

"That doesn't seem to really deter me one bit," I tell him honestly.

"Right back at you, Sweetie."

Oh. "Didn't you say we were better together than apart?"

"Yes. Yes I did."

"Then we'll make the right choice."

He sighs. "We're going to hold each other to that."

When I get home from school the next day, Alec's truck is parked in the driveway but when I come through the garage door inside, Alec appears to be nowhere in the house. Then, as I look out into the back yard, I see why.

A huge quilt is spread out on the lawn and Alec's stretched out next to a picnic basket, baseball hat across his face, seemingly fast asleep. I stand looking down at him through the kitchen window, watching his even breathing. Does he think being out in broad daylight will keep us on the straight and narrow? I think back on some of the highly inappropriate places where I've done the deed – in the complete throes of insanity - and shake my head at Alec's underestimation of me.

But I am different now.

Yes. Yes, I am.

I kick off my sandals and wander out to greet this man who makes my heart smile. Rather than wake him, I lay down next to him and curl up against his side. He always smells so good to me. "Hmmm," he says, obviously very much awake and turns towards me, throwing his arm across me and pulling me in close against his side. "Just what I was hoping for," his voice is thick and sleepy, "a woodland sprite to come and keep me company."

"Woodland sprites are tiny, delicate creatures," I murmur, pointing out significant discrepancies in his assumption.

"Woodland sprites are also full of mischief and prone to unexpected flights of fancy," he lifts he baseball cap and squints at me with one eye. "And, in addition, they are absolutely fantastic kissers."

"You've kissed woodland sprites before?"

"Well," he says, "I *thought* I did. But I *could* be wrong. I better check you out to see." We spend a long period of time rolling around and kissing on the quilt. I don't know if *I'm* a woodland sprite, but, if the litmus test involves kissing skill, then Alec must be king of them. When I tell him so, he gives me a sexy wink.

"You hungry?" he asks me as he sits up, drags over the picnic basket and opens it up.

Truth be told, I worked through my lunch so that I could leave with the dismissal bell. "I'm starved."

Out comes fresh crusty French bread, Brie cheese, salmon, grapes, apples, some kind of pasta salad, and, of course, the inevitable pastry bag. Sitting cross-legged (on what turns out to be his only bed quilt) we laugh and talk and feast.

I tell him about my conversation yesterday with Paulie and how shockingly well it went. "I don't think we had such a civil conversation during our entire marriage." Alec arches his eyebrows at me. "What?" I say.

"I heard it in your voice," he says all smug-like. "I knew something went down."

"Nothing *went down*," I say to him with superior hauteur. "It was the first time I called you unprompted after school *plus* I asked you out. You're just not used to me being so ..." Suddenly, I'm at a loss for words.

"Pushy? In-your-face? Take-charge? Assertive? Out-spoken?" He rattles off the list with a grin.

"*Available*," I finally settle on. "Usually, I play hard to get."

"You're as hard to get as a fishhook with a juicy worm attached."

Frowning, I think what he's trying to say about me. I need clarification. "Am I the worm or the hook?"

He looks at me intently and then sighs. "I love you, Elaine. I've been needing to tell you that for a while now."

That's a pretty tremendous change in subject, don't you think? "Why?"

He snorts out a short laugh. "Figures. No reciprocal declaration. Now I'm going to have to present my case." He's leaning on his side, propped up on his elbow, tearing off pieces of left over bread and throwing the bits to a rather brave and curious squirrel.

"Because you wear garter belts," he says glibly, "and Wonderbras, although that hasn't actually been *confirmed* yet."

"Unlike the garter belt."

He smiles at the obvious fond memory. "Oh, yeah. Unlike the garter belt."

"Keep going."

"Because you always smell good enough to add to one of my pastries, a personal fantasy I've had *forever* – well, at least since I've been baking which has been quite a while now."

"You'd like to bake me in a metal pan at 350°?"

"No," he says with a growl, tossing the bread aside and pulling me down so that I'm on my back looking up at him. "I'd like to be able to enjoy my favorite chocolate pastry with just a *hint* of almond essence mixed in. *That's* what I mean."

I look up at him and blink. *Oh.*

Alec looks down at me, absolutely serious. "Do I really need to explain why I have fallen in love with you? Do you really need to hear it, Elaine? I've been pretty honest with you all along telling you why I enjoy spending time with you, what I like about you. Falling in love was kind of inevitable, don't you think?"

Now it's my turn to sigh. *Oh, yeah. Falling in love was kind of inevitable.* I reach up and touch his face briefly. He's got salt and pepper beard stubble going on and it's rough and sandpapery against my palm. "No," I say with a deep sigh, "you don't have to spell it all out for me. I can see it most of the time just in the way you look at me."

"A lot of the time it's just lust you see," he says with a twinkle in his eyes.

Shaking my head I say, "I don't think you'd lust after just anyone."

Seriously he says, "Oh yeah? Why not?"

"You seem to be the type of guy whose got to have a little heart action going on before you head on to the other kind of action," I say with absolute certainty. He's not frivolous with his emotions. Can't everyone see that?

"Your quick wit and irreverent sense of humor got me first. That sparked my interest. Then it was your open and honest way of dealing with just about everything. It was refreshing, compelling, almost addictive." He's touching my face now, smoothing back my hair, examining the earrings I put on this morning. He looks at me intently. "But it's your heart that made me fall in love, Elaine. Despite the fact that you protect it with miserly tightness, it's so big, so giving that it kind of spills out all over the place no matter what you do." He leans in close and I can see the ring of darkness around the lighter brown of his irises. *"I want your heart, Elaine. With a passion I thought I'd lost a long time ago. I want to be a part of it. I want to be the one you give it too. I want to be the one that reverently carries it around within my own heart."* He takes a deep breath, almost as if he's trying to ratchet down the intensity and get a grip on himself. He stares out across my back yard. "I've never wanted such a thing before, Elaine. Not ever. In fact, it's something I've avoided at all costs. I understand if I'm going too fast for you. I understand if, given the course of your life, you need a lot more time to confirm that I'm not ..." he squints but still doesn't look at me, "someone who's going to be *completely toxic to you and your hard won mental stability.* I'm sure I've been exactly that to a number of women in my past." He snorts. "Hell, I could probably give you names and phone numbers."

At my continued silence, still not looking at me he says, "I want you to understand that just because I've put it all out there for you, I've no expectations that you're going to immediately reciprocate, okay? No pressure."

For a time we're both silent and, if I were a betting woman I'd guess that there were some very high odds that the X-man might have been wishing he'd not put his heart *so far* out there. I reach up and cup his face, making him, finally, look at me. "I can't actually pinpoint the moment I knew I loved you," I say.

The tension seems to seep out of him bit by bit and, finally he turns to kiss my palm.

"But do you know when I *started* falling in love with you?" I ask him softly.

He's got the tenderest expression, staring down at me. "No, when?"

"When you kept Liam's Batman mask on when you were introduced to Olivia. That's when."

He grins at me, a heart-stopping smile that brightens his whole face. Leaning over, he kisses me with a sweet, solid possessiveness that makes my toes curl. "Do you think," he asks me with a really wicked grin, "if I ask Liam really nicely - and even offer him a big bribe – he'll let me borrow the Batman mask when we decide to tear up the celibacy page?"

And I can feel Your presence here with me, suddenly I'm lost within Your beauty,
Caught up in the wonder of Your touch, here in this moment I surrender to Your love. [38]

Chapter 17: Setting Fires At Three A.M.

I t's pretty poor that Paulie, husband #2, has experienced full
disclosure on my part while, Dean, husband #1 and recipient
of far more fallout from the inception of the nitroglycerin
secret, is still in the dark. *Especially* when Dean did so good for so long at
keeping his lips sealed about what he *did* know. Wednesday after work
sitting in the silence of my classroom, I bite the bullet and call ex #1.
Except the recording, after the annoying tone, tells me the number has
been disconnected. How come nothing's ever easy where Dean is
concerned?

So here I am, calling my ex-mother-in-law for the second time in
less than a month. "Hello, Miriam? It's Elaine," I say as brightly as
possible, hoping that Miriam doesn't know a number of Elaines and I'm
forced to say stuff like, 'your ex-daughter-in-law' or 'Dean's ex-wife' or
something like that.

"Elaine," Miriam says in that breathy kind of voice that always
makes her sound a little like a poor Marilyn Monroe voiceover double.

We make the trivial small talk necessary before I drop the obvious
bomb of either a.) Can I have Dean's new phone number? or b.) Can you
tell me where Dean is currently working? She's silent for a few minutes so,
rather than get into a big question fest as to why I need this information

again, I say, "If you're uncomfortable giving me that information, would you please just ask him to get in contact with me as soon as he can?" I add, "It concerns the girls," hoping that the statement is general enough not to draw particular attention to Olivia and yet specific enough that she realizes I'm no longer warm for her son's form.

"He's just moved again so I don't know his new number." Translation: He's just had to move to escape the creditors *again* and he can't get phone service because of his poor credit. "But I do know that he's got an *excellent* job over at the new condo development on Milltown Road, between Routes 22 and 202. He's one of the *foremen*," she feels compelled to add. "Do you know which construction site I mean?"

I assure her I do and decide to drive over immediately and see if I can find him. Why invest in a sleepless night of tension when I can carve another hole in my stomach this very instant? The development is a massive expanse of dirt roads and buildings in various stages of skeletal development. Most of the action is centered on a new series of units that are being sealed in with fiberboard and then wrapped in a protective coating of insulating Tyvek. I park my car and carefully work my way to the first hard-hatted man I find. "Can you tell me where Dean Kelly is?" After getting the thorough once over, the guy turns, does an ear-piercing wolf whistle and shouts, "YO! KELLY!" From high up on the roof, I see Dean straighten, push his hard hat back a bit, and lean forward with a squint. I wave. So? What else should I do?

Dean looks at his watch and then holds up his hand once, twice, three times, four times and then looks at me. Twenty minutes. I give him the thumbs up and go back to my car to grade papers. Hey, a teacher always makes the most of the free time she has.

Lost in the power and frustration of spelling and grammar tragedies, I practically jump out of my skin when someone taps on my driver's side window. There's Dean, all blonde, blue-eyed, and tan, looking at me with serious concern. I guess it makes sense. Never, in the past thirty plus years of our acquaintance have I ever come to his place of work. I'd probably need oxygen if he showed up at my classroom.

Rolling down the window I say, "Relax, no one died. No one had a critical car accident or anything either. Your mother just didn't have a number for you and I wanted to speak with you."

Squatting down beside me so that we're almost eye level he says, "Okay. Shoot."

I sigh. "Well not *here*, if you don't mind. Could we go someplace? A restaurant? A coffee shop?" I'm not going to suggest a bar, which makes me sniff. No hint of stale alcohol excess that no substance on the face of this earth can mask. He's exceptionally clear-eyed, too. That's a plus. He must be working his way to another big penny.

Scratching his head, Dean says, "I could use a burger or something. Want to go to Wendy's?" Never let it be said that he didn't know how to show a girl a good time. But I understand the plusses as well: no bar to tempt.

"Fine, I'll meet you there."

It being just four in the afternoon, we pretty much have Wendy's all to ourselves. Dean orders two Baconators™, a large fries, and a large vanilla Frosty. I have bottled water. I know what I'm going to be talking about and it's not conducive to food consumption of any kind. We pick a table that looks out over the parking lot and the highway filled with frenzied commuters who have cut out early in hopes of missing evening rush hour.

"What's up?" Dean says through a mouthful of Baconator™.

"I need to talk with you, Dean, about Olivia and all of this mess. I …, well …, I haven't talked with Olivia and told her all of this yet, but I just felt that I needed to tell you the … truth and everything."

Dean swallows, wipes the back of his hand across his mouth and says, "You don't have to tell me anything you don't want to, E. It's all in the past. Done. Water down the sewage pipe."

Nice analogy. "Don't you want to know the whole story?"

To his credit, he thinks for a moment or two and then slowly shakes his head. "It's not going to make any difference to me, really. Olivia's always going to be my daughter no matter where she started."

He's absolutely serious, and for the first time I feel a powerful rush of *thankfulness* that Dean Kelly is Olivia's surrogate father. How astonishing is that? How many men could sit there, say such a thing, and – here's the impossible part – *mean it*. He may be an alcoholic, unable to stay sober for more than eighteen months at a stretch, but drunk or sober he's always loved his girls. Regardless of the facts of life.

"Maybe *I do* need to tell you this, Dean. Maybe I feel you have a right to know. The last time we saw each other you talked a lot about the guilt that you had and, well, it's really not fair for me to leave you with that and not the truth as well." So in fits and starts I go through my whole messy story *again* including my mother's apparent culpability and even Paul's fringe involvement with it all. Dean listens, never pausing in his consumption of probably close to six million calories.

When I'm done, we sit in silence, he sipping down to the very slurpy bottom of his vanilla Frosty and me sipping on my bottled water. Finally, Dean says, "When are you going to tell Livvy?"

I shrug. "I don't know. When I get my courage up, I guess."

Shaking his head, Dean says, "It's not a question of your courage, E, and you know it. It's a question of when Livvy is ready to hear it all. Lots of stuff can screw a person up. This has got to be near the top of the list of bad stuff to deal with. How messed up do you get when you know that you're the product of a rape?"

Oh, God. And I guess I am kind of praying again. I've never put all the facts together in that order. My face must show my horror because Dean reaches across the table and grabs both my hands, "She's a strong, opinionated woman, just like you, E. Livvy's been feisty since the day we brought her home from the hospital refusing to nurse and wanting only to be bottle fed. Hell, remember she potty trained herself at sixteen months? We'd only just breathed a sigh of relief that she'd *finally* starting walking and before we can catch our breath she's screaming like a banshee in the bathroom wanting to use the toilet. *Not the potty seat* my mother got her, mind you, but the damn toilet. Remember, I had to make her a special stepstool so she could climb up there and do her business?" He smiles

177

fondly. "She's always been a tough little bit. Did a Dad proud. If anyone can handle something like this … Livvy can."

I smile in fond remembrance over the child he's brought to mind. I can picture the stepstool – bright blue with Olivia's yellow handprints stuck all over it. "She wasn't always so tough."

Dean looks at me like I've finally lost my mind. *"She sure as hell was. I may have been sober only fifty percent of the time – or less, but even I* remember that much." He ticks off things with his finger, "The world's pickiest eater. My mother still says most of her gray hair was from trying to get Olivia to eat a full meal. Remember what it was like finding clothes that she'd wear? Remember she ran away *at three years old,* in the dead of winter, because you wouldn't let her finger paint? Didn't the neighbor bring her home?"

I nod. She'd been barefoot in just a tee shirt and her pink flower-power underpants.

"She *pulled* her own front tooth out before it was really loose just because her friend Janine had already lost her tooth."

I look at Dean. "And was absolutely livid that the Tooth Fairy only left her fifty cents."

He nods. "When we split up E, I didn't know how you were going to manage on your own with her. Erin was so easy compared to Olivia. I, well, I know I wasn't solid or consistent, but at least I was *there* most of the time in one way or another. My mother said after you left, 'She'll be back Dean. You mark my words.' I remember shaking my head and thinking well, if you *didn't* come back, that was sure as hell an indictment as to how bad living *with me* was."

When I go to open my mouth and say something Dean says, "It's okay, E. You were better off away from me. Neither of them drink, right? That's a plus right there. Erin's got a great marriage, right? There's another plus. Both the girls have done great professionally. Have you ever read the statistics of kids who grow up in homes with alcoholics?" He shakes his head. "You were right to go. That way, when I *did* see them, I was at least sober or close to it. They don't remember me falling down drunk and passing out in my own vomit. Or pissing myself in the front hallway. Or falling up the porch stairs and knocking my two front teeth out and not even realizing. *You were right to go, E."*

I sigh to myself, lost in thought over how terrible it really was dealing with Dean's alcoholism and knowing it was only going to get worse trying to raise two children right in the midst of it. "I don't know when I'll tell her, Dean." *Hi honey. Just wanted you to know that on top of all the other horrible demons you're dealing with you should know that you were the product of rape. I love you. Have a nice day.*

"You'll know the time." He reaches up and pats my cheek. "I know you think you didn't do a good job with her, but the reality is you did the best job possible with what you had to work with." He leans towards me and says real slow and clear. *"And. We. Always. Loved. Her. With. All. Our. Hearts. Even. When. We. Were. Tearing. Our. Hair. Out. Because. Of. Her."*

Sometimes, his flashes of insight and brilliance are blinding. We *did* love her. Would I care about all of this if I didn't? *No, I'd be my mother then.*

"How long?" I ask, changing the subject, but Dean keeps up.

"Almost a month. This time I'm determined to be different."

I sit up straight. *I'm different*, I think. That seems to be the greatest, newest buzzword all of a sudden. "Do you go to church, Dean?"

Shaking his head he says, "Nah, those places are too stuffy." He holds his arms out wide. "Can you see me in a place with incense, organ music, and prayer?"

Actually, I could. Why not? "I'm going to a place in Somerville. It's called Agape Shop. Rock music, people in flip flops and jeans, and afterwards there's this pastry shop that serves up coffee and the most fantastic desserts."

Stretching his arms out across the back of the booth, his tee shirt tightens and shows off his muscles. He seems completely puzzled. "You'd want me there?"

I shrug. "It's not my personal domain, Dean. And, if it helps you be sober ... *be different* ... isn't it worth a shot?"

He nods, slowly. It seems to make sense to him. "When's the service?"

"Saturday and Sunday nights, seven p.m."

"Maybe I'll try it."

"Maybe I'll see you there, then."

Driving home from Wendy's, I think about Baconator sandwiches (because *now* I'm starving) and my life. I shake my head in amazement at the changes. Suddenly, my head's not so bursting of all the crap I keep dredging up and refusing to let settle to the bottom and disappear. Things I cannot change must be let go. I cannot change my past. That's not to say I don't wish I *could*, but I'm not expecting that miracle anytime soon. (And if you're listening God, and you're going to give me a miracle, I've got other more important things to ask for, okay?) Other things I would have listed – all from my past – a stunning collection of disasters and failures – I will no longer allow to crowd my judgment because they are not realities, they are just rocks around my neck. I'm setting fire to all my mental guilt storage containers – every darn one – and will make a pledge to myself and anyone else interested in hearing that I Will Not Repeat Any One Of Those Mistakes Again.

God willing. (Another Club phrase I never used to appreciate. Now maybe I should have it tattooed on my forehead.)

The only important, critical *reality* is that I'm still barely on speaking terms with my oldest daughter and I would like that to change. I am different now. I am on the right track now. I've got Superior Help now. Wasn't there some verse in the Bible that talks about God not being a God of chaos? Just like Maxwell Smart, Secret Agent 86, I'm joining CONTROL and am no longer a card-carrying member of KAOS.

It's okay. You can laugh. It's a lot better than crying.

Friday afternoon, when I get home from school I sit on my living room couch reading the mail. It's mostly catalogs trying to tempt the early Christmas shop-by-mail shoppers of which I'm usually not. One minute I'm reading about Hammacher Schlemmer's R2-D2 Home Theater System available for the remarkably affordable price of $2799.95 (I wonder what the shipping costs for that are?) and the next thing I know I'm staring at the ceiling, which is lit only by the twinkling lights of my cable television box. I stumble up and head into the kitchen where the microwave tells me it's two eleven. *In the morning? I've slept almost eight hours and it's still the middle of the night.*

I think about Alec, doing his pastry-baking and decide perhaps he could use an additional set of hands. On his pastries, I mean.

I wash my face, brush my teeth, comb my hair and decide to change out of my school clothes (which I've slept in for eight hours in addition to working a full day in them – yuck). I choose jeans and a tee shirt that says *My significant other goes MEOW* (another Callie gift).

Maybe he's the kind of guy that doesn't like his woman to encroach on his domain, I think as I drive over on the unbelievably quiet streets. *Maybe he's a monster like that Hell's Kitchen chef and I'll be appalled at what I see.*

The front of Agape Shop is dark and silent, but as I idle in the middle of the street trying to peer into the windows I think I see lights in the rear of the store. Sure enough, when I drive around back, the kitchen entrance door is propped wide open and light illuminates the parking lot. Walking towards the light, there's also rocking music pulsing into the night. *Don't the neighbors mind?* I wonder and then remember who is the upstairs (and only tenant): Alec.

Who is singing at the top of his lungs when I step through the back door, head thrown back with enthusiastic abandon. He's even got a little wiggle going on:

> *I'm a one trick pony, if you will.*
> *I got a one track mind with a heart that's real,*
> *And don't forget I've got tunnel vision,*
> *For something much bigger than superstition.*
> *Call me hard headed for the One that changed me.*
> *Say what you will, it will not phase me.*
> *No need for anything up my sleeve.*
> *There's just one thing that I'll ever need.*
>
> *You are my one and only*
> *You are my one and only*

Joining The Club

Oh, I'm a one trick pony

If I hear just one more time
That I should try and be more open-minded,
I think I just might scream.
The world says this is all there is,
Yet I believe the One who says there's life after this.
Now tell me, how much more open can my mind be? [39]

"You're a one trick pony, huh?" I say when there's a lull enough in the tunes for Alec to hear me. He jumps like I've goosed him and I lean against the door, laughing at the look on his face.

Alec blinks, like he can't process that I'm actually standing in front of him. Switching off the CD player up on the shelf, he walks toward me with predatory intent and asks, "What are you doing here at two forty-five a.m.?" Before I can answer I'm grabbed and hauled up against his flour-covered apron and kissed thoroughly. Even my butt gets a squeeze or two.

"I guess that means you're glad to see me," I say when we come up for air.

"Are you kidding? This is wonderful ..."

Looking around, I take stock of the fact that no one else is present. "Where is everyone? I thought you were the big boss man." I give him a look. "If you're the only one around, that doesn't mean you're the boss, Alec, it only means *you're the only one around.*"

Grinning he makes the Herculean effort to lift me up so that I'm sitting on the counter looking at him. "You think so, do you?"

I nod. "You shouldn't have picked me up. Did you strain your back? Are you suddenly gripped with severe hernia pain? I have a chiropractor - "

Stepping between my legs he holds my face in his hands. "I'm absolutely *terrific.*" He forces himself to take a deep, calming breath. *"I can't believe you're here."* I get a kiss again, the kind that makes you think of a host of other things and I'm not talking brownies. Little alarm bells go off in my head suddenly and I think of another reason maybe I shouldn't have come here: *maybe we're going to end up ripping up the celibacy page and flipping right over to the chocolate sauce and almonds page* … One of Alec's hands slips down to curve around my waist and pulls me tightly towards him while the other hand slips down and rests just above my … heart. I feel like I'm being sucked up in some monstrous force of nature that I can't control.

I put my hands on either side of his waist and pull back enough so that he stops kissing me. We are in Big Trouble. "Are we the only ones that are going to be here?"

Another deep sigh and then he rests his forehead against mine, eyes closed. "No," he says. "People start showing up at three a.m. I always get here first because I set the recipes and choose the selections for the day. Sometimes that takes a while, depending on my mood."

I rub my hands up and down his sides. "Your mood doesn't seem to be that much concerned with the selections for the day right now."

Still with his eyes closed he shakes his head a tiny bit. "It's not."

"Maybe I shouldn't have come."

"It's just, well, I was thinking about you." He snorts. "Hell, I think about you all the time. I think about stuff you've said and done and then I imagine future conversations and future adventures with you …" Suddenly his brown eyes pop open and they're looking into my green ones. I smile and he must see mine crinkle in the corners because he chuckles. "I knew that people were due here any minute so I figured we were pretty safe. I just, well I just kind of let go a little and didn't worry about holding back so much. Knowing that people would be showing up any minute."

Holy cow. That was letting go *a little?* I roll my eyes and shake my head. "Audiences haven't deterred me much in the past, Alec. Just ask the 1975 Bridgewater High School Panther's Football team that interrupted Dean and I during half time. Dean wasn't on the team or anything. We were just making use of the locker room …" I kiss him lightly. My face must blush a bit as I remember the whistles, catcalls, and comments that were made. "You play with fire, young man, and you probably won't be able to put out our conflagration."

Stepping back, he runs his hands through his hair. "You're right." Outside we can hear car doors slam and distant conversations. Alec sighs again and then rolls his eyes at me. "Just in time, huh?"

I nod and jump down off the counter. "I'll say."

"Uh," he says with a wicked grin, "you might want to dust yourself off a bit." I look down and there is flour *everywhere*. On the front of my shirt, in between the legs of my jeans … I spin around trying to see my butt and I can't. I hear Alec laughing.

"Help!"

Walking over he brushes his hand against my front, making everything worse. "Not there! My butt!"

"Never let it be said I don't help ladies when in distress," he says as he makes motions to brush me off but in reality just gets to grab a couple more feels before people walk in the door. By the time two smiling people walk in, I'm sure I'm neon red and Alec is laughing so hard he can barely say hello.

I'm allowed to make and get coffee for everyone, spray and flour a billion trays and pans, and fill muffin tins with those little paper cup things. Otherwise, I'm obviously in the way and disturbing the flow. But it's fun to watch. Alec *is* the big boss, politely but firmly giving instructions, making decisions, and answering questions. Soon the wonderful aroma of hot baked goodies is wafting through the kitchen out into the still dark night. I offer to be the official taste tester and everyone laughs. It seems that working with the pastries day in and day out tends to lessen their appeal. I can taste test all I want they tell me. At last, I've found a job I'm born for.

At five-thirty a.m. there are numerous racks of freshly baked pastries. Today's special selections include miniature peach cheesecake tarts (it wasn't muffins they were making using the muffin papers), chocolate brownie *cake*, and peanut butter and jelly finger bars.

"That's it," Alec says to me, untying his apron and hanging it on a hook by the door. "Now, if it was any day but today, I'd be off to do my meter reading."

I'm bone tired. How can he do this all the time? Seeming to read my mind Alec says, "You get used to it. Don't forget, I've been doing this for many years now."

"Now what?" I ask him as we walk out into the parking lot. It's still dark, but there's a slight glimmer towards the east.

"Why don't you go home and sleep for a bit? We could get together for lunch," he says to me.

"Want to come home with me?" I ask it innocently enough. Honest I do.

He looks at me, perhaps trying to determine my ulterior motives. "Yes." He shakes his head. "No." He sighs. "I'd better not, Elaine. Now, thanks to you and your all too willing account of your past sexual escapades I can't even watch a football game without thinking wicked thoughts about you."

That makes me grin. Widely.

"Go on, keep smiling, woman. See where it gets you."

"I've decided I'm going to be like Maxwell Smart. You know that secret agent character from the television show *Get Smart?*" He nods, a small grin playing on his lips. I'm entertaining him again, I can see. Ah well, at least someone appreciates me, right? "I'm no longer part of the evil agency known as KAOS. I'm now part of CONTROL. Isn't there a Bible verse about that?"

"About Maxwell Smart?"

I put my hands on my hips. "About chaos."

He thinks and then winks at me. "Jeremiah. Chapter twenty-nine, verse eleven says, '*For I know the plans that I have for you, plans for welfare and not for calamity to give you a future and a hope.*⁴⁰' Calamity's a lot like chaos, isn't it?"

I look down at Callie's bangle on my wrist. Something I've been trying to faithfully wear every day. "Duh. I've got that one on my wrist." I hold it up for Alec to see.

"Who gave you this?" he says carefully examining the engraved words etched on the outside.

"Jealous?" I give him an evil smirk.

"Should I be?" he fires back, but he's grinning.

"Nah. Callie gave it to me. She's already married so you can relax."

"Phew. I was worried."

Reaching into my jeans pocket I take out my car keys. "Besides, I'm already taken. Didn't you know that?"

"You are, are you," he murmurs. "Just how taken are you?"

"Not the physical kind of taken," I say, amazingly straight faced. "No, we're trying very hard to stay upright and fully clothed, although with each passing day it seems to get harder and harder. No, the kind of taken I'm talking about involves deep inside heart stuff."

He steps in and crowds me against the car, putting his warm hands low on my hips. "Oh yeah? That sounds pretty serious."

Shaking my head I assure him, "It can't be serious. We've only known each other about a month. Well," I feel compelled to correct myself, "we've known *of* each other for over a year and a half but during that time I thought he was pretty nasty and damned annoying. And he thought I was sharp tongued. Can you imagine? Had some foreign word he used to describe me ..."

"Criticóna," he says helpfully.

"Yeah, that's it."

"How long does it usually take for you to get serious with someone?"

"I suppose you're not referring to putting out as I usually do that by the second date."

"Well, if knowing someone a month isn't long enough to be considered serious, then I'm forced to believe that putting out on the second date isn't particularly serious either."

I sigh. "You're right. It's happened quite a lot."

Alec smothers a laugh. "What do you consider serious? What are the qualifications?"

"I don't think I've ever had specific qualifications. I'd meet someone; if I liked him enough I'd invariably put out by the second date. If we dated for more than about six weeks, we usually got married. So, I'd guess the serious part hits somewhere between four and six weeks."

He's looking at me, I suspect trying to gauge if I'm serious or not. I look back, wide open and honest. *Sorry honey. It's the truth. When has there ever been a time when I've not been shockingly, brutally honest about my warped history and me?*

"So," he says slowly and carefully, "*if I play my cards right*, and make it to the six week mark – even without you putting out – does that qualify as a serious relationship for you?"

"Honey," I say to him in my best Mae West imitation drawl, "if we make it to six weeks and are still on the celibacy page we're either bound for the world record books, the insane asylum, or the nearest justice of the peace."

Oh refuge of my hardened heart, oh fast pursuing lover come,
As angels dance around Your throne, my life by captured fare You own.[41]

Chapter 18: Mother Bear Instincts

"Mom? This is Erin. When you get a chance will you call me as soon as possible?" I stand in my kitchen listening to the answering machine, frowning when I realize that Erin called me at exactly four thirty-eight a.m. There is no reason on the face of the earth to call someone at that hour with good things to say. Crap. Glancing at the clock, I see that it's now six fifty-four a.m. Crap. I pick up the phone and dial.

Dan answers, his voice rough with sleep. "Hello?"

"Dan, it's mom. I've got a message on my answering machine from Erin. Is everything okay?"

"Uh, well ... no, Mom." I hear Erin's voice in the background. "Here she is."

"Mom?"

"Erin! What's wrong? Is Liam okay?"

"Yeah, Mom, Liam's okay. It's ... Olivia. She was here, tonight, terribly upset about something. She wouldn't say what it was about ... She'd been ... drinking! We had a fight ... Dan took her keys ... All she kept saying was that 'Now it all made sense,' and 'Now she finally got it'. She'd apparently been to your house to 'face you down once and for all' but you apparently weren't there ... ? Maybe you just didn't hear the bell?

Anyway, Dan and I tried to get her to go to sleep in the guest room but sometime after four a.m. she just left! *Walked.* I ..., well I called you to give you a head's up and let you know ..."

As Erin talks I'm walking around my house looking out the windows front and back. Everything looks quiet and peaceful. Checking caller I.D. I see that I have no less than *eleven* hang up calls from Olivia's cell phone, all within a sustained time between three and three-thirty a.m. I blow out a big breath. "Are you okay?"

"Yeah, just tired. Dan says that Olivia's a big girl and that I need to just keep reminding myself of that."

"It's hard to do that when you're worried about someone you love."

Erin's quiet for a moment. "Yeah. It is."

"Try to go back to sleep. I promise to call if I hear anything and you promise to do the same, okay?"

"Okay." I hear tears in my daughter's voice when she says, "I love you, Mom."

"I know you do. I love you, too, Erin. Give Liam and Dan a kiss for me."

Hanging up the phone, I stand in the kitchen and lean my head against the cool wood of the cabinet. She has to have found out. *Lot's of stuff can screw a person up. This has got to be near the top of the list of bad stuff to have to deal with. How messed up do you get when you know that you're the product of a rape?* I hear Dean say to me. *Hello, my name is Olivia. I am a child of rape.* Who would have told her? Not Paul. Maybe, weeks ago I would have believed him capable of something like that, but after our last exchange I find that hard to swallow. Not Dean. Besides if he had his truck would be parked on my front lawn again.

And then I know. The only person who would have had no compunction about tearing open such a gaping cavern in someone's heart. Especially since the last time I spoke with her, I'd left with the distinct upper hand. Mother never liked it when I bested her in verbal battles. She didn't like it when I was a teenager, and she apparently doesn't like it now.

Alec arrives as planned at twelve-thirty p.m. holding a huge bouquet of red Shasta daisies. His grin slides off his face like jello off a plate when he gets his first look at me. "Elaine?" he asks, struggling with the storm door and the flowers trying to get inside my house. "What's wrong?"

I look at him in complete, abject misery and he reaches up to cup my face. "Sweetie?"

On autopilot I take the flowers from him and walk into the kitchen, going through the motions of getting out a vase, cutting the stems, and arranging them for display. Alec stands quietly beside me, silent and waiting for me to get myself together enough to form words. I appreciate that he doesn't hurry or push me, and his calm, solid presence is really nice. Rubbing my back he says, "You didn't go to sleep."

Since I'm still in my flour-covered jeans and tee shirt he's not that impressive a mind reader. Still, I shake my head 'no.' "What have you been doing?"

"Sewing." I watch him glance down and inspect me, and I'm sure he takes in the inevitable bits of thread here and there. Indeed, reaching up he pulls a strand of gold thread from my hair.

"Can I see?"

He's never seen my workroom, and although I've told him about my sewing therapy we've not talked much about it. I turn and wander upstairs to the smaller of three bedrooms. Alec follows and I look at the room trying to see it from his perspective. I've got my sewing machine and a large worktable. Besides those two pieces of furniture, the room is completely taken up with plastic containers carefully stacked against the walls with labels like "solid-blues," "plaids-red/orange," "random-violets." He maybe doesn't realize that they are anally arranged in colors of the rainbow spectrum starting from true primary blues nearest my machine and ending with rich violets by the door where we stand. I could find a color and a pattern with my eyes closed in the dark. Above the plastic containers are rows and rows of thread and bobbins in matching, similarly organized colors.

"Whoa …" he says more to himself than to me as he wanders in and inspects my tool board with its vicious collection of scissors, shears, and rollable cutting blades. Turning to me he says, "This is serious stuff."

I nod. "My escape. Some people do crack. I sew."

He wants to ask me what's going on, I can see the concern in his eyes, but again he stops himself. "Tell me what you're working on."

"It's almost always quilts," I tell him dismissively like they are easily and readily available at the local Walmart.

He fingers the piece I've still got anchored in the machine and then, as if he can't believe what he's looking at, bends down to look more closely. Glancing up at me he says, "You've *sewn* this?" I nod. "Elaine, this is … exquisite."

"When the girls were little, I used to sew their clothes. I couldn't always afford to buy them new, but I could afford to buy cheap pieces of material. Olivia was … difficult with clothes, particular about fabric and color and style. It became almost easier to listen to her list of what she wanted and to go and sew it than to drive all over creation trying to find the exact item she required. I eventually got good enough that she didn't worry about her clothes looking 'homemade.' In the end I killed two birds with one stone: Olivia was marginally satisfied and I discovered a satisfactory escape from reality." I shrug. "It became rather addictive.

"By the time Richard came on the scene I was into sewing together leftover pieces of material to make kind of like my own patterned creations. It was money saving and cost conscious to sew together scraps, have a new length of material, assemble a new … thing."

Alec gestures towards the piece he's now sitting at the sewing machine examining. "This is hardly a new … thing you've cobbled together from scraps you've found around the house."

Duh. I know that. "I really got into the blend of colors, the flow of patterns, the textures of the fabric. It became a game starting out with a pile of scraps and then trying to make them come together into something that was more beautiful once it was all together." Here's something I've never told a soul: "Sometimes I dream ideas and patterns and, until I've got

191

the fabric and built the piece I have trouble sleeping." I smile. "I can sew all night sometimes."

"There's more to this piece though, all the stitching ..."

"Yeah. The assembled pieces of fabric, no matter how pretty and harmonious started to be not enough. I began doing decorative appliqué stitches on the top in patterns that seemed to fit with the mood of the ... item. If there were visible pictures or obvious themes – like a children's quilt for instance, then I would do appliqué stitches on top in maybe the ABC's or a rocking horse or a ball bouncing across ... It has to be subtle because I don't want the appliqué to take away from the flow of the fabrics ..."

His eyes are starting to glaze over so I shut up. He's studying the piece in the machine. "These appliqués seem to be ..." he looks up at me, "musical notes."

"Yeah. It's a few bars from the song you were singing at that church concert on our first ... date. I asked James for the name of the song and he copied the sheet music for me."

"Sacred Delight" he and I both say in unison.

"There was a verse in the song that really hit me: *Is it true I'm Your heartbeat, and You chose to die than to live without me?*" I get a rush, like I always do when I think about what those words are saying. I point to the piece. "The music notes you see are the few bars for those words."

Alec looks around the room, searching for something he can't see. "What do you do with all the quilts you make, Elaine?"

I shrug. "I give them away."

"You give them away?"

Nodding, I try to explain. "At one point I thought maybe it could be a business. I even had some people offer to pay me if I'd make them something specific. But I discovered then it wasn't any fun. It was such a chore to come in here and work towards a specification and a deadline." I shake my head. "Sewing lost all its appeal."

I go over and sit on the cutting table. "So, I operate on inspiration alone. If I think of something then I do it. If a person motivates me then I usually give it to them. Anonymously, of course."

"You give this stuff away anonymously?!"

"Have I impressed you with my need for adulation? Over the course of time you've known me have I ever actively sought out recognition?"

He doesn't respond with the obvious answer. Instead he asks, "Do you only sew when you're upset?"

Interesting question. I think for a moment. Then slowly, hesitantly, I nod. "Some of my best work is when my world is going up in flames around me." I give him a pointed look. "These past few weeks I've done *less sewing* than ever."

"So the fact that you're up here bleary eyed with lack of sleep, sewing this magnificent piece must mean something's really gone wrong." Ahh, what a wise man he is. He's brought us right back to the primary point of all this.

"I think Olivia talked with my mother. I think my mother told her *everything.*" I take a deep breath and feel my 'bleary eyes' sting with tears. "Olivia's last known whereabouts was walking – too drunk to drive so Dan had taken her keys – somewhere at about four-thirty this morning."

Alec gets up and walks over to me, pulling me into his tight embrace. "What should we pray for?" he asks with solid matter of factness.

Another good question. I think, but it's not too hard to voice what I so desperately want. "Peace for her, courage for me ..." A shaky sigh escapes. "Tolerance when she hears what I have to tell her and wisdom for me that I can communicate all I need to communicate *and* still get across to her that I love her above and beyond everything else."

"Okay," Alec says as he kisses the top of my head, "that's what we'll both pray for."

I fall into a netherworld of waiting. Horrible anticipation morphs into gut wrenching concern when the silence from Olivia continues through all of Sunday past our never-before-missed dinner at Erin and Dan's. She doesn't answer her cell phone. She doesn't answer her home phone. We decide as a family to have Dan travel over to check out her condo and, since he's got a key, he actually lets himself in and looks all around. Nothing. Nada. Not a blessed thing. We can't even tell the last time she was there. Dan listens to her seventeen phone messages, most of which are from Erin and myself, and discovers nothing.

Monday, I call in sick to work and wait until nine a.m. to call Olivia at work. All I get is her voicemail. Dialing again, I get her assistant and am told, "Ms. Kelly has taken a leave of absence due to a family emergency." Hanging up I decide on the plus side I now know *at least she's not dead.*

Erin, it turns out has done similar things. She's home when I call to leave an updated message on her answering machine and she has been told similar things from Olivia's assistant, Margaret. Except Erin's been told one additional thing: *As per Ms. Kelly's orders, under no circumstances is any specific information regarding Ms. Kelly's leave to be given out to family members.*

Erin and I are silent on our respective ends of the phone line. Finally, Erin says, "Are you okay, Mom?"

I roll my eyes and thunk my head against the kitchen cabinet. "I've always loved you both equally, Erin. Despite evidence to the contrary."

"What evidence to the contrary?" she says surprised.

I sigh. "Remember that last disastrous dinner when Olivia spelled out all of my horrible attributes as a mother: blatant favoritism, selective memories, one-sided loyalties ... ?" I can't go on.

"Mom, Olivia is ... dissatisfied with a lot of things. You sit down and talk to her and she'll give you a list of things she's upset with at work, a list of things she hated about her last five boyfriends, a list of things she dislikes about her condominium, heck, give her a chance and she'll give you a list of things she dislikes about me, too! I think, although I try not to remember because it doesn't do either of us any good, in the past she's said things like I'm a pleaser, I have no backbone, I'm too much under Dan's control, and I should be more assertive at work and go back to get an advanced degree so I can become a principal." Erin sighs. "She's *always* been like that, Mom. I've met some of her friends. She tends to gravitate towards people who are … like her or *lesser*. She doesn't usually associate with people who are happy or content." After a moment's hesitation, Erin says quietly, "I like to say I love her because she's my sister, but I don't like her very much. If we weren't blood related, I don't think we'd ever have become friends. I like being around her when Liam's on the scene because that seems to be the only time she's really … relaxed and happy."

"Do you believe I loved you both equally?"

"Sure I do! And Olivia believes that, too." I snort into the phone. "Mom, she's said to me on more than one occasion, 'I don't know why you and Mom put up with all my bull. You guys love me too much.' Not only *is* she hard, *she knows* she's hard, too."

"Has she told you?"

Erin's silent for a beat, trying to catch up with my train of thought. "About Dad not being her biological father?" Erin sighs. "Yeah, Mom, she told me."

"I think she went to see … my mother. I think my mother … told her some … terrible truth. I think … it was told in a way that was probably cruel and unfeeling." I feel a big wave of a sob roll up from my soul at the hurt and humiliation that Olivia must be going through. *I know … I know …* Sliding down, I'm sitting on the kitchen floor I begin to rock back and forth, moaning and crying.

"Mom? Mom! *MOM.*" Erin's talking to me in my ear.

I sniff. "I'm here."

"*It's okay*, Mom. All this will be okay. If Olivia has heard some … hard things, then she just needs time to process that, I guess. You've lived with this … knowledge … all your life. She hasn't. She's strong and tough and wise and capable. *You made us both that way.* You taught us to stand up for ourselves, question things that didn't make sense, and the only thing bad about bad mistakes is repeating them. If this … terrible truth … is what's set all this in motion, then as long as it's *the truth* then, well, we'll just deal with it one way or another, okay? We love Olivia. *She knows that.*"

After we hang up, I go upstairs … and sew.

My phone rings at about one-thirty. "I'm outside your front door," Alec says. "Let me in."

"Not by the hair of my chinny-chin-chin. I'm still in my pajamas, have been crying on and off all day, desperately need a shower, and on a scale from one to ten I'm a nine on the probability of doing dangerous harm to others."

"I brought pastries."

"You always do."

"I've got videos."

"Are they horror?"

"No. They're psychological dramas. I figure seeing someone worse off than yourself would be a plus."

My silence makes him sigh. "Are you sewing?"

"No, today's a crack day. Sewing just doesn't cut it."

"I have a confession to make."

"What?"

"I memorized the code to your garage. I can get in whether you let me in or not. As we speak, the garage door is already going up. Listen. Can you hear it? Either get yourself showered and changed or not, but I'm coming in."

In the distance I hear the rumbling of the garage door. "That's not fair."

"All's fair in love and war and I'm in love with you so I've got the edge. Here I come ..." I drop the phone, run to my bedroom and lock the door. But I start stripping to climb into the shower.

Forty-five minutes later I'm squeaky clean. Wandering down into the kitchen I smell coffee brewing and hear the television in the living room. Leaning against the door jam I look at Alec lying on my couch. "I'm glad you're here."

"I know. Women tell me that kind of stuff all the time."

"How was your day?"

"Longer than usual. I was worried about you and wanted to get here as soon as I could."

"How'd you know I took the day off?"

"I didn't until I pulled in the driveway and saw your car in the garage. I was just going to lie on your hammock until you showed."

"Oh."

He sits up. "Can I ask a bizarre favor?"

That peaks my curiosity. "Sure."

"Can I take a shower? I really reek and I'd feel a lot better about myself if I could hose down." He points to a small gym bag in the corner. "I came prepared."

"You're not afraid I'm going to accost you?"

He gets up and pads over to me, tenderly taking my face in his hands. "Sweetie, you look like you barely have enough energy to stand up. I think it might be the only time I'm well and truly safe."

"The almond soap is in the blue bottle," I say and give him a light kiss on the mouth.

Alec calls me, once he's out of the shower, and asks me to come up and show him what I've sewed today. I've completed the 'music' square as he calls it – an intricate orange, red, and yellow eighteen by eighteen inch square appliquéd with gold threaded notes – and added it to a pile on the right of my machine. Once he realizes there are more finished squares he practically vibrates with curiosity. "Can I see the other ones?"

I shrug and nod. There are twenty-two completed squares and three more I've got planned in my head. Alec takes the time to lay them out on the floor and they make a colorful collection of cloth stepping-stones right out of the room and down the carpeted hallway. Because of my anal way of working, the squares have been stored in the correct order. Alec, laying them out carefully, has displayed them in descending order. He studies them for a long, long time. Sometimes he looks from standing level, sometimes he kneels down to see more closely, and more than once he leans in and traces the patterns of appliqué I've worked into each piece. At the last one, all greens and leafy material patterns he looks up at me and smiles with intense satisfaction. "It's the story of your life," he says with complete certainty. "Here's your birth, the force of life all green and new

197

and alive." He steps down a few squares. "This is Olivia." It is a vividly beautiful square of red and mahogany with splashes of rich velvet and expensive silk. "Here is Erin." Calming blues and soft turquoises intertwined with baby-soft brushed cottons. Both of the girls squares are appliquéd with hearts and suns and moons and stars sewn in gold. He skips over a few and then stares down. "That," he points to a sharply geometric patterned square of clashing colors and patterns, "is your marriage to Paul, and that one," he points to a dark, somber square which is predominately dark gray but with splashes of every color in the rainbow peeking through, "is your marriage to Richard." He kneels at the square I was working on the first time he saw my work and then frowns. "This isn't me," he says shaking his head with certainty, "even though I was the one singing the song ..." He looks to me for explanation.

He's right, it's not him. "It's the start of my interest in spiritual faith. It's rooted in song. Pink is the color of hope for me – baby girls and all that – so that's the reason for the predominate color."

"So I'm not on here," he says and I smile because he seems disappointed.

"Not until we're serious," I tease.

"We're serious, Elaine," he growls. "Don't give me this 'between four and six week' crap."

"Callie's not there either," I point out.

He looks again. "Hey, yeah, she's not."

"She's not getting a square, either."

"Why not?"

"The joining strips," I explain as I bend down to begin picking up the squares, "will be appliquéd with elaborate green vines that are strong and dependable. Sturdy enough to swing from, hang onto, or even wrap yourself up in. That will be Callie. She's woven throughout most of my life. She's more than a square."

"You know," Alec says, deep in thought about what I've described to him, "throughout the Bible is something called 'The Scarlet Thread of Redemption.' It's the belief that from start to finish, through the good and the bad, there is the scarlet path of Christ's coming foretold, anticipated, longed for, and promised. I always thought that my life had a scarlet thread through it. Little points along the way where I had a glimpse of what I could have and could be, and not until very late in life did I choose to really look at it and accept it." He looks at me. "Do you think that each of your squares has a glimpse of something like that? Even the dark ones?"

I don't honestly know. But it's something to think about. And I say so.

"*Am* I going to get a square?" he asks, following me into my sewing room where I carefully store away the squares.

Sometimes the truth hurts. "I don't know! I've got it all planned in my head already. There are three more to do and this was planned way before you came on the scene. You know, it's the first time I've ever done a quilt with the intention of keeping it myself." When I peek at him he's frowning and looks *very* upset. "It was not my intention to let love or romance into my life ever again, Alec," I point out defensively. When he keeps glaring at me, I finally give him a little smile. "I have to admit that I've been rethinking some things. You know: joining the club, falling in love, being so different and all ..."

Late in the afternoon, as we lounge on the couch and Alec fights much needed sleep to instead be my cheerful and supportive knight in shining armor, I murmur, "Where could she be?"

"Where would you go? What do you do when you're upset? You can disagree with me if you want, but Olivia seems to be similar to you in a lot of ways."

I scroll out my mind's collection of disastrous life occurrences. "I need to be alone when my world falls apart." I think about huddling in my bedroom for two full days, with my dresser pulled in front of my door to keep my mother out after the rape. I remember pinpoints of pain and sorrow and disappointment and my immediate reaction is always to withdraw, hide, seclude myself as much as possible. Which, admittedly, was pretty difficult with two young children after I left Dean and two observant teenagers after I left Paul, but that didn't keep me from wanting to and trying to. I had a lot of alone time after Richard killed himself. I filled it with work, therapy, and sewing, with Callie's constant intrusion only because she wouldn't let me close her out.

"Why?" Alec prompts when I make no effort to elaborate.

It takes a while for me to be able to answer. "Because I need to think it all out. I need to pick through all the rubble. I need to figure out the truth and the lies and what I own and what I don't."

"Are you better for it afterwards?"

"Usually, yeah," I manage reluctantly. "It took me a decade to get over Richard though ..."

I feel him shake his head. "I don't think that's true."

"How do you know?" I say a tad too defensively.

"When I came on the scene, you were a strong, confident, outspoken women. Sure you had a pile of baggage, but I've said more than once, *everyone does,* that's lived a life. Did that woman I encountered just happen the very week you met me at the concert?"

"No."

"How about that first time you let me into your home to read your meter, all ... cold ... and feisty? Was it around that time?"

"No ..."

"What would people at work say: your students, parents, and colleagues? Would they say that this strong, confident, outspoken woman just materialized within the last few, say three or four years?"

I'm forced to shake my head 'no.'

"Correct me if I'm wrong, but from what I've learned about you, you've *always* been pretty strong, confident, and outspoken ... even when you were a belligerent adolescent finally beginning to call your mother out for all the lousy ... crap ... she'd put you through. Taking time to evaluate things when stuff goes wrong is *wise.* That's how we grow and mature." I feel him shrug, because I'm leaning against his shoulder. "You might prefer to be alone when bad stuff hits the fan, but I don't see any evidence of you *ever once* being knocked down so badly you never got back up again. That takes a *strong woman,* Elaine." He leans in, shifting me so he can put his arm around me, and whisper, in my ear, "Do you know what is the most impressive of all the strong things you've done, Elaine?" He jostles me a little. "Do you?" I shake my head, because I honestly don't have a clue what he's going to say. "You have loved your daughter Olivia, *a child of rape*, with as much passion and ferocity as a mother bear does. You've hung on tenaciously, looked repeatedly at yourself when things went bad, and *never once* thought all the millions of negative, horrible, damaging things that a lesser woman in your situation would have done regarding Olivia."

He kisses me and lets me process all of this for a few moments. "She's somewhere, she's hurting, she's crying, she's thinking a million different things, and she's *remembering*. She's remembering her life with you. She will not remember hate, disgust, regret, or sorrow in regard to you. She'll remember love, persistence, and patience. She is your daughter, Elaine. You raised her to be like yourself: confident, outspoken, honest, and damn smart. She's wise to take this time alone. We'll keep praying for her, *together*, and give her all the time she needs."

"That's two more things I'm doing now that I'm different."

"Which are …?"

"Worrying *together* with someone and praying."

"See what a good influence I am on you?"

Did the angels know You knew my name before I existed?
Did you tell them out of all You made why You gave me Your image? [42]

Chapter 19: Excellent, Thought-Provoking Questions

One week passes. Two weeks pass. Three weeks pass. *Six weeks pass.* My life has a gaping hole where Olivia should be. I allow myself one call a week to Olivia's work and am always told the same thing: *Ms. Kelly has taken a leave of absence due to a family emergency.*

Alec goes with me to Erin and Dan's for Sunday dinners to provide moral support and, in his words, 'keep on Liam's good side in regard to the Batman mask.' He's waiting at my house each day (inside since he knows the code, already showered with fresh coffee brewed). We eat an early dinner together most nights and then he goes home to go to sleep and I go upstairs and sew because sleep isn't so easy for me these days. I'm close to finishing my quilt, but not quite. The two of us function like an old married couple right down to having no sex.

Work provides the necessary escape. I conduct Back-To-School Night, review double-digit multiplication and division, place value, and graphing, teach map skills and introduce all of the north- and southeastern United States, and carry out the novel study for *In The Year of The Boar and Jackie Robinson* as well as *Sounder* practically with my eyes closed and my hands tied behind my back. I see Paulie twice and he smiles, waves, and leaves me – *blessedly* – alone.

I go to Sunday evening church with Alec and we sit together, in the back in what has become our spot. Alec and I venture out to a 'Jesus Book and Gift Store' and have great fun looking at and finally selecting a Bible for me to call my own. I finally choose an excellent two tone maroon and brown leather bound edition (it looked a little like a quilt ...) that is nowhere as big as Alec's. On my own, each night and each morning I read random sections and begin to underline things I like just like Alec does. And finally, at Alec's encouragement – and Tonya's (of 'God Rocks' tee shirt fame) - I even begin attending a Thursday evening Bible study that's held in the Agape Shop's cozy coffee shop.

And I pray. I can't seem to stop myself. Alone I seem to have a running dialogue with God, sometimes aloud, and sometimes silently. I'm sure that people passing me while I'm driving must assume I'm talking on a cell phone when they see me conversing with such great animation. I come to a lot of conclusions about things that the ladies at Bible study seem willing and interested to hear about.

Like I wonder at first, why do I need to bother to pray if God already knows everything? Isn't that like explaining to the master baker what ingredients are in the pie and why? So I think and think about this and talk aloud to God about it, and I decide that it's not *God* who needs the reminding but *me* who needs to get to the point where I care about these things in the same way He does. Once God and I are on the same page about stuff, then I can do the acting, since now He's got someone listening to His directing.

My attitude's different now. And I like it. I find I look at people and things differently when I pray. I give God the big green light and tell Him to have at it and remodel me any way He sees fit. I start to think that sometimes when I notice something I've never noticed before or respond to something in a way I've never responded before that it's *more* than me being different, maybe it's *God* actually controlling my head and my heart, and my very big mouth. That gives me chills.

Marlie, true to form, has done a thorough personal check on Agape Shop, and much to the intense relief of both of us has given it the Big O.K. Two weeks into Olivia's disappearance, she gives me a plaque that is now sitting on my classroom desk. It says: *What is faith, after all, but believing in advance what will only make sense in reverse?* [43] Every single, blessed day I read those words and pray for my girl.

Halloween rolls around and, for a brief few moments we take a break at school and allow the kids to be ... well, kids. The girls have fun with their extensive multicolored hair sprays and false eyelashes while the guys try to look cool and suave in their vampire and billy-bob false teeth. When my assistant principal appears in my doorway I think it's just to steal a cupcake, but she grins and says, "I'll cover for you. You've got to go to the office."

As she's unaware of the Olivia fiasco, all I can think as I rush through the endless corridors is that something's finally turned up! At last! Answers! I catch myself gasping out my standard prayer, "Please guide my words! Make me wise! Let Olivia know I love her!" Bursting into the school office, I run to the counter. "Marie!" I say breathlessly to the school secretary, "I'm here! What did you need me for?"

Expecting her to gesture towards one of the numerous blinking phones she gives me a highly curious expression, points behind me and says, "You have a visitor."

I turn around to see Alec sitting on one of the plastic office chairs looking significantly embarrassed and highly uncomfortable. For, you see, he's dressed in a *gorilla costume*.

I can't help it. My mouth just drops open and stays there.

"I didn't realize security was so tight," he says standing up and walking towards me. He's got the enormous gorilla head tucked under one fake fur encrusted arm. "I thought I could walk in, find your classroom, hand you these," he holds up a bouquet of a dozen red roses, "and then walk out. Except," he glances over my shoulder at Marie who I can hear snickering hysterically, "the Gestapo here wouldn't let me pass. Not even when I begged and said it was just a surprise to cheer you up."

"All visitors must report to the office first," I intone in a robotic, brainwashed sounding voice. "No masks of any kind, no weapons of any kind, no costumes of a sexual nature, no costumes of an offensive nature ... *such as a Gestapo uniform*," I hiss at him, "have ever been allowed in a public school in probably the past ten years. Since 9/11 it's been even more strict."

He looks sheepish. "It's been a long time since I've been in school, Elaine."

I reach out to take his big, furry hand. "Come on down with me. You've come this far. At least you can have a cupcake."

I sign him in and get him a visitor's badge, which we stick to his black plastic bare chest (right above the plastic nipple). We walk silently through the hallways past many classrooms filled with screaming, sugar-rushed kids. Although there's a "healthy food" rule in effect too, it's kind of Scrooge-ish to ban all sugar on Halloween.

My assistant principal, Victoria, is sitting on the front table in her power suit and three inch heels eating a strip of red licorice. She grins and walks towards us when we come into the classroom. Extending her hand to Alec she says, "No hard feelings I hope, Mr. Kong," making me start to laugh ... finally.

"Great," Alec mumbles, "a whole school of women with warped senses of humor," but he shakes her hand and manages a "thanks," too.

"Hey, Ms. Cummings! Is that your husband?"

"No, Nicholas, he's my bodyguard. You know how famous I am. Class, this is Mr. ... Kong."

"Hey Mr. Kong!" come a chorus of voices. I'm sure half of them don't even clue into the joke. Alec laughs and shakes his head.

"Licorice? Juicy Juice? Brownie? Cupcake?"

"I'll take a brownie. Can you unzip the back of this thing? It's like a hundred and fifty degrees in here."

While he strips off the gloves, I hunt for the invisible zipper and finally release him from his furry prison. He's not kidding, it is hot in there. Comfortable in seemingly any situation, within minutes Alec's sitting on a desk surrounded by a bunch of male and female admirers while he plucks out a catchy tune on one of the kid's violins. "I've always got instruments in the back of the room, Mr. Kong," I call out to Alec, "because *someone* always forgets to bring his or her instrument home after orchestra day."

"*Some of us* actually *never* take them home at all," Andrew says speaking from actual experience. I shake my head and chuckle. Hey, I'm not his mother.

"He's cute, Ms. Cummings," Violet says. Her right eye is twitching because her false eyelash is put on incorrectly.

"With or without the gorilla suit?" I ask, eating a Rice Krispie treat.

Violet rolls her eyes. They're all used to my sense of humor, just like my own kids. Sigh. Which makes me think of Olivia and down I go …

Forty-five minutes later, the only thing remaining of my most recent classroom Halloween party is an overflowing garbage can, an empty gorilla suit, a dozen roses, and a very sexy fifty-three-year-old man who's middle name is Xavier.

"How come Xavier?"

Alec doesn't even blink at my train of thought which is just a little bit scary when you take the time to think about it. "Mom's Spanish. Family's originally from Pamplona, Spain. Mom's also Catholic. Saint Francis Xavier was a Roman Catholic missionary credited with winning more souls to God than any other saint save Saint Paul. I guess she wanted to make sure that I had some big shoes to fill."

"Hmmm," I say. I walk over to him leaning against my bulletin board entitled 'How To Survive A Year With Ms. Cummings' which contains a list of things you should do like Do write your name on all papers, DO carefully complete your homework, and DO be kind to everyone as well as a list of things you shouldn't do like DON'T text (I take your phone and call Cambodia), DON'T laugh at my jokes (it only makes me tell more), and DON'T ask me 'what should I do now?' (to which I'll insist you tap dance on the front table). I am proud to say that truly warped children that I have corrupted to my will, eventually, tap dance on the table to the cheers of all, me included.

I touch Alec's face, his beard stubbly face, his too long salt and pepper hair, his laugh lines on either side of his brown eyes, his wonderful, kissable lips ... He sighs and lets his eyes drift shut at my touch. It's been over six weeks since Olivia went away and I am tired of living in this limbo. I miss her just as much, am worried about her just as much, want her to come home just as much, but I need to start living again. At least, that's the feeling I got this morning during my pray-a-thon on the way to work. I loop my arms around Alec's neck and look into his big brown eyes. "Thanks for coming here to school in a gorilla suit."

He stares at me for a moment and then he grins wryly, "Yeah, well. Don't think I'll ever do something like *that* again."

With a kiss, I say, "No one ever came to school to see me in a gorilla suit, you know."

"Well, I *hoped* that was the case, but given your colorful past I wasn't exactly positive ..."

I pretend I'm thinking, trying to remember. "There was that Chippendale dancer I dated after Paul and I divorced ... but no," I shake my head positively, "he never came to school in costume."

Alec's looking at me, like he does, when I've told him something he has to work to get his brain around.

I roll my eyes and with a heavy valley-girl accent I say, "He was like, completely, like, so totally vapid. He like, never got to the second date so like, consequently I never -"

But he's kissing me so I never get to finish saying, "put out with him."

He ends up hugging me for a lot longer than we kiss and it's so nice. For someone like me who has spent the last ten years solo, I sure do enjoy this man's company. "So," Alec says to me, still with his arm tightly around my waist and his hand tangled in my hair, "I thought the gorilla suit, besides being an excellent Halloween costume, would be a guaranteed unique way to ..." But he stops and looks at me instead. I look at him, staring at me and then I look left and right and finally behind me. Nope, it's just the two of us here in the empty classroom.

"Unique way to … what?" I finally say.

He sighs and stares at me some more. I get a feeling of sick dread in my stomach. A unique way to … tell me he's dying? Tell me he's moving to Siberia? Tell me he's decided we should stop seeing each other? Granted it *is* a unique way to tell someone those things but I'd prefer just the straight dope. Sighing again, he reaches into his pocket and pulls out … *a ring.*

Holding it up to me he says, "I thought it would be a unique way to propose. I didn't want to repeat anything the other three did, so I figured me, and a diamond, and a gorilla suit … now *there's a combination that doesn't usually come across too often.*" There in front of the bulletin board line that says, "DO make every effort to ask excellent, thought provoking questions" Alec kneels and says to me, "Elaine, will you marry me?"

Now if seeing Alec in a gorilla suit was a shock, seeing Alec on one knee proposing is completely overwhelming. A myriad of responses roll through my head, most of them completely obnoxious and inappropriate, which is what I always gravitate towards in situations that are completely out of control. Getting up, Alec takes my hand. "I know its kind of bad timing with you worrying about Olivia. We can wait until that gets settled or whatever you want. I just, well, I've waited fifty-three years to finally find you, Elaine! I don't want to waste any more time, you know?" He sighs at my continued silence. "And despite the gorilla suit and the roses and the ring, you can take all the time you need to decide what you want to do."

"The idea of spending the rest of my life with you sounds pretty wonderful, actually."

"It does?" he says with a big, hopeful grin.

"It's the marriage part that bothers me. I've struck out three times, Alec. *Three times.* Doesn't that scare you? It sure scares me!"

He's shaking his head even before I finish. "No. NO. It doesn't scare me. We're both on new, level, firm, *right* ground, Elaine. I'm not looking at the past. I'm looking at the future. *I want a future with you.* It sounds like," he takes the time to make me look at him because I've turned away, "you'd like a future with me, too." He waits until I sigh and nod. "We're better together than apart, right?" I nod again. We've already had *this* discussion. "We've *both* got love and Life now, don't we?" He's blurry now, because I'm tearing up but I nod again. He kisses me. "You said 'world record books, the insane asylum, or the nearest justice of the peace'. I pick justice of the peace. How about you?"

"I've already done the insane asylum," I say as the tears trickle down my face, "and I've never, ever been interested in setting world records."

"Is that a yes? *I need to hear you say yes, Elaine.*"

"Yes, Alec Xavier Monroe," I sigh and lean into his warm embrace, "I can't believe you really want to do this, but I'll marry you. I hope you realize what you're getting yourself into."

"I think we both know. That's why we're smiling."

Walking out to the faculty parking lot with Alec, I suddenly think of something I've never thought of before. "I've got to drive by Olivia's condo," I say suddenly so wired I can't stand still. Alec insists on following and we buzz through the back streets until we're parked in front of Olivia's home. Without saying a word or waiting for Alec to get out of his truck, I walk up to the front door and peer into the side windows.

"What are you looking for?" Alec asks me.

I'm all agitated. "Mail. Alec, there's no mail! Either she's picking it up or she's having it forwarded. I could ... write her something ... Maybe, she'd get it." I swallow. "Maybe she'd read something if I sent it to her."

Alec turns me around. "What would you tell her, Sweetie?"

Doesn't he get it? "I've got to explain all the ... truth. I've got to give her all the facts ... It's one thing to keep the horrible truth from her because it's too awful to hear. But part of my worry is I don't know exactly *what* truth my mother told her. Mine or hers. What if she's got some of the horrible truth but it's not all accurate? Doesn't she deserve to hear all this awful stuff from *me?*"

In talking with the landlord he confirms that the mail is being forwarded but "is not at liberty to give out the new address." I suspect that mental or physical threats to his person would not bring about successful results so I behave as civilly as possible and leave.

Driving home, with Alec right behind me, I pray. "What do I do, God? Should I write to her? What should I tell her? How could I possibly explain on paper what I've never been able to say out loud?" Pulling into my garage, I sit in my car lost in prayerful thought.

Alec finally opens the car door and squats down next to me. "How good are you at writing?" he asks me. I study his face and he's not teasing, he's serious.

I shrug. "I don't know. I've never won a Pulitzer."

He chuckles and shakes his head. Laying a warm hand on my thigh he says, "Can you write as well as you can sew?" When I look at him questioningly, he smiles. "Pretend you're sewing Olivia a quilt, Elaine. Think of your story in those kinds of blocks. But instead of sewing the quilt, write down all the things that need to be told in each square. Let your chapters be your squares. Start by making a list and then build the story together piece by piece. Maybe you don't have to tell a whole life story." He shrugs. "Maybe you would concentrate on just these last few months. You've had Paulie, Dean, Callie, James, Me, Liam, Erin, Dan, and even Richard make some pretty strong appearances recently. Why not see if thinking of it that way would make it easier to consider?"

"You're still bent that my life's quilt doesn't have you on it." I lean out of the car and clunk my head into his. "Maybe, you'll just have to settle with sleeping *with me* under that quilt. Did you ever think of that?"

He pulls me towards him and kisses me. "Every night, Sweetie. Every darn night."

Moments pass while I think of chapters of my life's story entitled 'Skeletons In My Closet,' 'My Nitroglycerin Stash,' and 'Batman Is My Hero." But I think of something else and …

I start to tremble because still, after all this time and after all the people who have heard the truth, the reality is that there is a piece of the nitroglycerin secret that I've held back … from everyone. Alec can see me starting to lose it and he pulls me out of the car, pressing me against it's side and holding me tightly. "Sweetie … Elaine …! Hey, if writing this down is too much then forget it! You need to do only what you *can* do. I know you've been praying a lot these past weeks. Let the Lord talk to you and tell you how best to proceed …"

But I'm really gone now. I try to slide down to huddle on the garage floor but Alec won't let me, holding me tightly and rocking me gently. "It's okay, Sweetie," he's saying to me over and over again, "it's going to be okay, Love …" He keeps repeating that over and over again clueless as to what to do with me I suppose.

"I …, I …, went to a … clinic …" I finally manage to say, "right after I was married to Dean … to get an abor-," I choke on the word and then force myself to say it, "*abortion.*" I feel a moan work its way out of my throat and try again to curl up on the floor but still Alec holds me tightly against him. "I filled out the forms and … met with the doctor … and listened to all they had to tell me and even made an appointment to go back and have the pro … procedure." I feel a loathing for myself deep down from the depths of very heart and soul.

"You didn't go back though, Elaine, did you?"

I don't answer him. I remember those days like they happened just yesterday. I remember being stunned that I could actually feel more emotionally destroyed at the prospect of … the procedure … than the … circumstances … that brought me to the need for one …

Alec's arms tighten around me. "Come on, Elaine. *Say it.* Why didn't you go back?"

"I was a coward."

Shaking his head, he says without hesitation, "No. That's not the reason."

He's so sure? How the hell does *he* know? I feel a wave of blistering anger towards him. Words boil up in me to hurt him and I open my mouth … But I stop. I'm loosing that peace I'd so recently found; I feel it trickling away so fast it makes me shiver. The peace of my difference. *I can't loose it.* It's too wonderful. Having a crisis with Alec in my garage, God helps me keep my mouth shut. Then God gently reminds me of *all* the emotions I felt over those days ... and days just recently, too. I think of Alec's explanation of the scarlet thread of redemption and how he said *I always thought that my life had a scarlet thread through it. Little points along the way where I had a glimpse of what I could have and could be ...* Was it God who gave me all those powerful emotions those days so long ago? Did He give me a clear glimpse of what could or could not be so that I was forced to face the future of my choices in one way or another?

"Having the abortion wouldn't have made the hurt go away. Having the abortion would have only made it worse," I finally say.

"Why's that?" Alec throws out with a burst of frustrated air. "At least you wouldn't have to face a daily reminder of the rape. Day in, day out, looking into the face of a child who was living, walking, breathing proof of the most horrible time in your life? Why not get rid of the child? Why should your whole life be turned upside down over something that you had no control over? Why should you have to suffer for the rest of your life?"

In the midst of his tirade, I've pulled back to look at him while he speaks. He says these horrible, awful words looking me right in the eye. "Why not, Elaine?" he says quietly to me while I stare at him.

It's another excellent, thought provoking question. With a rush, I remember *all* the emotions of those days. Sighing, I say, "I realized I didn't care where the child came from. It was someone whom I could love and who would love me back *forever*. Having an abortion wouldn't have erased the rape. It just would have scarred me even more. It would have just left a *second* empty, black, gaping hole in me that I could never escape or forget. A baby," I sigh and start to cry, "a baby was something good that came out of it. I decided that maybe the baby was more of a miracle than a curse ..."

"Now *that's* the truth," he says with a satisfied tone of voice. Alec holds me while I cry but I'm no longer hysterical, I'm just exhausted from it all. "And *that* is true love."

Love doesn't give up like that, Love doesn't say enough's enough,
Love doesn't just walk away when the going gets tough, I know 'cause I Am Love. [44]

Chapter 20: A Different Point Of View

I t's obviously a wedding party that pours out of the Somerville
city hall building and spills down the front steps. The bride is
wearing an attractive cream-colored suit, her short hair curls
wildly in the stiff November breeze, and she's clutching a small bouquet of
autumn mums held together with long, bright red ribbons. The groom,
looking smart in his dark three-piece suit, has a bright red mum pinned to
his lapel. The groom's smile is so wide it's visible to the woman watching
the whole event almost a block away sipping coffee inside a local shop.

Others join the bride and groom on the city hall steps. There
appears to be about twenty in attendance, including a miniature version of
Batman completely decked out in a cape, pointy-eared mask, and bright
yellow utility belt which causes the observing woman to chuckle. From the
way the bride and groom duck, it seems that birdseed is being thrown and
Batman's definitely got the greatest stash in his utility belt compartments.

The group processes down the street laughing and smiling. Like
paparazzi chasing famous movie stars, cameras click and cars slow down to
gawk at the show. The wedding parade works its way past the woman and
then disappears into another coffee shop across the street called Agape
Shop, which bears a sign on the door that says 'CLOSED BECAUSE OF

WEDDING.' In one of the store's big picture windows is a photograph of the happy couple with the caption 'Alec and Elaine: Together At Last!'

Olivia Kelly could no more attend her mother's wedding than stay away from it. Having spent the better part of the last three months coming to terms with things she never knew as opposed to things she'd *thought* she'd known ... well, the puzzle that was her mother never ceased to be compelling.

Once the letters had started arriving, irreverent, tightly worded stories that spoke of guilt and love, hope and despair all interlaced with her mother's unique brand of twisted humor and in-your-face honesty, well, what could Olivia do but read them? Like her mother, Olivia was a person who needed the truth ... so she could decide to face it or hide from it.

Staring at Agape Shop, separated by two layers of window panes and a busy city street Olivia could just barely glimpse the celebration going on inside. Liam's bright yellow Batman belt appeared regularly in the window, and her mother's off white suit showed brighter than the other darker clothing.

So, her mother had found a new man and God. Not necessarily in that order, mind you ... Olivia sighed and took a sip of her coffee.

This complicated relationship Olivia had with her mother was rooted in love ... The fact that they had difficulty adequately expressing it to each other didn't negate each other's desire for happiness in a relationship.

These past months of self-analysis and discovery had taken their toll on Olivia. The 'Discover You're a Child of Rape' diet – loose twenty-five pounds in three months, guaranteed! She'd needed the time, though. Still needed a lot more, but in doing a before-during-after comparison she was markedly improved.

The addition of her mother's letters into the already seething mass of emotions – almost two months into her quest to find herself while at the same time maintaining her sanity - had, surprisingly, helped quite a bit with the original indigestible pile. With the arrival of the letters, which arrived chunk by chunk, came the ability to sort and organize, process and begin to understand, think and muddle through.

Olivia had gone through the whole process of grief: shock, denial, anger, guilt, depression, and loneliness. At the end, she'd resolutely buried her old self and was now in the process of rising from the ashes. *At all costs.* Currently, Olivia supposed she was in the 'acceptance' stage. That supposed last stage: hope, was an as-of-yet impossible one to consider.

Mommy? How come we never go see our other grandma? We see daddy's mom but how come we don't see yours?

My mother likes to be … alone, Olivia. Some mommies like to spend time with their babies to kiss and cuddle and laugh with. But some mommies don't.

So I've got the kiss and cuddle kind and you had the don't kind?

Yeah, something like that.

Why are you here again? Hasn't your mother ordered you to stay away? Do you know that she came here to this house and threatened *me? Told me to 'keep my mouth shut' around you. Doesn't want you to know the big, ugly truth.*

What truth? That's what I'm trying to find out. That's what I need to know!

You don't need *to know anything, young woman. Absolutely nothing. But since you asked I'll tell you. Never knew a good man when she was looking him in the eye and never knew a bad man when he was between her legs. Until after the fact. Until trouble was already growing, so to speak. Stupid just like me, too. Not enough courage to end it all and start fresh. Had to go ahead and* have *the baby, let it steer her life in a direction that was anything but what she wanted or planned. Now, you're mother will tell you she was* raped, *something that never occurred to me to claim. But then you've got to admit that it certainly is a convenient way to deflect the blame, isn't it?*

Olivia had driven around for hours that first night trying to unscramble her horrifying thoughts. She had stopped and tried her fath -, *Dean's* way of dealing with things but alcohol had only made her weepy and clingy. First, she had tried calling her mother and finally she'd ended up at Erin and Dan's. Both the drinking and the seeking out of family were regrettably huge errors in judgment, especially after Dan took her car keys. What had she been thinking? Like Olivia wanted to sit around and have a *civil* discussion with *anyone*? Hello? Was she out of her mind? In the end, first chance she had to escape she'd walked close to eight miles home to her condo, collected her computer and called a cab. *Arrivderci.*

I need to be alone when my world falls apart. I need to think it all out. I need to pick through all the rubble. I need to figure out the truth and the lies and what I own and what I don't.

Children of rape are called 'The Forgotten Victims.' *Can you be a victim if you don't know?* Olivia had wondered cynically to herself. Which made Olivia wonder *how* her mother had ever managed to keep such a horrible secret to herself. Olivia spent that first week, holed up in a local motel barely eating or sleeping doing Internet surfing reading, processing, remembering and crying …

Hello, my name is Olivia Kelly and I'm a child of rape.

Don't equate us to the act that brought us here.[45]

Olivia had gotten out pencil and paper, subtracted back from her birth date, and then calculated what her mother had endured *at the age of fifteen.* She'd then forced herself to remember, to the best of her ability, how *her* life had been at the age of fifteen. Flashes of memory had revealed that at fifteen, Olivia had been busy being a raging nightmare of a teen, having already concluded – based on extensive evidence mind you – that the mother she was saddled with was incapable of making wise decisions for *anyone.* There was a time in Olivia's life that if you gave her the opportunity, she could give you quite an extensive list of evidence to support her conclusion, too.

I've tolerated your lousy maternal instincts, your blatant favoritism towards Erin, your one-sided loyalties to what only you deem to be important, and your convenient memories regarding your extensive array of personal disasters!

216

Which led to the inevitable question: If discovering you were a product of rape was so mind altering, how explosive was enduring the act itself? Words and statistics that had never entered her mind until now dominated Olivia's waking days *and* sleepless nights.

"One in six women are sexually assaulted, 44% of all rape victims are under the age of 18, every two and a half minutes somewhere in America a woman is being sexually assaulted ..."[46]

"Only 37% of all rapes are reported to the police, pregnancy rate associated with rape is estimated to be 4.7%, there may be 32,101 annual rape-related pregnancies among American women over the age of 18.17..."[47]

"Rape victims often experience anxiety, guilt, nervousness, phobias, substance abuse, sleep disturbances, depression, alienation, sexual dysfunction, and aggression. They often distrust others and replay the assault in their minds, and they are at increased risk of future victimization ..."[48]

My subsequent relationships – both married and otherwise – regularly drove home the point that no matter how bad the situation was, being myself would only make it worse. The magnitude of my vitriolic anger, low self-esteem, and gargantuan guilt makes me a perfect candidate for going postal one day. Good thing I'm not a mailwoman.

The need to sort through all of the horrible putrid garbage and determine what was truth was critical. Considering her mother and her ... grandmother, Olivia was forced to acknowledge that her mother had never, shied away when faced with the truth.

These last ten years of singlehood I've discovered the real, honest to goodness Elaine Marie Cummings nee Kelly nee Richardson nee Brockman. I like her, don't get me wrong about that, but she's definitely best served up in small, carefully managed dosages for the most successful results. Like strong cough syrup. Or Milk of Magnesia. Not intended for small children, not to be taken regularly, and never to be mixed with alcohol.

Without having actually done it, Olivia imagined asking her mother, "Am I the child of a rape?" and felt resoundingly that her mother would have answered 'yes.' The fact that her mother had never spoken of it, implied it, or ever in their many, many heated confrontations ever gave any hint regarding such a horrible thing only seemed to make the truth that much more clear and easy to believe. One of the things that had always grated on Olivia had been her mother's willingness to wave all of her disasters like a banner for anyone interested enough to look. No matter how Olivia tried to spin it, the reason for never speaking of the rape could only mean that it was to *protect* rather than to *hide*.

That, of course, and the hatred that had poured out of Olivia's grandmother's eyes and words. Comparing what was said out of love versus what was said out of hate always makes the distinction of truth that much easier, doesn't it?

Watching my mother talk down to me regarding my continuing course of bad choices and then hearing her disparage my violet eyed baby girl's less than auspicious start was something I chose to tolerate only once.

The waves of guilt, once they arrived, almost knocked Olivia down when she remembered the things she'd said and implied regarding her mother and her character. Again, piles of inaccurate assumptions culled from years of adolescent know-it-all and angst had painted what turned out to be a completely inaccurate picture of her mother. The embarrassment of having a mother who had married *three* times, a mother who had been on welfare, a mother who had lived in her car with two children for a period of time, a mother who had had a mental breakdown after the suicide death of her third husband, a mother who was always too loud, too brash, too shocking, too unpredictable had been something Olivia had struggled with *forever.* Seen in the light of the truth, these qualities took on an immensely different appearance … and few of them were negative.

Lately, in these past years, Olivia had watched her mother's hesitancy towards her and had added another thing to resent. Why couldn't her mother just be as open and as casual as she was with Erin? Why did her mother always have such a guarded, careful expression on her face when they talked about things as simple and as easy as the past week's work? What had Olivia done to cause her mother to close herself off so completely that there was no more warmth or caring between the two than would be between casual acquaintances? Was Olivia so *lacking* in comparison to Erin and her perfect husband and perfect son? Was she so *different* in the way she acted and reacted to life's situations?

God only knows what prompted the paternity test. Ever since a high school science project had determined that blond haired, blue-eyed Dean Kelly and light brown haired and green-eyed Elaine Marie Cummings could not have *possibly* produced black haired, violet-eyed Olivia Kelly there'd been a nervous buzz in the back of her mind. While Olivia really hadn't been surprised when the paternity results had verified the scientifically obvious, it had never crossed her mind where this would eventually lead. In pressing her mother to reveal her actual biological father, Olivia had simply been searching for the reason why Erin had always seemed to fit and she never had. And when her mother had refused to divulge a name, well, suddenly it all fit into place: Mother had never wanted her in the first place.

"It is not just a name. It is the entire directional force of my life since your moment of conception." Doesn't she get that if it were just a name I would have sung it from the highest rooftops long ago?

Truth - or at least the snippets of selective disclosure that Grandmother had hurled at Olivia - only led to more questions, the most pressing: why did her mother go ahead and give birth to her? Why *didn't* she just terminate the pregnancy and move on? If Olivia's mother had truly

219

never wanted her in the first place *and the pregnancy was the result of rape*, she would have had every valid reason under the sun to abort. Olivia's initial rationale that she had never been wanted in the first place no longer fit the picture when faced with the brutal reality of her conception and subsequent birth.

The lives [of children conceived through rape] and the courage of their mothers says clearly that everyone has the right to live, regardless of how they were conceived. It is also the testimony of many women who have become pregnant through rape that giving life to their child was the best thing they could have done to bring something good from such a terrible crime. [49]

I realized I didn't care where the child came from. It was someone whom I could love and who would love me back forever. Having an abortion wouldn't have erased the rape. It just would have scarred me more. It would have just left a second empty, black, gaping hole in me that I could never escape or forget. A baby was something good that came out of it. I decided that maybe the baby was more of a miracle than a curse ...

By the time her mother's letters had started to arrive, pages and pages of handwritten bits, Olivia had already spent enough time reading and researching on the Internet that she had begun to appreciate what her mother had managed to accomplish – *on her own, despite the odds*. She'd finished school, gotten a job, secured housing, managed to feed, clothe and love – yes love – both girls. Her outspoken, irreverent, in-your-face style of living was probably both a defense mechanism *as well as* the characteristic trait that had kept her putting one foot in front of the other.

"I love you, Olivia. Do you believe that?"

Sigh. These past weeks and months, Olivia had worked diligently to prove the fact that her mother *had not*. And yet each instance, good and bad, led to the conclusion that no one but a *loving* person would have behaved as her mother consistently did. Olivia could find no memory of hate, anger, disgust, or impatience directed towards her on her mother's part. In actuality, the only negative feeling was the emotional distance that seemed to have grown over the past few years – directly in proportion to Olivia's increasing dissatisfaction with life in general.

Eventually, to escape the motel atmosphere, Olivia had called in a favor of a colleague and rented a small beachfront cabin on the Jersey shore. Telecommuting had allowed her to meet most of her work-related responsibilities, and yet as the weeks passed it had become crystal clear that being a financial planner was not something she really liked doing *at all*. As of this week she'd given her one-month notice (with vacation time she was paid through the end of the year) and she'd enrolled in the local state college to get her certification in ... teaching math. Never wanting to "copy" Mother or Erin, Olivia had stifled that interest. And to what end exactly? To make herself miserable? Just yesterday she'd gotten a letter from the district of Bridgewater who were interested in hiring her to teach high school math *and* in financially assisting her successful completion of the alternate route of teacher training. It would seem that her life at long last was finally coming together positively. She might even manage a smile now and then.

The only thing left was facing her mother.

Alec, crazy man that he is, has proposed, Olivia. I've kept him waiting longer than any man – amazing huh? – but he's been rather insistent that Thanksgiving Weekend would be the perfect time for us to tie the knot. We're going to be married by the Justice of the Peace in Somerville on Saturday morning at 11:00 and then go back to Agape Shop for a blessing by our minister Crystal (a ridiculous name for a minister, I agree) and then enjoy some non-Alec made pastries. (Hey, I don't want him tired on our wedding night, are you kidding?) My life is suddenly, wonderfully good, Olivia. It only misses you. Would you consider coming? Please?

Pushing aside her coffee cup, Olivia glanced over at Agape Shop only to see Liam apparently licking the picture window. Shaking her head at the continual antics of her nephew, she watched as her mother came into view. A serious discussion ensued, no doubt outlining the horrors of germs versus the joy of doing something outrageous and naughty. God, Olivia loved that little guy. How could anyone not?

Stiffening, Olivia watched as Liam pointed out the window, directly at *her* as she sat frozen in her seat. While at first her mother seemed to take no notice of Liam and his finger, Olivia watched her mother suddenly stand up and look out the window as if in a trance.

Well, Olivia thought, *that takes care of whether I have the courage to make an appearance today.* Slowly standing so that she was in full view, Olivia watched her mother turn and respond to Alec who had come to stand beside her. Alec, in turn, looked toward Olivia through the windows and smiled. Slowly, precisely, he laid his fist to his heart and thumped his chest and then, amazingly, blew Olivia a kiss. Leaning in, he whispered something in his new wife's ear, kissed her pointedly on the mouth, led her to the shop's front door, opened it, and pushed her outside.

The only thing that came out of that time in my life that had any redeeming value or potential for joy was you, Olivia.

When Olivia had read that line she had cried and cried. She'd remembered her mother saying those words to her. More importantly, though, Olivia had remembered the words she'd said to her mother prior to her making that statement. *There could be no doubt that her mother loved her. None whatsoever.*

Any courage deserted Olivia as she stood and watched her mother fight the traffic and walk slowly toward her. For a few charged moments, they both stood looking at each other through the storefront window. Her mother seemed to be about ready to burst. Olivia was about ready to bolt. She'd always hated drama, tears, and the loss of one's dignity. This current situation was a guaranteed triple play.

Finally, with a rush of leaves and autumn wind Elaine Marie *Monroe* walked into the shop. "The pastries are *a lot* better across the street," were the first words out of her mouth and she was already crying when she said it.

"There's no need to cry about, it Mom, they're not that bad over here. Besides, I've only had the coffee."

"Coffee's a lot better across the street, too," her mother said and then as if she couldn't help herself she rushed to say, "I need to hug you, Olivia, whether you like it or not, so brace yourself." Before Olivia can respond she's pulled fiercely into her mother's almond scented embrace. "Thank you, Olivia," she choked out. "Thank you for coming."

"I didn't come. I was a coward. I sat here the whole time. If not for Batman's superior eyesight, you never would have discovered me."

Her mother pulled back and looked at her. "You've lost weight, are you ... okay?"

Olivia nodded. "I'm better. Much better. I've needed time to ... *pick through the rubble.*"

Her mother caught the reference to one of the many letters. "I couldn't not write, Olivia, not once I knew you were having your mail forwarded. Pitifully, it took almost six weeks for me to figure that out. I never was the sharpest tack in the box."

Olivia looked pointedly at her mother. "You usually were the *only* tack in the box of paper clips, Mom."

Her mother tilted her head to one side and smiled. "I guess that would make me the sharpest, huh?"

"I'm sorry for -,"

"NO. *NO.* If we want, later, another day, another time we can both sit down and have a good cry and we can ask hard questions and give painful answers. Maybe we can make a pledge over melted Snickers bars or something that we will commit to forgetting all of our mistakes and misunderstandings and just ... look forward, okay?" Her mother began to drag Olivia to the shop's door. "Please, come across and join the celebration. We were just going to begin to take photos. Alec and I have to catch a plane at six, so everything's got to be over by four."

Olivia looked across, hesitantly, at Agape Shop, and couldn't help bursting into hysterical laughter.

Her mother, looked across the street, groaned in abject humiliation. "Look what I've married Olivia! *Look what I've married!*" For standing outside Agape Shop, still in his three-piece suit was Alec, only he'd added a black cape, a yellow utility belt, and a plastic Batman mask to the look. Standing next to Alec holding tightly to his hand was Liam, dressed with the same accessories.

Olivia struggled to get her laughter under control and said, "You never were normal or ordinary, Mom."

"No, honey, you're right. I think I'm destined to always be different."

About The Author

Susan McGeown is a wife, mother, daughter, sister, friend, aunt, uncle (don't ask), teacher, author ... but, most importantly, a "woman after God's own heart." Living in Bridgewater, New Jersey, with her husband of over fifteen years and their three children, writing stories is just about the best way she can imagine spending her free time. Each of Sue's stories champions those emotions nearest and dearest to her: faith, joy, hope and love.

Philippians 1:20-21

For I fully expect and hope that I will never be ashamed, but that I will continue to be bold for Christ, as I have been in the past. And I trust that my life will bring honor to Christ, whether I live or die. For to me, living means living for Christ, and dying is even better.

Footnotes

1 "Faith Enough," Jars of Clay, *Who We Are Instead* Album
2 Walt Whitman
3 Proverbs 17:17, The Message
4 "Martyrs and Thieves," Jennifer Knapp, *Kansas* Album
5 "By Surprise," Joy Williams, *Joy* Album
6 "Faithful To Me," Jennifer Knapp, *Kansas* Album
7 "Nobody Number One," Over The Rhine, *Ohio* Album
8 "Leaving 99," Audio Adrenaline, *Worldwide* Album
9 "Walk On," Susan Ashton, *Along The Road* Album
10 "Sacred Delight," Sunday Drive, *Sunday Drive* Album
11 "Shine," The Newsboys, *Shine* Album
12 "Here With Me," Mercy Me, *Undone* Album
13 "Taking My Time," Ashton, Becker, and Dente, *Along The Road* Album
14 "Along The Road," Ashton, Becker, Dente, *Along The Road* Album
15 "Clay and Water," Margaret Becker, *Falling Forward* Album
16 Romans 7:18-21, New Living Translation, selected parts
17 Romans 8:28 New Living Translation
18 Romans 3:23-25, New Living Translation, selected parts
19 Romans 9:31b, New Living Translation
20 Romans 9:39-39, New Living Translation
21 "Faithful To Me", Jennifer Knapp, *Kansas* Album
22 Psalm 56:3-4, 8, New Living Translation
23 "Valleys Fill First," Caedmon's Call, *Long Line of Leavers* Album
24 "Leaving 99," Audio Adrenaline, *Worldwide* Album
25 Hebrews 11:1, New Living Translation
26 Jeremiah 29:11-13, New Living Translation
27 "Open Skies," David Crowder Band, *Illuminate* Album
28 "One Trick Pony," Mercy Me, *Coming Up To Breathe* Album
29 John 14:25, New Living Translation
30 "Like A Child," Jars of Clay, *Jars of Clay* Album
31 "Oh My God," Jars of Clay, *Good Monsters* Album
32 "So Long Self," MercyMe, *Coming Up To Breathe* Album
33 "Salt and Light," Ashley Cleveland and Michael Tait, *Roaring Lambs* Album
34 "Well Pleased," FFH, *Voices From Home* Album
35 "Beauty For Ashes," Shane & Shane, *Upstairs* Album
36 Isaiah 61:3, 10 New Living Translation
37 "The Servant Song," by Richard Gillard
38 "Here With Me," MercyMe, *Undone* Album
39 "One Trick Pony," MercyMe, *Coming Up To Breathe* Album

[40] Jeremiah 29:11, New American Standard Version

[41] "Hymn," Jars of Clay, *Much Afraid* Album

[42] "Sacred Delight," Sunday Drive, *Sunday Drive* Album

[43] Philip Yancey, *Prayer: Does It Make Any Difference?*

[44] "I Am Love," FFH, *Voice From Home* Album

[45] http://www.righttoliferoch.org/nforgotten.htm

[46] http://www.rainn.org/statistics/

[47] http://www.paralumun.com/issuesrapestats.htm

[48] http://www.feminist.com/antiviolence/facts.html

[49] http://dakotavoice.blogspot.com/2006/09/children-conceived-of-rape-testify-to.html